P

Prince of the Hollow Hills

By Margaret L. Carter

Writers Exchange E-Publishing
http://www.writers-exchange.com

P

Prince of the Hollow Hills
Copyright 2021 Margaret L. Carter
Writers Exchange E-Publishing
PO Box 372
ATHERTON QLD 4883

Cover Art by: Jatin

Published by Writers Exchange E-Publishing
http://www.writers-exchange.com

Chapter One

***I** knew all along that a union between mortal and immortal could lead only to loss and grief.*

May the Powers of Light guide me to kindle a spark of hope from this tragedy.

The portal contracted to a circle of light and vanished like a bubble popping. Cloying heat replaced the wine-crisp air of home. Kieran emerged into a cleft between walls of rock, so close together his shoulders almost brushed them on each side. Behind him, the walls narrowed still farther until they met, while ahead the space widened until the stony niche gave way to forest. He blinked in the glare of this world's sun, dazzling even filtered through leaves. The moist, green scent of a summer day filled his nose. Four strides took him into the open, on a mountainside covered with trees and undergrowth. Not an ancient forest, he perceived. If he could rely on his slight knowledge of time's flow on this plane, most of these trees had stood no more than seventy years. He drew a deep breath. Artificial odors, some kind of acrid fuel burning, tainted the air not far away.

Even a distant whiff of that pollution made him queasy. He ought to welcome that taint, though. It pointed the way to human cities, and he would need human help to reach his destination. *Adair's foolish passion created this catastrophe. Now I have to repair the damage he left.* Kieran reined in his first impulse to charge headlong to the rescue. The sooner he found the child, the sooner he could leave this death-shadowed place.

Given the erratic connection between the time-streams of the two realms, Halwyn might already be far ahead. Also, the portal could be opened from this side only for the next few days and would then lock itself for two moon cycles, so Kieran had no time to waste. Still, he knew better than to rush forward in blind panic. He leaned against a tree, sensing the flow of its life under the bark. A red bird with a crest on its head fluttered down to alight on his shoulder. He willed it to fly away, for he needed to concentrate on more distant objects. With his eyes closed, he extended his inner senses in search of the child. Faintly, at the farthest edge of his perception, stirred a hint of the infant's half-formed awareness. Perhaps Halwyn would find that trace impossible to pick up and would blunder around long enough for Kieran to make contact first.

He counted on having two advantages over his enemy. First, he had visited the human realm several times before, although only briefly. He had some sketchy knowledge of this region and its customs. Halwyn probably had little more than a spell of tongues to enable him to speak the language. Secondly, Kieran had pledged brotherhood with his cousin Adair. *And now I must pay the price for my blood brother's folly.* He suppressed the pang that pierced him at the memory of his kinsman and forced himself to focus on the urgency of the present task. The mingling of their blood would surely forge a bond with Adair's child, a link that would allow him to track the babe more reliably than the enemy could. Kieran would have to follow that trail if the mother had left her previous home. Once he found her, could he persuade her to yield the child to his protection?

Leaves rustled under his feet as he walked away from the portal. A sigh escaped him. Already he longed for home. Although cast out from his family, at least on the other side of the gate he had his own domain with its gardens and orchards and with lesser creatures who depended on him as their lord and protector. Here he could look forward to nothing but discomfort and danger, along with the ordeal of wrenching an infant away from its mother.

No need to agonize in advance over that prospect. The next hour presented enough problems. Following the fuel odor would lead him to a road used by hordes of metal carriages. A simple mind-control spell would induce one of their drivers to transport him. His stomach churned at the thought of that ride, boxed in by a framework of iron, but he had no time to indulge such weakness. *My cousin got used to it. So can I.* Bracing himself, he cast a glamour to veil his true appearance and started hiking downhill. He had failed Adair. He would not fail Adair's child.

The bell over the shop door jingled. Behind the counter, Fern glanced up and suppressed a sigh when she saw her sister Ivy walk into Danforth's Den of Mystery, wearing denim shorts, a halter top, and a cloth baby sling. Her flame-red hair, cascading down her back, curled slightly from the June humidity. A visit to the bookstore in the middle of a weekday afternoon probably meant she had a problem. The tense set of Ivy's mouth confirmed the impression that she wasn't casually dropping in to show off the baby. In the pouch on her chest, Baird blinked at the change of light from outside to inside.

Fern came out from behind the counter, wondering what her sister wanted this time. Beverly Danforth, her boss and best friend, straightened up from the corner where she'd been shelving paperbacks. "Hi, there, how's the little guy?" Brushing book dust off her peasant blouse and calf-length skirt, she bustled over to the counter and tickled the baby's chin. His mouth opened like a baby bird's. "Aren't you getting big for only two months? How're you feeling, Ivy?"

"Okay," Ivy said with a faint smile. "Can I talk to Fern for a minute?"

Bev ran her fingers through her short, brown hair, pushed her wire-rimmed glasses up on her nose, and made an elaborate pretense of scanning the deserted shop for customers. Even on a Friday afternoon, the tourists didn't flock here in droves. Located in West Annapolis away from the downtown historic district, the store got most of its business on weekends. "Sure, you can borrow her for two minutes or even three."

Fern took a seat at one of the tables in the coffee bar area by the front window. Ivy crouched to pet a plump tortoiseshell Maine Coon lying in a basket on the floor, then sat down across the table from Fern. "I need a favor."

"If you're here about your tires, like I already said, you'll have to wait until I get paid next week." She didn't like to borrow from her savings account except in a true emergency.

"No, it's not that."

"Oh, no, what else broke, and how much is it going to cost me?"

"Why do you think I'm going to ask for money every time you see me?"

"Because you usually do. Not that I mind helping out when you really need it, like with the tires, but when are you going back to work? You should be in pretty good shape by now, right? Not that I'm pushing or anything."

"I'm planning to get back on the Ren Faire circuit at the end of the summer, and meanwhile I have a couple of gigs lined up downtown."

"So you can drop off Baird at my place while you're singing, I guess? Which is okay," Fern hastily added. After all, she didn't exactly have a whirlwind social calendar. "Haven't you given any more thought to getting a real job? After all, you've got a baby to think of now."

"Yeah, I noticed. When are you going to accept that my music is my real job?"

"I never said there was anything wrong with that, did I? Just that you can't depend on it to support you and Baird, especially with Adair--gone. Not to mention the hassle of dragging a baby around to one Renaissance Faire after another."

"Lots of couples bring their kids along."

"Couples. A single mom is a whole 'nother thing. And you aren't still expecting Adair to come back, are you?"

Ivy's eyes widened with a flash of anger. "You know I don't expect that. If he could have, he'd have done it already. Something terrible's happened to him, I know it."

"Yeah, right, another premonition." Ivy would grasp at any fantasy rather than entertain for a moment the idea that her lover might have bailed the same way their father had.

"Never mind, I didn't come here to rehash the same old arguments. I need you to take Baird to your place for tonight, maybe longer."

"Why?"

"He isn't safe at home. Somebody's after him."

"Who? What's going on?" Fern's throat tightened in fear. She stared at the baby, snuggled against Ivy's chest with a lock of her hair clutched in one tiny fist. "Did you get a threatening phone call or something?"

"Promise you won't blow me off? I really do have a premonition." The tension in her voice kept Fern listening, despite her scorn for the whole clairvoyance notion that Ivy put such faith in. "They're going to try to take him from me."

"How do you know that? Anything besides your second sight?" Otherwise known as imagination working overtime, in Fern's opinion. The mere mention of the subject made her stomach knot with anxiety. All that New Age mumbo-jumbo sparked nothing but negative memories in her.

Ivy shook her head, clearly annoyed by Fern's skepticism. "I just know. Take him to your house where he'll be protected, at least a little bit."

"What makes my place any safer than yours?" Torn between relief that no concrete danger existed and worry over her sister's paranoia, she strove to keep the exasperation out of her voice.

"I can't explain it," Ivy said with a sigh. "You wouldn't believe me, so why waste my breath?"

Reaching across to stroke Baird's downy hair, damp from the warm weather, Fern said, "So don't tell me. Look, you know I don't mind watching him, but I don't get off until five. You can bring him over for the night then. Come to think of it, if your house isn't safe, why don't you stay over, too?" One of them would have to sleep on the couch, but if that arrangement would make Ivy quit worrying about imaginary bogeymen, Fern could live with it.

"I'm afraid they'll find me. I can't risk having Baird with me when that happens."

"Who the heck is this 'they'?" The shop's bell rang at the entry of two middle-aged women, causing Fern to drop her voice to a whisper. "If you have any definite idea of who might want to hurt you, why don't you call the police?"

"Because I don't have a name or a description," Ivy whispered back, "and if you think I'm crazy, the police sure would. Can't you just do what I ask without arguing, for once?" She spread one hand over the baby's back in a protective gesture. Tears shimmered in her eyes. "I've lost Adair. I won't let anything happen to Baird."

"Hey, stop that." Fern leaned over to put an arm around her sister's shoulders. The familiar guilt coiled like a snake in the pit of her stomach. Somehow, Ivy could always make her feel like a negligent parent, even though the age gap between them was only six years. Fern could never quite ignore the ghost of their mother's voice in her head, ordering her to keep an eye on her little sister. "I already said I'd take care of him. Drop him off about five-fifteen."

Shaking her head, Ivy rubbed her eyes with the back of her hand. "Like I said, he isn't safe with me. I'll leave him at the day care center until you can pick him up. That should be okay for a couple of hours."

"Sure, if it'll make you feel better." The baby had never spent a night away from Ivy before. Fern hoped feeding from bottles instead of nursing for that many hours wouldn't upset his digestion. "Are you planning to collect him tomorrow morning or what?"

"I'll call you later, and we can figure out what to do next. I might have to leave home for a while. I don't know. Oh, and I have to give you this." From under the baby sling she pulled a chain she wore around her neck. Fashioned of lacy wrought iron, it supported a Celtic cross of the same metal. In the center of the cross, a crystal sphere held a four-leafed clover. Ivy had ordered the necklace custom-made at a downtown Irish-themed shop, along with a matching filigree bracelet also adorned with a clover inside a marble-sized glass ball. Now that Fern thought of it, she realized Ivy had worn the set of jewelry constantly for the past few months, an odd habit considering neither of them had ever paid much attention to religion aside from Christmas and Easter services.

When Ivy handed her the necklace, Fern stared at it in bewilderment. "You want me to borrow this? Why? You never take it off."

"I wear it for protection, which you might need soon. Better safe than sorry." The urgency in her voice, still thick with unshed tears, underlined her sincerity. This plea meant more than a lighthearted "can't hurt" ritual of knocking on wood or circling around to avoid a black cat.

Rather than start another argument, Fern hung the chain around her neck, with the cross tucked into her blouse. "You know what I think about that stuff, but if you insist, I'll wear it. What about you, though? Sounds like you're the one who needs protection."

Ivy touched her left wrist. "I still have the bracelet." She stood up. "Now I've got to go. I've been out with Baird too long already. I have to get him to the day care. Almost forgot, I put something else in the baby bag you might need. The instructions are on the bottle." She cut off the next question with, "No time to explain, and it's another thing you wouldn't believe. Maybe we can talk about it later." She bent over to give Fern a hug, with the baby snuggled between them. "Thanks, sis. I know you think I'm nuts. So, well, thanks for humoring me."

Fern kissed the top of Baird's head, patted Ivy on the back, and watched her sister carry the baby out to the car parked at the curb.

When she resumed her spot behind the counter, Bev said, "Do you think there's really anything wrong, or just postpartum nerves?"

"That's got to be it. Who'd want to hurt Ivy or Baird?" Fern busied her hands with rearranging a stack of promotional fliers left by a local author. "You know she's always thought it's cool that second sight is supposed to run in our family. Sometimes she lets the idea trample on her common sense." She broke off when the two women shoppers finished their browsing and walked over with a couple of books each, which she rang up.

After the customers left, Bev said, "You don't think in this one case she could be right?"

Fern rejected the comment with a vigorous shake of her head. "Every time she came up with an incident she thought proved we had clairvoyance or whatever, it could just as well be explained as coincidence. Today is no different. Like you said, she's nervous because she's alone with a new baby."

Early in her school years, Fern had learned to keep quiet about her random flashes of intuition. Mentioning them had brought her nothing but trouble. What was the point of telling the next-door neighbors their lost dog was lying hurt in the crawl space under a vacant house, when she couldn't explain how she'd known and so had been accused of wounding the dog in the first place? A few episodes like that had taught her to keep her mouth shut. Life had gone smoother after she'd taken the next logical step and convinced herself those feelings and premonitions had no grounding in reality. Neither did Ivy's.

"If she's that scared of staying home alone with him," Bev said, "maybe you should take her out of town for a few days. You know you can use my place on the Eastern Shore whenever you want. You still have your key from our last trip, right?"

Fern nodded. The tempting image of Bev's beach house floated into her mind. "I don't know. I'll wait and see if Ivy calms down by tomorrow. I shouldn't bail on you just when the tourist season is getting into full swing."

Kneeling beside the half empty box of books on the floor, Bev said over her shoulder, "You work too hard. We do have other staff coming in this weekend, you know."

"Yeah, but as assistant manager, I have to set those college kids a good example."

Bev laughed. "Girlfriend, sometimes I can't believe you hit the big three-oh just this year. I think you were born middle-aged."

"You know where I'm coming from. I don't want to turn into my mother. Bad enough Ivy's doing that."

Hands on hips, Bev shot her a mock-scolding glare. "You can't style your whole life around being the opposite of your mother. Don't you remember how to have fun?"

"I have plenty of fun." Fern walked over to the coffee bar and fidgeted with the cups and napkins that didn't really need straightening. "What do you think I do on my days off?"

"Besides laundry, cleaning, and helping Ivy with the kid? Rent videos and eat ice cream in your pajamas, I bet."

"So what's wrong with that?" She felt herself flushing, irritated at the defensive tone that crept into her voice. The cat, Tilly, stretched, crawled out of her basket, and strolled over to rub against Fern's leg. She bent to give the cat an absent-minded stroke.

"Nothing, if you don't mind living the life of a nun, only without the cloister and the neat black outfits."

"I don't think they allow rocky road ice cream in convents. And I don't have time for a guy, even if I could find one who'd accept Ivy as part of the package." Look who was talking, anyway. Bev spent most of her waking hours at the store.

"Well, you need some kind of company in that apartment. Tilly's going to have her kittens in a couple of weeks. Why don't you take one of them when they get old enough?"

"Come on, you know I can't afford a purebred cat."

"And you know I'm talking gift, not sale."

Though she wouldn't admit the feeling to Bev, a kitten sounded even more tempting than a weekend at the beach. Fern knew she would enjoy a warm bundle of fur on her lap while she watched her Saturday night chick flicks. The last thing she needed, though, was one more living creature dependent on her. The last pet her family had owned, an elderly, gray-striped tomcat, had fallen sick one night while Fern had been babysitting for her little sister, with their mother at a poetry slam in a coffeehouse over an hour from home. With no way to transport the cat to a vet, Fern had phoned her mom to rush home and then helplessly watched his breathing grow more labored and fade into silence. Her mother had walked in the door a few minutes too late.

"Thanks, but I don't want the responsibility. I already have what amounts to a fifty percent share in a baby. I can't handle another one, even if it's not human."

With a despairing headshake, Bev withdrew to the back room for another book crate. For a woman only one year older than Fern herself, she thought, Bev acted like an overprotective aunt.

When the front door jingled again a second later, the man who stalked into the shop didn't act like a customer. He didn't spare a glance for the books. Instead, he marched straight to the counter. Tall and lean, he wore sleek-fitting, black jeans with a short-sleeved, blue polo shirt. Though his long hair, tied back with a leather thong, was entirely silver, his face, pale with a hawk-like profile, showed no signs of old age. Despite his grim expression, he didn't look much more than thirty.

Fern caught herself staring into his eyes, an unusual shade of light brown that looked almost amber in the shop's overhead lighting. She swallowed and forced out the words, "May I help you?"

"I'm looking for a woman." He pulled out a wallet and flipped it open. Glancing down, Fern saw a private detective's license. She blinked, trying to focus on the details, but he snapped it shut before she could even make out the man's name. "I need to speak to Ivy MacGregor. Have you seen her today?"

The abrupt tone of the question put her on guard. "Yes, as a matter of fact, she was here earlier this afternoon." His cold gaze induced a slight wariness that kept her from volunteering her relationship to Ivy.

"Do you know where she might be now?"

"Not a clue." Fern felt sure her attempt at a cheerfully casual reply fell flat. He would probably pounce on her lie like Tilly on a wind-up mouse.

"Then perhaps you know where she lives." Though relentless in its persistence, his voice was almost a pleasure to listen to, like the pealing of a bell.

Fern shook her head to dispel the ridiculous image. He sounded like any other man with a melodious tenor voice. "I can't tell you that."

"But do you know?" His tone shifted from inquisitorial demand to smooth persuasion. "If so, it's important that you tell me. I must find her. I need to give her a warning." He leaned on the counter, capturing her gaze again. The music of his voice made her feel as if her head were floating a few inches above her body.

"About what?"

"She is being pursued by a man who intends to lay claim to her child. He's a relative of Adair Hunter."

The name broke the trance Fern was drifting into. She dragged her eyes away from the detective's. "What do you know about Adair?"

"That he has disappeared and that his family wants the boy. They've sent someone to kidnap him. You must help me warn Miss MacGregor before it's too late." He leaned still farther over the counter, until it almost seemed he meant to grab her.

The echo of Ivy's claim that Baird was in danger knocked the breath out of Fern. Her fingers crept to the necklace her sister had insisted she wear. She drew the chain out of her blouse and nervously twirled the Celtic cross. "I can't help you." Her voice sounded thin and shaky to her, with none of the determination she wanted to project.

The man straightened up and took a step back. "All right. I'll return and talk with you tomorrow, if I don't find her before then. If you are her friend, I'm confident you'll reconsider your...reticence." He wheeled around and walked briskly out of the store.

Bev emerged from the back room and stepped up to the counter beside Fern. "What on earth was all that about?"

Fern shook her head. "Says he's looking for Ivy. Strange detective, come to think of it. If he's that anxious to get in touch with her, why didn't he give me a card with his number in case I reconsider, as he put it?"

"I heard him mention warning her."

"Yeah, well, I can do that, and for all I know, he's what she needs warning about." After that cryptic conversation, Ivy's premonition sounded a little more plausible.

Fern pushed the thought aside. Getting sucked into that kind of nonsense would turn her into a nervous wreck like Ivy, not to mention distracting her from her concrete goals. An aspiring businesswoman couldn't waste time on occult woo-woo stuff. She dialed Ivy's cell phone and got no answer. After leaving a message, she tried her sister's apartment phone, with the same result. With a sigh, she recorded another message and hung up.

"I'm sure it's nothing to worry about," Bev said. "She's probably on her way home."

"Who says I'm worrying?"

"Don't try to kid me, hon. You've made a second career out of worrying about her." To Fern's relief, they had to drop the conversation when a flock of teenagers wandered in to buy mocha lattes. After a pause to pet the cat, they headed down the street toward a nearby music shop, leaving the bookstore, it seemed, even quieter than before they'd come. Fern dialed both of Ivy's numbers again. Still no answer. "Why doesn't she turn her cell on?" she grumbled.

A few minutes later, while restocking a rack of brochures about Naval Academy tours, she glanced up at a flicker of movement in the corner of her eye. She caught sight of a man on the sidewalk peering in through the display window. Her chest constricted at the sight of his platinum hair, rippling almost to his shoulders. She dropped the pamphlets she was holding and rushed to fling open the door. "Adair!"

The man whirled around to stare back at her. Anger welled up like bile in her throat. She charged at him with clenched fists. "What's the idea of vanishing off the face of the earth like that? You've got a newborn baby who needs you, not to mention the woman you claimed you loved!"

He grabbed her forearms to fend her off. From her modest five-foot-five height, she tilted her head to gaze up at him. Eyes of a deep moss-green snared hers. But they held a cold determination she'd never seen in Adair's.

Realization hit her like a punch to the head. She pressed her hand to her chest, where her heart thudded frantically against her breastbone. "No. I'm sorry. You're not him. But you look so much like him." This man had the same greyhound-slim, graceful build as Adair and the same chill beauty, like a marble sculpture, but the bleak lines of his face suggested a harsher outlook on the world. He wore a long-sleeved, loose shirt that looked too warm for midsummer, with sleekly fitting trousers of the same smoky gray material.

When he let go of her arms, she stumbled. He clutched her elbow to steady her, and a shock like static electricity sparked on her bare skin. "My name is Kieran," he said. "We have met before."

Freeing her arm from his clasp, she said, "Oh, right, that one time at Ivy and Adair's place."

He nodded. "You're Ivy's sister, yes?"

"Fern MacGregor. Yeah, I know, Fern and Ivy. What can I say? Our mother was a late-blooming flower child." He arched his eyebrows in apparent bewilderment. She let the implied question pass, not in a mood to discuss twentieth century social movements. "And you're Adair's cousin."

That fact triggered a more detailed memory of their brief meeting. No wonder Kieran's hawk-like profile looked familiar. Though short, that encounter had been memorable. "We all had lunch together, and then you dragged him out back for a shouting match."

The visit had occurred in September, early in Ivy's pregnancy. They'd shared a simple meal of homemade vegetable soup, fruit salad, and whole-grain bread. Before lunch, with Ivy and Adair busy in the kitchen, leaving Fern and Kieran together on the tiny, fenced patio, she'd tried to start a conversation with him. He hadn't volunteered any information about himself, but the two of them had agreed on how frustrating their younger relatives' carefree lifestyle could be. "Adair does not seem to grasp the seriousness of his family responsibilities," Kieran had complained.

Fern had sympathized, with the comment that Ivy and Adair made a perfect match that way. "She's always been a little out there."

"Out where?" His voice held a faint accent, nothing she could identify, only a hint that English wasn't his first language.

"Someplace I've never visited," she'd said with a wry laugh, "but I guess it's wherever Adair comes from."

Only after lunch had the pleasant atmosphere deteriorated into a fight between the cousins. Fern and Ivy had sipped iced tea at the kitchen table in silence, while the argument raged outside on the patio in a foreign tongue Fern hadn't recognized.

At the time, she'd appreciated Kieran's exotic good looks in a purely aesthetic way, of course. She'd enjoyed watching his long, graceful fingers peel and chop the apples, pears, and peaches Ivy had assigned the two of them to cut up for the salad. When he'd licked peach juice off his fingers, she had let her thoughts stray into fantasies of how those hands and lips would feel on her skin. She wouldn't have considered replacing fantasy with action. She had goals that left no time for pursuing any male, especially one she hardly knew, no matter how gorgeous. In fact, she'd thought Kieran's maturity made him even more attractive than Adair, who she couldn't deny was the most beautiful man she'd ever met up to that point, even if he had seduced her sister off the straight and narrow path. She had actually started to like Kieran, until she'd overheard that fight on the patio and Ivy had later translated the gist of it for her.

She still appreciated his physical attributes, but this was no time to goggle at a luscious man. She wanted to know what he'd come here for and why his cousin hadn't shown up. "You do know Adair disappeared before Ivy had the baby?"

In a cool, cautious tone, he said, "Yes, and that is part of why I need to speak to Ivy as soon as possible."

"If you know where he is and why he left, she deserves to be told." His expression turned still more remote. "Where can we discuss this?"

"What's to discuss? Right here is fine with me." She waved toward a bench on the sidewalk in front of the shop in the shade of a crepe myrtle tree. She took a seat, and as soon as Kieran joined her, she said, "Okay, what's the story?"

"I need to speak to your sister as soon as possible. I thought I might find her here."

"What made you think that?" Fern wondered how he even knew where she worked. "As you can see, Ivy isn't here. She's probably home by now."

"Then I had better look for her there."

"Are you going to tell me what this is all about or not? Where the heck is Adair?"

His mouth tightened to a grim line. "I'm sorry, I believe Ivy has the right to hear that news first. As for the other reason I've come, it is on account of her child. He is in danger."

Her breath caught in her throat. Counting Ivy's premonition, this warning made three in one day. "From whom?" she asked.

"That is connected to what happened to Adair." He stood up. "I'm going to your sister's home. If you see her before I do, please give her my message."

What message? I've met more informative clams. Instead of voicing that protest aloud, Fern limited herself to a cautious nod. The detective, if he really was one, had warned her against one of Adair's relatives trying to snatch the baby, and here a relative had shown up a few minutes later. Until she found out which if those men, if either, she could trust, she'd better volunteer as little as possible. She wouldn't mention the first visitor to Kieran, much less bring up Ivy's dire predictions. Why let him know she had a crazy sister? He might pigeonhole Fern as nuts, too. Even though she didn't expect to have much future contact with him, she didn't want to leave a negative impression with the first man who'd made her pulse flutter in months, if not years. It was just a matter of pride, not like she had any reason to care what he thought of her.

He said a curt goodbye and walked up the street toward downtown. No car, then. Maybe he'd arrived in a cab. When she reentered the store, Bev said, "Who's the hunk? Have you been holding out on me, girlfriend?"

An annoying blush warmed Fern's cheeks. "I wouldn't exactly call him that," she mumbled. "He's Adair's cousin. This is only the second time we've met." She phoned both of Ivy's numbers again and still got no answer. Hanging up, she said to Bev, "Ivy needs to know those guys are looking for her. Why isn't she answering? She's had more than enough time to drop off Baird and get home."

"Listen, if you have a feeling she's in trouble, you'd better check on her."

"I don't have those kinds of feelings. That's Ivy's thing, not mine." She couldn't let her friend and employer get the idea that she based her actions on gut instincts instead of rational thought.

"Still, you should go to her place and make sure she's okay." Bev held up a hand to ward off the protest Fern started to make. "We're not exactly overrun with business here. Go on, I'll see you tomorrow."

Fern let out her breath in a long sigh and stooped to retrieve her purse from under the counter. The heavy necklace thumped against her chest, bothering her, so she took it off and stuffed it into her bag. The humid heat of the afternoon settled onto her skin the minute she stepped out the door. In her car, she switched on the cranky air conditioner and waited for it to do its feeble best to relieve her discomfort. Her thoughts churned with anxiety. Little as she wanted to grant any validity to Ivy's foreshadowing of disaster, she had to admit that if two other people claimed Baird was in danger, the warnings might have some basis in truth. Which one of the two should she be watching out for? The alleged detective who hadn't offered his name? Or a close relative of a man who'd deserted his pregnant girlfriend?

Shoving these speculations to the back of her mind, Fern pulled her compact car away from the curb, made a U-turn at the corner, and headed for the historic district. She followed the narrow road between the high, gray walls of the Naval Academy campus on one side and the red brick buildings of St. John's College on the other, then inched around the traffic circle next to the city dock, with its upscale shops and million-dollar boats. Ivy lived only five minutes away in Eastport, across Spa Creek from downtown Annapolis. Fortunately, when Fern approached the creek, clogged with sailboats as usual in summer, the low drawbridge didn't open. That delay would have thrown her into screaming hysterics.

She drove a few blocks in the light midday traffic, through shady streets lined with respectable but faded-looking houses built between the World Wars, to the almost-new townhouse complex where Ivy rented a two-bedroom apartment. The car's erratic cooling system had barely cranked up to speed by that time. A sheen of sweat coated Fern's arms and forehead when she parked in front of her sister's unit. Ivy's shabby, blue sedan with the baby seat in the back sat in its usual spot. Fern strode up to the door and rang the bell. No sound came from inside.

A movement in the corner of her eye made her jump. Wheeling around, she found Kieran at her elbow. "Don't sneak up on me that way. What are you doing here?"

"Looking for Ivy, as I told you." He wore tight-fitting gloves of thin, supple leather or kidskin, a strange accessory on a summer afternoon.

"You just got here? You haven't seen her yet?" He shook his head.

When he didn't volunteer any further information, she turned away from him, opened the screen door, and knocked on the wooden panel. Still nothing. She tried the knob. Although expecting to need her key, she found the door unlocked. The air conditioning, set low enough to generate exorbitant electric bills, made a shiver course over her bare arms when she stepped inside. "Ivy? You home?"

Kieran followed her into the apartment. She pretended to ignore him.

She hurried through the deserted living room to the kitchen. Nobody there. The silence pressed on her like a hundred-pound weight. She checked the downstairs half bath, then rushed through the living room and up the stairs, with Kieran right behind her. Bathroom, empty. Baby's room the same, of course. Her heart raced with mounting anxiety. *Something's wrong, terribly wrong. Ivy's prediction is coming true.* Fern squashed that thought like a spider. These feelings of impending catastrophe weren't real. She couldn't let them control her actions.

When she reached the open door of Ivy's bedroom, she discovered her sister sprawled on her back, with arms and legs flung at awkward angles, eyes shut, and her long hair fanned out behind her head. Oddly, a wrench lay beside her right hand, as if she'd dropped it when she had fallen.

God, no, not again! An all-too-vivid memory flashed into her mind--the image of her grandmother lying on the kitchen floor in almost the same position. At the age of sixteen, Fern had rushed home from school, a weight of imagined doom crushing her chest, to find that what she'd "imagined" was horribly true. Her grandmother had never regained consciousness, and Fern and Ivy had lost their last real home.

Collapsing to her knees, Fern groped for a pulse at Ivy's neck and wrist. No pulse, no breath, and in the artificially chilled room, the flesh held little warmth. She swallowed the scream that tried to burst from her throat. Instead, she picked up the bedside phone and dialed 911, gave the operator the information, and left the phone, with the line still open, on the bed. She glanced up at Kieran, who stood in the doorway with his face frozen in a stunned stare. *Why doesn't he do something?* She dismissed him from her thoughts and focused on her sister. She straddled Ivy's body and started CPR, but the intuition she'd always tried to deny told her there was no hope. Still, with tears trickling down her cheeks, she kept pumping until she heard the wail of a siren, and a minute later two uniformed men clattered into the room. When she stood up to meet them, Kieran was gone.

Chapter Two

Over an hour after following the ambulance to the hospital, Fern finished the clipboard full of paperwork, left the emergency room, and rode the elevator to the parking garage. Her head reeled as she belted herself into the driver's seat of her car. Dead on arrival, most likely from a stroke, the ER doctor had said. What healthy twenty-four-year-old woman had a stroke? An autopsy, required after an unexpected death, would reveal more, but the doctor seemed sure a sudden cerebral hemorrhage had killed Ivy. A freakish accident. Fern closed her eyes and tried to make the buzzing in her brain shut up. For her own safety, she probably shouldn't confront traffic in this condition. But she had to get Baird from the day care center. She was the only one he had now.

Oh, God, he's all I have, too. Tears stung her eyes, and she felt her face crumple. She bowed her head on the steering wheel and yielded to loud, throat-rasping sobs.

She didn't allow them to continue for long. Wiping her face with a handful of tissues, she put her sunglasses on and started the ignition. Since she didn't trust herself to merge onto the freeway for the couple of exits between the hospital and Eastport, she drove the surface streets. She reached the church that housed the day care in less than fifteen minutes.

The staff had her name on file as authorized to pick up Baird, and she'd installed a baby seat in her own car when she'd bought one for Ivy, so the mechanics of collecting him and his bundle of supplies went as smoothly as ever. When Fern slung the heavy diaper bag over one shoulder and lifted the baby to the other, he rubbed his face on her shirt with muted snuffling noises and clutched her sleeve. She had to swallow a lump to keep tears from her eyes.

The middle-aged black lady who'd handed him over said, "Are you okay, hon?" Fern just nodded. At the moment she didn't feel up to explaining that her two-month-old nephew was now an orphan.

Or so she assumed, she reminded herself while buckling him into the car seat. His father had simply disappeared five months previously. From the beginning Ivy had sworn Adair must be dead, for she insisted he wouldn't have deserted her. Most of the time Fern had kept her doubts on that subject to herself. If Ivy didn't want to believe her lover could behave the same as their own long-gone father, Fern didn't care to waste energy arguing the point.

She considered stopping by her sister's place to gather extra diapers and formula, but Ivy's warning leaped to mind. *He isn't safe at home,* she'd insisted. The voice of reason asked what danger could possibly threaten him. The townhouse had shown no signs of an intruder, and the doctor had sworn Ivy had died of natural causes. Still, Fern's infuriating intuition prodded her to follow her sister's advice. She rationalized that she had enough baby gear to last overnight, and anyway she didn't want to face the empty apartment right now. She wasn't about to admit that a sense of urgency, as if an invisible follower watched the car, pressed her to hurry home.

By the time she pulled into her driveway, Baird was asleep in the backward-facing car seat. He must have filled up on a bottle at the day care. *Nothing but bottles for you from now on, poor little guy.* He only stirred and whimpered when she unfastened the belt. Cradling him in the crook of one arm while dangling her purse and the larger bag from the other, she paused under the tree to gaze down at him. In coloring he looked exactly like Adair, with no visible trace of his mother's genes. He had platinum hair, almost white, instead of Ivy's flame-red or Fern's dark auburn. Of course, babies' hair often darkened later, but his milk-pale skin, again unlike his mother's and her ruddy complexion, suggested otherwise in his case. Instead of the blue-gray eye color Fern and Ivy had shared, or the midnight blue typical of white newborns, he had green eyes like his missing dad's and Kieran's. Not hazel, but true moss-green, a color Fern had never seen on anyone outside Adair's family.

Enough woolgathering. She wanted to get him out of the heat and settled before he woke up. While she walked down the slope of the yard to the side basement entrance and rooted in her purse for the key, again that sense of an unseen watcher made the back of her neck prickle. She felt clammy sweat there even though her pixie-cut hair left the nape exposed to what little breeze there was. She turned the knob and nudged the door open with her hip.

Cool fingers grazed her elbow.

Stifling a shriek, she whirled around. A slender man towered over her. Kieran again. Baird blinked and made squeaky pre-crying sounds. She hugged him closer to her breast and rocked, fixing her gaze on the man.

Kieran glanced around, then down at the baby. "Can we go inside? The child is not safe out here."

"What are you talking about? Ivy said something like that, too. If you're just going to come out with cryptic warnings again, why should I listen to you?" How did she know the threat didn't come from Kieran himself? If he made a hostile move, she couldn't fend him off, protect the baby, and dig out her cell phone to call for help at the same time.

He cast another glance over his shoulder, as if expecting a tiger to pounce from the shade of the trees. "I'll tell you all I can, once we've taken shelter."

Without quite realizing she'd stepped over the threshold, Fern found herself in the living room. Kieran entered right behind her, closed the door, and locked it.

"So this is Adair's son." He peeled off his right glove and fingered Baird's silken hair. The baby stirred and nuzzled Fern's breast. "I can see his father in him."

The gesture brought Kieran so close she could feel his breath on her hair. Shivering, she stepped back. "I don't want him to wake up," she whispered. "I'd better put him to bed." She headed down the short hall with the bathroom at the end and one bedroom on each side. The smaller one, which she used as an office, had a portable bassinet in the corner by her desk. She laid the baby on his back. His eyelids fluttered but instantly closed again.

When she straightened, she found Kieran hovering behind her. He'd taken off both gloves and apparently stashed them in a pocket. The alarmed leap of her heart angered her. "What do you want?" she said in a fierce whisper. She tiptoed into the hall and closed the door.

He followed her to the living room. "I'm trying to help you protect the boy."

"Why should I listen to you? You're the one who tried to talk Adair into leaving Ivy. She told me that last fall, after the fight you had." She glared at him. "Guess he finally decided to take your advice."

"Not exactly. I was trying to persuade my cousin to return to his parents. He refused to leave your sister because she was expecting a child. He could have brought her with him if he'd chosen to return home. He would not consider it."

Fern stared at the man, trying to penetrate his cool gaze. "So where's home? And what happened to him?"

"He's dead. Murdered." He showed no sign of noticing Fern's gasp of shock. "We have no time for this. Adair's killer is searching for the child at this moment. He killed your sister."

She collapsed into the nearest chair with her hands pressed to her temples. Her head felt about to explode. "Nobody killed her. She had a stroke. Just a once-in-a-million brain hemorrhage."

"Yes, it would appear that way at first glance. A healer might mistake it for bleeding inside the skull." Kieran paced over to the window and peered around the edge of the drapes.

Fern couldn't imagine what he expected to see, since that window showed nothing but the house's small, shady side yard and the wall of the house next door. "Are you saying this mysterious person murdered Ivy some way that made it look like she had a stroke? I don't believe it."

He strode toward her, shaking his head as if in despair at her obtuseness. "Didn't you say your sister mentioned a danger to her child? Why do you have difficulty believing she was attacked?"

"Oh, God, I tried to tell myself she had some kind of post-childbirth paranoia." Fern's brain whirled in confusion. "I still think it might be something like that, considering the stroke diagnosis. If she had brain damage, she could have been imagining things when she talked to me this afternoon. The house didn't show any signs of a break-in. And why would anybody want to kill her or Baird? It's all too far- fetched." *But what about that other man who came to the store?* a persistent voice whispered in her head.

"That reminds me, how did Baird survive?"

"She'd left him at the church day care center she uses. She asked me to pick him up and bring him home with me."

"Of course, she would have known a holy place would offer some protection. She must have also known he would be safer here than at her home." He started pacing again, as if he might explode otherwise.

"Here? Why?"

"This town is surrounded on three sides by running water." He made the comment as offhandedly as if referring to the excellence of the local police force. "Enough questions. I've come to take the child where he will be truly safe."

"Hold it right there." She jumped to her feet. "You're not taking Baird anyplace."

"I intend to deliver him to Adair's father, who can protect him. You can't."

She dashed to the entrance of the hallway and stood in the gap, arms folded. "You're crazier than you look, if you think I'll hand over my nephew to a man I don't even know."

He closed the space between them in a couple of long strides and stared down at her. His green eyes turned icy. "You doubt that I am Adair's cousin?"

"No, of course not, and I don't doubt you mean well." As irrational as it seemed to trust her intuition in a crisis like this, she felt Kieran sincerely had Baird's welfare at heart. "That doesn't give you the right to snatch an orphaned baby and run off with him, even if he is your second cousin or whatever. Now that Ivy's dead, he belongs to me. He knows me."

"He will learn to know and care for his father's kin quickly enough."

A new fear pierced Fern. Suppose Adair's parents sued for custody? If they had money to hire a hot-shot lawyer, they might convince the authorities they could give Baird a better home than she could.

"You never even answered my question about where home is." Her breathing turned shallow and erratic. Kieran loomed over her. She stood her ground, even though she knew he could pick her up and lift her out of his path if he felt like it. She caught a whiff of his breath, an aroma like nutmeg and cloves.

"You'd better not know exactly where, in case the assassin finds and questions you."

"I'm still not sure I believe in your assassin. Why am I arguing with you, anyway? You're not taking Baird. If you're so insistent that Ivy was murdered, I'll report it to the police."

"And what will you tell them?" He made no move to push her aside and invade the bedroom, but he didn't back off, either.

Fern's shoulders sagged. "Good point, when I don't know a thing except vague warnings. After the autopsy, if there's any indication Ivy's death wasn't natural, the police will get involved. I know they won't listen if I call them before then." She clenched her fists, hating this sense of being cornered and helpless. She reached out to brace her palms against the walls on either side. "Unless your mysterious killer shows up first. Meanwhile, I'm half tempted to call the authorities to get rid of you."

He said with a humorless smile, "You may try. Your determination to protect Adair's son is admirable." He skimmed her jawline with one long finger. She shivered and flinched from his touch. The smile vanished. "But if you wait for the killer to appear, it will be too late. I must take Baird away from this house before the enemy finds it. After all, I did."

"Yeah, come to think of it, how did you? Did you follow me from Ivy's?" She remembered that creepy sensation of a watcher. Kieran or the phantom enemy? "Damn it, have you been stalking--" She didn't realize she'd raised her voice until the baby's wail cut her off. "Now you've gone and woken him up." She turned and rushed to the office, close to tears from confusion and frustration.

When she leaned over the bassinet, Kieran caught up with her. "I woke him? You were shouting, I believe." His voice actually held a trace of humor.

"Well, you made me do it." She picked up Baird, who waved his arms and legs. The crying subsided to hiccups. She bounced him in her arms. "He needs changing and feeding. Stop crowding me." To her mild surprise, Kieran stepped out of the way. She took a disposable diaper from a box on top of a file cabinet and laid the baby on a blanket on her desk in the narrow space next to the computer. He would soon grow too big to fit there, she reflected. Suddenly, the full awareness of the job she'd taken on rushed over her. For at least eighteen years, longer if her experience as Ivy's big sister was any guide, she'd have sole responsibility for this little boy's welfare. Shaking off the weight of that thought, she changed Baird's diaper in a brisk rhythm that had already become familiar.

Kieran watched from a safe distance. "He appears healthy."

"Of course he is." Fern snapped up the legs of the baby's one-piece sleep suit. "And I'll make sure he stays that way." She draped a receiving blanket over her left shoulder, hoisted him up, and held him there with one hand while she picked up a bottle of pre-mixed formula with the other, unscrewed the cap, and attached a nipple. She carried baby and bottle to the kitchenette, where she zapped the milk for a few seconds in the microwave, then shook it to distribute the heat evenly.

"What are you doing?" Kieran asked.

"Getting ready to feed him, of course. Don't you know a thing about babies?"

"Very little. But I do know we have no time to waste, so please hurry."

"You expect me to explain that to a two-month-old?" Moving to the living room, she sank into the single armchair, set at an angle to the couch. When she shifted Baird to a reclining position in her arms, he nuzzled her breast and whimpered. An ache settled deep in her chest. Again tears welled in her eyes, and again she blinked them away. To keep him safe, she couldn't let grief distract her. "Sorry, sweetie, you have to settle for this now." She popped the rubber nipple into his mouth.

Kieran, who'd kept shadowing her, leaned against the archway leading to the kitchenette, watching. "He has Adair's eyes." She thought she heard a note of wistfulness in his voice. "How did you learn how to care for an infant so efficiently?"

"Because I don't have any of my own, you mean? I've been helping with Baird since he was born. Ivy and I didn't have any other family. She needed all the help she could get."

After watching the baby suck for another minute or two, Kieran started pacing around the room, glancing out the window and tilting his head as if listening for something. Finally, he said, "How much longer will this take? He cannot stay here."

Fern sighed. "Are you harping on that again? This baby is not going anywhere without me."

Kieran swooped down upon her and grabbed her shoulders. "Haven't you been listening to me? We're talking about this child's life!"

She suppressed a shudder. She wasn't sure whether his firm grip made her stomach churn from fear or an unwelcome stirring of interest. *I can't be attracted to this man. My sister just died.* "I care about him more than you do. That's why I'm not letting him out of my sight."

His face leaned close to hers, the deep green eyes holding hers captive for a few tense seconds. "Very well!" He released her and stood upright, flinging up his hands in a gesture of exasperation. "Come along, then. I have no objection to your company."

"What? Me, drop everything and run away who knows where with you? You've got to be kidding."

His cold stare turned into a frown. "This is no joke."

"I know it isn't." Her head drooped. "Ivy and Adair are really dead."

"Then you believe me about Adair, at least?"

"Yes. I don't know of any reason why you'd lie about that. But as for some shadowy killer stalking a two-month-old baby--"

"He's no shadow. His name is Halwyn. He is also a cousin of Adair's and mine." Kieran's grim tone erased any doubt in her mind about his belief in the threat.

One of Adair's own relatives was trying to wipe out his family? What kind of weird clan had Ivy become involved with? The nipple slipped from Baird's mouth. When Fern tickled his lips with it, trying to coax him to drink the last couple of ounces, he showed no interest. "He must be full." She lifted him to her shoulder and patted him until he burped. "Good boy!"

Meanwhile, Kieran wandered to the front of the room. He circled around the picture window and edged over to the door, with a glass pane covered by a cafe curtain. Peering around the curtain, he tensed. "Look."

Fern tiptoed to his side, careful not to place herself in direct view of the picture window. His apprehension was infecting her. She plucked the curtain aside just enough to peek through the door. From this angle, she could barely see the driveway and a small segment of the front yard. A figure stood at the end of the driveway where it met the sidewalk. A man, she thought, but she could see only a fuzzy silhouette, not a sharp image. She didn't need a clear view, though, to know this must be Halwyn, the supposed killer. She felt the pressure of his stare, although from that position he would be watching the front of the house, not her apartment.

"That's him, isn't it?" she whispered to Kieran.

"Yes. We can't face him in direct combat. It would endanger Baird. I must escape with the child. Now."

"Wouldn't this be a good time to call the cops?"

"He would flee as soon as they approached, to return at some other time when you and the child are vulnerable. And you would have no description to give them, no idea of where they might search for him, true?"

"You would," she retorted, still whispering, as if the man could hear them from his vantage point practically on the street.

"I couldn't give them any information they could use. Halwyn has none of the identity papers your law enforcement relies upon so heavily."

So if Kieran was telling the truth, his family must have come from a foreign country. Adair's last name had been Hunter, but he could have changed it from something more exotic. "Okay, how do you expect to escape with him standing right there?"

"You have a vehicle. If we managed to reach it, Halwyn would be unable to follow, at least for the moment."

"We?"

"I cannot drive," he said. "Even if you were likely to lend me your car, which I doubt. In any case, you've made it clear you won't trust the baby to me. Therefore, we must escape together."

She stared at him. "And where do you plan on going? No, skip that for now. How do you expect to get to the car with him standing there?"

"We'll wait for a distraction." Kieran stepped back from the door. "Gather whatever you need for the baby and prepare to follow my lead."

Shaking her head in bewilderment, Fern carried Baird to the office and laid him in the bassinet. Why was she even listening to this man? She had no doubt of his relationship to Adair, and she was willing to believe, provisionally, that he thought he was doing what was best for Baird. That didn't guarantee Kieran wasn't a complete nut, maybe certifiably paranoid.

On the other hand, the stranger, Halwyn, really was staking out her house, and the creepy feeling that emanated from him affected her very differently from the exasperated confusion that Kieran inspired. Fern had never believed in "the Sight" the way Ivy had, but at a time like this the old "better safe than sorry" principle urged her to listen to her feelings. She cautioned herself not to mention those feelings to Kieran. If he got the idea she was mentally unstable, he would have ammunition for that custody battle she feared.

She tucked a couple of extra outfits into the baby's bag, along with the few bottles of formula she had on hand. While packing, she noticed the sling carrier folded in the bottom of the bag. Good, she might need that. Next to it, she found a glass vial, not much bigger than a bottle of nail polish. A rubber band around it secured a penciled note--: *Use this when you think things aren't what they seem.*

The barely legible scribble suggested the message had been written in a frightened hurry. Fern pulled off the scrap of paper and read the label underneath--*For clear sight.* She shook her head sadly. *Magic eye drops.*

How typical. More New Age drivel. After zipping the tote closed, she stuffed a box of disposable diapers and a couple of bottles of formula into a shopping bag. With both bags looped over her left arm and her purse slung over the other shoulder, she picked up Baird and headed for the living room. He squirmed and smacked his lips without actually waking. Thank goodness he'd been a sound sleeper from birth.

She paused at an end table beside the couch to pick up the phone. Kieran glared at her. "Now what are you doing?"

"What do you think? Calling the police the way any normal person would do."

"I told you that wouldn't work."

"I'm doing it anyway. This is my house, after all." She raised the receiver to her ear and heard no dial tone. She jiggled the cradle, not sure what that procedure was supposed to accomplish, and wasn't surprised when nothing changed. Seething, she rummaged in her purse for her cell phone and punched 911. A recorded voice announced that the call couldn't be completed. She dropped the phone back into the purse and frowned at Kieran, who waited near the door with his arms folded. "Nothing's working."

"Now will you stop wasting time and come along?"

"Okay, just in case that guy's actually as dangerous as you claim." *I'm really doing this,* she thought. *Evacuating my own house on a strange man's word. And he's about the strangest I've ever met.* After snatching up her keys, she passed the shopping bag to him. "Here, carry this. Now what? Is he still out there?"

"Halwyn is not likely to leave as long as you and the child are here. Are you prepared?"

"As I'll ever be." She still wondered where Kieran thought they were going but shelved the question for the moment.

"You aren't wearing the pendant you had in the bookshop."

"It was bugging me. I'm not used to heavy jewelry."

"Wear it now. You need the protection."

"I can't believe you're into that crap, too. What is it supposed to protect me from, vampires?"

His level stare delivered a silent rebuke to her sarcasm. "Please."

"Oh, all right." She dug the necklace out of her purse and put it on.

He opened the door halfway. "Stay behind me, as close as you can manage. Be ready to run."

Fern set the doorknob to lock automatically when closed. Though she didn't like leaving the deadbolt unlocked, she couldn't do anything about that if they had to sprint for the car. The question of when she would see her home again flickered across her mind. She squelched it and concentrated on Kieran. He put on his gloves and slipped through the doorway, while she stuck close to him with the baby hugged to her chest.

The man at the end of the driveway took a couple of strides toward them with his right arm raised. She didn't see a weapon, but she registered the posture as a threat. At the same instant, she recognized the man as the detective who'd questioned her at the shop. If he really was a detective. Credentials could be forged. Kieran had said the other man didn't carry valid "identity papers". Or maybe Halwyn had told the truth and Kieran was lying, except that Halwyn hadn't given her his name, a suspicious detail in itself. She couldn't think of a reason to trust either of them very far. Never mind that she had a good feeling about Kieran and a bad one about Halwyn. She couldn't depend on something as tenuous as instinct in a crisis like this.

Directly in front of her, Kieran waved a hand in the direction of the watching man. From the tree overhanging the driveway, three birds swooped down. They flew straight into Halwyn's face. He flailed at them with both hands. They ignored the blows, flapping and pecking like winged Furies out of a Hitchcock movie.

Fern didn't have long to stare at the attack in stunned disbelief. Kieran reached back to grab her wrist. "Now!"

They dashed for the car. Halwyn reached into a side pocket, raised his right hand to shoulder level. He pointed an object at Kieran. Some kind of gun? She couldn't get a good look at it. A spark flared from the end of the thing. At the same instant, one of the birds dove at Halwyn, pecked his wrist, and veered off. Kieran dodged sideways, jerking Fern with him. She staggered and just managed to keep on her feet. A squirrel darted from the base of a tree near the sidewalk and ran between Halwyn's legs. He tripped and fell but immediately levered himself up on hands and knees.

Before he could stand, Fern and Kieran reached the car. She scrambled into the driver's seat, while he got into the passenger side. As soon as he closed his door, she punched the lock button. After flinging the bags into the back, she buckled Baird into his car seat behind Kieran, who twisted around to watch her. "What are you waiting for, woman? Go!"

"And have him fall out and break his neck? There, it's done." The shaking of her hands matched the tremor in her shallow, rapid breathing. She jammed the key into the ignition and started the car.

Panic and disbelief spurred her. She pulled onto the street and headed out of the historic district without a coherent thought except to get away from the impossible scene in front of her house. The sudden turn threw Kieran against the door. "Put on your seat belt, for heaven's sake."

"What?" He looked down at the belt as if he'd never seen one before and fumbled with the buckle until he got it fastened.

She glanced in the rearview mirror and saw no sign of Halwyn running after the car. The slow-moving traffic on the narrow street made her want to scream. She forced herself to draw a deep breath and relax her fingers' cramped grip on the steering wheel. "What was that? Some kind of high-tech gun?"

"Of a sort." Kieran stared straight ahead, his voice low and strained. "We can discuss that later. Now we must cross running water."

Waiting for the traffic light at a T intersection across from an enclave of Naval Academy housing, she said, "Why? What does that have to do with anything?"

"Please stop arguing. Trust me for the moment, if you can." He sounded as if he were trying to keep from fainting or vomiting. His right hand clutched the armrest.

"Okay, running water. Sure." Maybe he really was crazy. In the absence of a better plan, though, she decided to humor him for the moment. When the light changed, she turned right, toward the Severn River. A minute later, they crossed the bridge. Rush hour hadn't quite started yet, so the traffic moved smoothly onto the tree-lined highway running north to Severna Park and other towns between Annapolis and Baltimore.

"This is when we park someplace and call the police, right?" Kieran sighed. "And what will they do?"

Fern thought for a second. "Tell us to meet them back at my place to give a statement, I guess."

"By that time, Halwyn will be long gone."

"I wouldn't be surprised if one of my neighbors saw what happened and called the cops already."

"If so, they will find nothing. As I said before, you and the child will be in your home unprotected when he comes for you again. You must not return there."

Chapter Three

"You have a point. The man did shoot at us." And Kieran hadn't physically threatened her so far, a mark in his favor. "All the more reason to report him to the authorities. Hand me my purse."

Kieran did so, with the comment, "It won't do any good."

She dug out her cell and tried 911 again. Still no signal. Silently fuming, she dropped her purse at Kieran's feet and kept driving. They soon passed from the wooded stretch of highway just beyond the bridge to the more congested commercial area of Route Two. She navigated the heavy stop-and-go traffic while pondering what to do next. Kieran had a valid argument for not going home right now, but they could hardly cruise the streets forever. First, she decided, she had to check in with a couple of people. She pulled into the parking lot of a strip mall.

Kieran looked no less pale and strained after she switched off the motor. "What are you doing now?"

"Calling my boss, for one thing, which I should have done already. If I can get the stupid thing to work this time." When she leaned over to retrieve the phone, she glanced back at Baird, whose eyes opened. At the sight of her face, his toothless mouth widened in a smile, and he gurgled a stream of vowel sounds. Forcing a return smile, she patted his stomach and let him grip her finger for a second. "Let go, now. I've got stuff to do." When Kieran turned his head to watch, Baird switched his attention to the man, who looked slightly disconcerted by the baby's curious gaze.

She hit the speed dial number for the bookstore and was puzzled when the phone worked fine. The crisply businesslike voice on the other end mellowed as soon as Bev heard Fern's voice.

"Bev, I have real bad news. I won't be in for a few days. Ivy died this afternoon." Maybe she shouldn't have blurted out that statement, but she couldn't think of a subtle way to work up to it.

"Oh, God, Fern, I'm so sorry. Was she in an accident? Are you okay? What about the baby?"

"He's fine. She was alone, and it wasn't anything like that. The hospital thought she had a stroke." She gulped down the fresh lump that congealed in her throat.

The shock in Bev's voice echoed Fern's own baffled reaction to Ivy's sudden death. After a few more words of sympathy, Bev said, "Of course you should take all the time you need. You haven't had a chance to decide about the--arrangements yet, have you?"

"No. They haven't told me when they'll release the--" She choked back a sob. "The body."

"Well, you call me if you need anything."

After disconnecting, Fern contacted her voice mail to check for messages, in case the hospital had phoned. Nothing. Then she called her landlady, who lived in the top two floors of the house whose lowest level Fern occupied. "Mrs. Perez, did you notice anything strange happening out front in the past half hour or so?"

"I don't think so, hon," said the elderly woman. "Like what?"

"Police? Maybe an accident? I thought I heard a disturbance of some kind just as I drove away a little while ago."

Although that answer sounded lame even to Fern, luckily Mrs. Perez didn't probe for details. "No, not a thing, and I've been home all day."

"Oh. That's good, I guess. Don't worry if I'm not around much this weekend. I've got a family crisis." She didn't feel strong enough to explain Ivy's death all over again.

After she put the phone away, Kieran said, "No one has called the authorities, I take it?"

"No, and that strikes me as really weird. I can't believe not one person saw that."

"You live on a quiet street. Perhaps no one happened to pass by and your neighbors were not home."

"My landlady was, and she didn't notice anything either."

"She might not have looked out the window at that moment." He rubbed his forehead with a gloved hand. "At any rate, do you now accept that contacting your police would do no good at present?"

"I accept that if Halwyn's vanished and nobody saw the fight, there isn't any use calling them unless he attacks again. What I can't understand is why you're so determined to talk me out of it."

Kieran shook his head. "That is too complicated to explain." The weariness in his voice made her feel almost guilty for arguing with him. Almost, but not quite.

"Are you all right? You look awful." Did he suffer from carsickness? That wouldn't surprise her after sitting in heavy traffic in the summer heat, with the car's air conditioner emitting more noise than coolness. Any extra money she earned went toward her savings account, not optional comforts.

"It is nothing," he said with a thin smile. "We have to find shelter and plan our strategy. Now that we've crossed the river, we should be temporarily safe from Halwyn."

What's all this about the river? She didn't ask aloud, knowing he would just evade the question again. "How temporarily?"

"After the energy he expended in attacking us, we can hope he won't find us until tomorrow. We need somewhere to rest."

Kieran certainly looked in need of rest, and Fern craved a few hours of peace, too. "Okay, if I can't take Baird home tonight, what do we do next?" The recent conversation with Bev had triggered a memory of something her friend had said that afternoon. "My boss has a beach cottage on the Eastern Shore. We'll go there." She silently resolved to try the phone again as soon as she had a minute to breathe. Kieran's objections to calling the authorities only sharpened her suspicion. "If I'm going to be away from home overnight, I'll have to get some more supplies. Come to think of it, don't you have a room someplace? Where are you staying?"

"Nowhere. I came directly to your home."

In a taxi, no doubt, since he obviously didn't have a car and had claimed he couldn't drive. "Didn't you bring any luggage?"

He shook his head.

Stranger and stranger. "Most people at least carry an overnight bag when they go on a trip."

"I did not expect to stay long enough to need anything. I expected to take Adair's son home with me at once."

"Why do you keep calling him that, as if Ivy didn't exist? He's her son, too," Fern said.

Kieran turned to face her, lightly touching her bare arm with his gloved fingers. "I know," he said softly. "I respect your sorrow for her death. But my own family must be my first concern."

Avoiding his eyes, she drew away from him. "Yes, I realize your family's in mourning, too, and I can understand why Adair's father would want custody of his grandson. But the situation wouldn't have been any different if Ivy were still alive. You're living in a dream world if you think she would have let you take her baby."

"She knew more about the situation, as you put it, than you do. She would have understood the paramount importance of sending her child to a place of safety. And if she wished to join him there, she would have been welcome."

"Ivy was more impulsive than I'll ever be, but I still can't imagine her packing up and leaving home on a moment's notice to go...where? Never mind, you won't tell me, will you?"

They got back on the road to drive across the Bay Bridge. Rather than asking him to confirm or deny her guesses, since she knew he would reply only with exasperating evasions, she concentrated on the drive to Route 50. Friday was the worst time to travel to the Eastern Shore, with all the summer weekend traffic to Ocean City. She hoped the usual Bay Bridge congestion wouldn't delay them too badly. Fortunately, they wouldn't have to go as far as Ocean City to reach Bev's vacation home. In the backseat, Baird screamed his outrage at being stuck in his car seat for so long. "Hush, sweetie, I know, there's nothing I can do about it." Once they turned onto Route 50, their speed picked up, and the motion and engine noise lulled him to sleep the way they usually did.

He didn't wake when they had to stop at the tollbooth. She noticed how Kieran clenched his fists in his lap when she merged into the lane leading onto the bridge. The running water thing began to make a tenuous kind of sense. He must have a bridge phobia. Lots of people did. The state police offered a regular service of driving cars across the Chesapeake Bay for people who were afraid to do it themselves. It seemed a little farfetched to think the phobia ran in the family and Halwyn suffered from it, too, but at least that idea provided some rationale for Kieran's strategy, not to mention his obvious anxiety. She couldn't really blame people who reacted that way. The first few times she'd driven over the span had made her nervous, too. While the highest point of the bridge gave a beautiful view of the bay, it was also a long way down. She almost felt sorry for him, an emotion she ordered herself not to indulge.

When they reached the other side, he let out a sigh and visibly relaxed.

Immediately after crossing over to Kent Island, they stopped at the Kmart to buy supplies. On the sidewalk in front of the store, Fern detached a shopping cart from its mates with an impatient yank. Kieran's cryptic remarks made her wonder if his and Adair's family had connections to organized crime. Maybe Adair had been in the witness protection program, hiding from the Mob. But if so, why couldn't Kieran produce a decent cover story? Maybe, given his stilted speech, he was an international spy instead. She almost laughed at that notion. While she didn't know much about espionage, she was pretty sure a genuine spy would have better training at fitting into the target culture.

Inside, she asked Kieran to push the cart. He gave it a tentative shove, and one of the front wheels locked. Shaking her head, she jiggled until it came unstuck, then steered the cart straight for him. "You don't go shopping much either, huh?"

"Very seldom."

Since she didn't see any carts equipped with infant seats, she had to carry Baird in the baby sling on her chest. He wiggled in resistance when she stuffed him into it. Kieran cupped his head and whispered a phrase she didn't catch. To her surprise, Baird blinked, smacked his lips, and relaxed into a placid half doze.

When Kieran responded to her questioning look with a bland stare, she decided it would be no use to quiz him. "Okay, baby stuff first." He followed her up and down the aisles, watching her toss diapers, a blanket, more formula, extra rubber nipples, tissues, and wet wipes into the basket. He stared at the shelves as avidly as an anthropologist enjoying his first glimpse of an exotic society. Maybe he came from an impoverished third world country?

Next, she headed for the women's section and bought herself a couple of changes of underwear and an extra T-shirt, followed by a detour a few aisles over to stock up on toiletries. She also bought a cheap gym bag to carry the stuff. "Since you won't let me in on your plan, if you have one," she said, "I figure I'd better prepare for a night or two away from home."

"You know my plan. You rejected it," he said.

"Yeah, forget that one. You'll have to come up with a Plan B. Now, what about you? If you traveled without luggage, you'll need some clothes, right?" "I suppose so."

"Do you have a credit card with you? Or some money?" She hoped she wasn't going to have to lend him the price of a basic outfit.

After a second's hesitation, he put one hand in a side pocket. "Yes, I have money."

"Great. The men's department is over there."

At first he wandered the aisles examining jeans, T-shirts, cargo pants, and running shorts as if he'd never seen such garments before. Deciding she had no desire to give him fashion advice, Fern took over the shopping cart despite the awkwardness of the maneuver and headed for the food department to collect an assortment of nonperishable snacks. It crossed her mind that Kieran might disappear while her back was turned.

She instantly dismissed the thought, though. He was too fixated on taking Baird with him. If by any chance the man did vanish back to wherever he'd come from, she would say "good riddance" and breathe a sigh of relief.

No such luck. He caught up with her at the checkout counter in the front of the store. He carried a bundle of clothes and a gym bag similar to the one she'd picked, so he must have figured out what he needed. Fern checked out with a credit card. Kieran, right behind her in line, paid for his purchases with a handful of twenty-dollar bills. *So he doesn't have a credit card. I know, he's an alien from outer space left stranded by the mother ship.*

She couldn't hold onto the whimsical idea for long. Her thoughts insisted on straying back to Ivy and Adair. Kieran's cousin had been a flesh-and-blood man, one who, as far as Fern could tell, had genuinely loved Ivy. Their love had created Baird, all that was left of either of them, and Fern had no intention of trusting his welfare to anyone but herself. The thought stirred up the sorrow that lurked just below the surface of her mind. She squelched it again. She couldn't take proper care of her nephew if she melted into a puddle of tears every other minute. Instead, she forced herself to focus on practical necessities, such as changing Baird before buckling him into the car seat again.

The stream of traffic heading down the Eastern Shore along Route 50 moved slowly but steadily, the Friday "reach the beach" traffic no worse than usual. Fern's own tension slackened a little when the commercial build-up on Kent Island gave way to open fields and wooded stretches punctuated by off-ramps leading to widely scattered towns.

After several miles of silence, she said, "If I'm going to run all over the state on your say-so, I want a sensible explanation. You claim Halwyn murdered Adair and Ivy. Why? And why on earth would he want to kill their baby?"

Kieran gave her a long stare, as if carefully constructing his reply, before answering, "It's a matter of inheritance."

"Inheritance? Money, you mean?"

"With Adair dead, if Baird also dies, Halwyn will stand next in line as my uncle's heir."

"That must be quite a fortune." She couldn't imagine murdering an innocent baby, let alone a close relative, for anything, not even millions of dollars.

"According to Halwyn, Adair forfeited his birthright by turning his back on the family. Halwyn sees himself as the rightful heir unjustly slighted."

"Does anybody really think that way nowadays? It sounds positively feudal."

Kieran spread his hands in a modified shrug. "It is our custom."

Definitely either a Mob family or the ruling dynasty of an obscure country stuck in the nineteenth century, she decided. "So what about you? You must be in line for the inheritance, too."

He glowered at her. "I don't want it. In any case, Halwyn is older and therefore my uncle's logical next choice."

"So if you know he killed Adair, doesn't your uncle suspect?"

"No, he trusts Halwyn." Bitterness tinged the reply.

"Oh, but not you, is that it?"

He turned toward the side window, his reflection a pale blur on the glass. "I don't want to discuss it." The hard edge in his voice convinced her she'd hit upon the truth.

About two hours after leaving Annapolis, they switched over to Route 333 and soon reached Bev's vacation house, near the small town of Oxford.

A two-bedroom, one-bath cottage with white siding in need of a paint job, it had a pocket-sized yard covered with marsh grass in the front and a stretch of sandy beach in the rear. Bev's great-grandparents had bought it decades before shorefront property became too expensive for anyone but the very affluent. The evening breeze off the bay made a refreshing contrast to the humidity back home. The horizon was turning pink with sunset when Fern pulled into the gravel driveway, switched off the motor, and leaned her forehead on the steering wheel.

"You need rest," Kieran said with surprisingly gentleness. "We should be safe here long enough for you to sleep in tranquility for one night."

"One night?" She lifted her head. "What happens tomorrow? No, don't answer that, not as if you would, anyway. Come on, let's get Baird inside."

She unstrapped the baby, leaving Kieran to carry the bags. She noticed that he paused to draw a deep breath of the sea air. "This is much more pleasant than your cities and highways."

"I can't argue with that," she said. Baird woke up when she transferred him from the car seat to her shoulder but didn't protest beyond a few muffled squeaks. She unlocked the door and walked into the living room and eat-in kitchen, then down the hall to the bedrooms, flicking light switches on the way. "How about opening some windows?" she said over her shoulder as she plopped the baby and her purse down on the bed in the room she usually occupied during her visits, sparely furnished with a double bed, a dresser bought secondhand and refinished, and a single straight-backed chair. She followed her own suggestion, welcoming the salty fragrance of the ocean and the rhythmic sound of the waves into the room.

Baird windmilled his arms and legs, drawing breath for a cry. "Yeah, I know, just a minute," she told him, turning him onto his stomach, placing a multicolored set of plastic keys a few inches away from him, and giving him a pat on the bottom. When Kieran walked in a second later with her bags, she thanked him and said, "Could you watch Baird for a minute? I'll be right back." At some point, she realized, she'd accepted that he had no plans to snatch the baby and steal her car. If he was still determined to take Baird to Adair's father, he wouldn't accomplish it by blatant force.

After a quick trip to the bathroom, she returned to find Kieran seated on the bed, leaning over Baird while the baby, still lying face down, clasped the index finger of his right hand. "He has a strong grip," Kieran said.

"That's what babies do," she said. "I've heard it's instinct, something to do with hanging onto tree limbs or mommy's fur. They outgrow it in a few months." Taking the empty bottom drawer out of the dresser, she set it on the floor and lined it with a clean towel she'd found in the hall linen closet. "Or so the books say. I can't claim to know from personal experience."

"What about your memories of your sister as an infant?"

"Not that clear. I was only six when she was born. It's not like I was old enough to baby-sit right away." Speaking of Ivy made her eyes sting. She forced a brisk tone. "Why don't you change him while I get a bottle ready?"

"Change--"

She suppressed a smile at his dismayed tone. "You watched me. It's not rocket science. You don't even have to worry about sticking him with a pin. There's tape."

He pried his finger loose from Baird's grip. Baird planted both of his palms on the bedspread and shoved like a man doing push-ups. He flipped onto his back. Wide-eyed, he stared at her as if amazed at his own feat.

"Look at that! He rolled over." She could hardly wait to tell Ivy--

Oh, God, I can't believe I forgot for a second! Tears blurred her vision and threatened to overflow this time. She tossed Kieran a disposable diaper from the bag and took out a bottle, which she carried to the kitchen and warmed in the microwave. When the machine beeped, she leaned against the counter and shook the bottle until she managed to choke down her tears.

Back in the bedroom, she found Kieran struggling to hold the side flap of the diaper in place long enough to fasten the sticky tab, while Baird kicked and squirmed. She stood in the doorway watching. If Kieran was so eager to take custody of his little cousin, let him figure out the procedure on his own. Fern smiled briefly at the thought that he probably wouldn't last an hour alone with an infant, much less long enough to get Baird to the family home, wherever that might be.

With the fingers of one hand splayed across the baby's torso, Kieran leaned down and murmured something in the unknown language she'd heard him speak with Adair on that brief visit months before. Baird stopped wiggling and fixed a wide-eyed gaze on Kieran's face. "That's better, little one." Kieran taped both sides of the diaper with brisk efficiency and stood up to drop the wet diaper in the trash can.

"Bravo." Fern saluted him with a light patter of applause. "I knew you could do it." With the bottle in one hand, she stepped toward the bed and held out her arms.

"No harder than binding a boggart," Kieran murmured absently. He picked up the baby in the curve of his elbow as she'd demonstrated earlier. Baird gurgled as if in greeting. "May I feed him while you rest? I assure you I won't disappear into the night with him." He tickled the baby's chin, and the tiny mouth opened.

Silently acknowledging that she wouldn't mind a break, she said, "Sure. It looks like you've cast a spell on him anyway." Baird continued to stare at Kieran as if hypnotized.

"Not a spell, only a meeting of minds."

She showed him how to hold the baby. "Here, make a cradle of your left arm and support his head in your right hand. See, nothing to it." He accepted the bottle from her and inserted it into Baird's mouth, gaping like a baby bird's in a nest. A faint smile played over Kieran's lips when Baird started sucking.

"Be sure to tilt the bottle so the nipple stays filled with milk and he doesn't swallow too much air," she said. Her chest tightened at the sight of her nephew staring into Kieran's eyes while clutching the man's silver-gray shirtsleeve.

Kieran finished feeding the baby. He gurgled and gave both of them a broad smile. She took Baird from Kieran, burped him, and carried him to the padded drawer. Because he didn't look sleepy, she laid him on his stomach with the plastic keys in front of him. He lifted his head, gazed at the bright toy, and stretched his arms out as if eager to grab the keys, if he could just figure out how.

Kieran knelt beside her and reached tentatively toward the baby. His fingers barely grazed Baird's silky, platinum hair. Baird squirmed, twisting his neck around to gaze at Kieran. The tiny mouth opened in a stream of vowels as if the baby wanted to start a conversation with his distant cousin.

"Amazing, how much he looks like Adair."

"Yes, he does," Fern said, though she didn't like conceding any link between her nephew and the people who wanted to steal him from her. "The hair and eyes are just the same. But the shape of his face is more like Ivy's." Ivy herself had always claimed such comparisons were silly, because she thought new babies didn't much resemble any adult. But Fern clung to the belief that she could see her sister in Baird.

"That may change as he grows," Kieran said. He gave the baby a light pat on the back, then pulled away as if afraid of damaging the small body. "If it is any comfort, my cousin truly loved your sister. He would not have forsaken his home and family for her otherwise."

"No, it's not any comfort. If that Halwyn guy did what you claimed, being loved by Adair got her killed." She wiped her eyes with the back of her hand to clear them of unwanted moisture. She had to maintain a strong façade in front of this intruder into her life.

"You need rest," he said. "Why don't you lie down for a bit? I'll stay awake for protection."

Reluctantly nodding in agreement, she turned the baby onto his back and followed Kieran into the living room. She couldn't deny the exhaustion creeping over her like a slowly rising tide. "Just for a few minutes, maybe." She stretched out on the couch, trying to ignore the vulnerability she felt with him sitting a few yards away, his gaze fixed on her. She closed her eyes, not to sleep, only to shut out the world temporarily. Kieran maintained absolute stillness on the other side of the room. Drawing slow, deep breaths, she ordered herself to relax and forget about his presence. He posed no immediate threat. She'd always slept lightly. Even if she dozed off, she would snap awake if he moved.

Kieran gazed at the sleeping woman. The spell he'd murmured under his breath as she closed her eyes had taken rapid effect. Ordinary noises would not wake her. Only some unusual disturbance could break the magical slumber. He rose to his feet and paused to scan her again in the twilight. Sleep softened the stubborn lines around her eyes and mouth. Traces of weariness etched her face. She needed rest, not to mention relief from the burden of caring for her nephew. Of course, she would not see it that way. Her love and anxiety for the boy rang clear in every glance and gesture. Kieran felt a pang of regret for having to separate them. But Baird's life took precedence over Fern's grief.

If possible, Kieran would have avoided the whole conflict to begin with by overriding her will and forcing her to surrender the child. His power, though, did not extend that far. He could bespell unsuspecting strangers to perform such trivial actions as stopping on the highway to give him rides. Forcing a woman already on guard against him to do something that violated her deepest wishes was a different matter. So he had placed her in enchanted sleep to give him time to escape with the infant.

First of all, he took a moment to set wards around the doors and windows of the house to alert him if the enemy approached. Halwyn might find their trail again anytime. As soon as Kieran began casting the spell, he breathed easier. If for any reason he wasn't able to flee with the child as he planned, at least Baird would not stay completely unprotected. An errant thought drifted across his mind. He couldn't help admiring Fern's devotion to the baby. Not only that, he had enjoyed her company the first time they'd met, in less dire circumstances. Her tart appraisal of the two "young people" had amused him, considering that compared to both Adair and himself, Fern, like Ivy, seemed as young as a freshly hatched chick.

He glanced at Fern again on his way to the bedrooms. While he understood Adair's attraction to a woman with Ivy's joy in music and enchantment, Kieran found himself intrigued by the tangy sharpness of a female who insisted on staying firmly rooted in the earth she knew. Suppose he offered her the chance to join her nephew in the Hollow Hills? Would she accept? He silently laughed at himself. With her aversion to all things she considered irrational, she would doubtless run screaming from any such proposal, if he could make her believe in the elven realm at all.

Nor did he want the responsibility for a human pet, which was how his kin would see her. Dismissing the absurd notion, he finished casting the wards.

When he walked into the bedroom, he noticed the baby lying awake, silently gazing up at him. Doubtless Baird had sensed the currents of magic in the atmosphere. *He is truly his father's son.* Kieran leaned over the makeshift crib and reached for the baby. "Come, little one," he whispered in his native language. "It's time for you to go home."

He picked up Baird and started for the living room. At the threshold, when he touched the deadbolt on the front door, Baird squirmed. When Kieran unfastened the bolt and turned the doorknob, the baby cried. Kieran cursed under his breath. The infant's rudimentary psychic sense had already grown keen enough to sound an alarm. He trusted Kieran enough to let himself be picked up, but not carried out of the house without Fern. A kidnapper like Halwyn, who didn't care about the baby's welfare, could override that undeveloped talent and put him into a coma for transport. Kieran, though, couldn't use magical brute force and risk hurting Baird. "Isn't there any way to convince you I'm doing this for your own good?" he whispered.

With a sigh of frustration, he tiptoed away from the door, just as Fern woke.

Chapter Four

A bolt of lightning flashed behind Fern's eyelids. Her eyes snapped open. Violet-blue light dazzled her. She blinked and sat up. The sparks faded, yet a glow remained at the edge of her vision.

She blinked again, and the glow vanished. It must have been the aftereffect of an already forgotten dream. Kieran stood in the middle of the living room holding the baby.

"What do you think you're doing?" She scrambled to sit up and switch on a lamp.

Shifting the baby to his shoulder, he met her eyes calmly. "He started crying, and I didn't want him to wake you. I thought walking him a bit might calm him."

By now Baird's wails had subsided to hiccups. He snuffled against Kieran's shoulder.

"He couldn't be hungry already, so he probably needs a dry diaper. That's always a safe bet." She took the baby and carried him into the bedroom.

Kieran followed her and stood beside the bed, rattling the plastic keys, while she changed Baird, whose hands flailed at the toy in unfocused grabbing gestures. "I didn't realize infants required such frequent attention."

Fern edged away from him, unnerved by the sensation of his breath ruffling her hair. Again she noticed the spicy aroma that hovered around him. "All day and half the night. Liquid goes in one end and out the other. Parents know what they're getting into, or should. I take it you've never had a child? Or even a baby brother or sister?"

He shook his head. "Parents might know what lies ahead and welcome the task. You didn't ask for it, though, did you?"

The question caught her by surprise. Picking up Baird and hugging him hard against her shoulder, she swallowed the lump that clogged her throat. "That doesn't matter. I'll manage. I can rearrange my life all I need to. This baby comes first." She'd hardly had time to think about what that rearrangement would entail. Day care costs, waking up night after night at odd hours, child-proofing the apartment, revising her savings plan to cover the fresh expenses--of course Ivy hadn't carried life insurance. *Never mind, I'll sort out all that later.*

Kieran's long fingers massaged Baird's back. "May I hold him again?"

For a second the question made her suspicious. She silently laughed at herself. If he planned to kidnap the baby, he wouldn't try it this way. The contact with Kieran's cool skin made a stray shiver dance up her arm. She stepped back, concentrating on the baby's face to distract her from the unwanted sensation. His green eyes locked onto Kieran's, the same forest-hued shade. She couldn't doubt their family relationship. Baird opened his mouth in a lopsided grin.

"He likes you," she said. "Of course, babies that age like everybody. They develop the fear of strangers later."

Kieran shifted his eyes from the baby's face to hers. "Indeed? You know a great deal more about infants than I do."

She shrugged. "I read a lot of child care books before he was born. I knew Ivy would need help, after Adair--disappeared."

At the mention of Adair's name, silence dropped between them like a wall of ice. She couldn't help thinking of Kieran's motive for tracking down Baird. "Maybe he'll go back to sleep now. It's worth a try." She carried the baby into the bedroom and settled him in the drawer, massaging his chest with her fingertips until his eyes fluttered shut.

Back in the living room, she found Kieran watching out the window like a sentry on duty. Her pulse leaped. "Any trouble?"

He shook his head. "Perhaps now that all is quiet, we should consider eating. You can't take proper care of him without caring for yourself."

She cautioned herself not to imagine she heard sincere concern in his voice. Nobody except Bev had worried about her welfare in more years than she wanted to recall, and this man she barely knew wasn't likely to be an exception.

"I'm not hungry." As soon as she said the words, she recognized them as untrue. Her stomach felt hollow, even though her throat constricted at the idea of swallowing anything. "I don't even know if there's any food here."

She went into the kitchen and took a rough inventory of supplies. As she'd expected, given the month or more since Bev's last visit here, the pickings were sparse. Only nonperishable items such as crackers and canned soup dotted the cabinet shelves. Finding that her insides didn't rebel at the thought of tomato soup, she heated two bowls in the microwave and set them on the kitchen table with iced ginger ale and a box of saltines.

Kieran, following her example, blew on the spoon before taking a dubious sip of the soup. His frown cleared at the taste. "Not bad, although very far from its natural state."

"Bev can't leave fresh food here for weeks at a time. What you see is what you get, cans and boxes. Would salt help?" She pushed the shaker toward him.

"No, thank you, my body can't accept it." Did he have a blood pressure problem? He looked awfully young for that. Between spoonfuls, he said, "We can't stay here for long."

"I should think not. I have a life, you know."

"Nor can you go home while Halwyn remains on the loose. He will pick up the trail soon enough, so we must find some refuge safer than this."

"Any suggestions? Besides Adair's father's home, that is?"

He sighed. "I wish you would see reason and accept my clan's protection for the boy."

"Baird. Quit talking about him like he's a trophy or something."

"A fitting name. It means 'bard'."

"No wonder Ivy picked it, then. She was so into music. You know she was a singer part-time, don't you? Except she called that her real career. She always thought of the day jobs as just a way to pay the rent." Whenever Ivy's day jobs had failed to cover unexpected expenses that popped up, she hadn't minded falling back on Big Sister Savings and Loan.

He nodded. "Doubtless that gift of music attracted Adair to her."

"Yeah, I wouldn't be surprised. They met at a Renaissance Faire where she was playing."

His eyebrows arched. "What kind of fair?"

"People dress up in costumes and pretend they're living in the sixteenth century. They have plays and minstrels and knights on horseback jousting and lots of booths full of high-priced craft items. Ivy played guitar and performed folk songs under the stage name Jenny Wren. Of course, the Faire circuit wasn't the only singing she did. She worked at local nightclubs and other kinds of festivals, too." Fern sighed. "It didn't seem to bother her that she didn't have a snowball's chance of building up any financial security. She took after our mother that way. A free spirit. Or a flake, depending on how you look at it." Fern suddenly remembered that almost her last words to Ivy had consisted of griping about her sister's cash flow problems. Tears trickled from her eyes. She fumbled for a napkin to dry them.

Kieran leaned forward, his gaze fixed on her. She had never met a man with such intense eyes before. The deep green amplified the effect. "I beg your forgiveness for stirring memories that worsen your grief."

"It's not like anything could worsen it. The only reason I'm not falling apart is that I haven't gotten over the shock yet. I was just thinking about the last time we really talked. We had a dumb argument about money. I was always hassling her about how she should start saving up for emergencies instead of depending on me. Like I didn't want to help my own sister."

"Family is of supreme importance to us, also. As boys, Adair and I were like brothers. I cannot leave his child unprotected."

"Then you should understand how I feel. All I can do for Ivy now is take care of her baby."

After they finished eating, she went into her room to check on Baird. He stirred and whimpered at her approach. She decided to feed him again, hoping a full stomach would keep him content for a few hours. This time she fed him herself, while Kieran patrolled the house like a restless tiger pacing off the dimensions of its cage. He joined her when she took the baby into the bedroom, as if, she thought, he worried that she might grab Baird and disappear while his back was turned.

"Will he sleep now?" Kieran asked.

"For most of the night, I hope. I'll get him into a clean outfit, first." The man's spicy aroma and the baby's powdery scent blended to tickle her nose. She made quick work of peeling off the sleep suit and pulling on a fresh one. Baird drowsed while she snapped up the leg openings. She replaced him in the makeshift bed. "It's a good thing he's not old enough to get upset about sleeping in a strange place." She switched off the overhead light and tiptoed into the corridor with Kieran. "You can use Bev's room across the hall. I left an extra towel and washcloth in the bathroom for you. Just give me a second to get some stuff."

She zipped into Bev's room to borrow a nightgown and robe, then retreated into the bathroom. After shedding the sweat-dampened skirt and blouse she'd worn all day, she had a quick shower and changed into the nightclothes. The lightweight cotton robe covered her from neck to knees, more than any bathing suit would. Why did her pulse flutter at the thought of letting Kieran see her in this dowdy outfit? Why did she think such frivolous thoughts at all, with her sister not dead twenty-four hours yet? She suppressed the twinge of guilt, which could only distract her from the vital task of protecting Baird.

Irritated at herself for blushing like a kid at the thought of Kieran stripping for a bath, she scurried down the hall, relieved not to bump into him. She bundled her dirty clothes with Baird's and tossed them into the combination washer-dryer in a corner of the kitchen. The pipes rattled with water from the shower that Kieran had just turned on. Resolutely ignoring the pictures her mind persisted in painting, she wandered into the kitchen, hungrier for distraction than food. She found the refrigerator empty except for the rest of the ginger ale and an unopened bottle of white wine, but the freezer held a half gallon of rocky road ice cream. Her mouth watered. Well, why not? She could use some comfort food, even if no other kind of comfort was available.

Seated at the kitchen table, she'd just started scooping ice cream into a bowl when Kieran appeared. He had changed into khaki shorts and a T-shirt. She succumbed to the temptation of scanning his bare feet and long legs, then up to his lean torso, hawk-like profile, forest-green eyes, and damp mane of platinum hair. He returned her scrutiny with a steady gaze that sent a shiver through her. She swallowed the inexplicable nervousness and said, "Would you like a snack?"

He stepped to the table and sat opposite her. He gave the ice cream the same quizzical look he'd given the soup. "Yes, I'd like to try some, please."

She felt his eyes on her while she got out another bowl and spoon. "I didn't find any chocolate syrup," she said while dishing out his serving. "We'll just have to rough it."

He spooned up a dollop of the chocolate-nut confection and ventured a taste. His eyes widened in what looked like pleased surprise. "It doesn't seem rough to me. Very smooth, except for the nuts." He swallowed the mouthful, took another, and swirled his tongue around the spoon.

Fern's heartbeat stuttered. She lowered her eyes to her bowl. "That's just an expression. It means, oh, living without luxuries."

"Like this house," he said. "It doesn't appear luxurious, but it offers shelter and comfort. You say it belongs to your employer?"

She nodded. "Beverly, my best friend from college. You saw her this afternoon. She runs that mystery-themed bookstore where I work. She hired me as assistant manager when she opened the place a few years ago. When I can manage to save up enough, I'm going to buy into it as part-owner."

That program would hit a few bumps in the road now, of course, with the expenses of Ivy's funeral and Baird's support. Fern sighed to herself. Having waited this long, she could handle a slight delay. Bev had offered to let her pay in installments, but Fern wanted to own her half of the business free and clear. The fecklessness displayed by Ivy, not to mention their mother, had instilled a habit of caution in her.

"My next project after that will be saving the down payment for a house. I'll need my own place even more now that I have Baird to think of."

"Won't bringing up a child alone present a considerable burden for you?"

"I don't think of it as a burden. There's a saying, 'He ain't heavy, he's my brother.' Well, Baird's my sister's baby. I'll do whatever it takes. Anyway, lots of women manage alone. Our mother did."

"Did your father also die?" *Like Adair?* was the unspoken implication.

"No, he skipped out on us. He and Mom never married. She always said they didn't believe two people needed a piece of paper to validate their love." Fern sighed and stared into her bowl for a second before scraping out the last of the ice cream. "I remember him in flashes from when I was little. He traveled a lot. He was a folk singer, like Ivy, but he made more of a full-time career of it. In fact, her guitar was one of his. That's about all he left us."

"So the musical gift runs in your family."

"Yeah, like flightiness, which Ivy got from both sides. I don't know how I escaped. Our father couldn't handle the idea of two kids, I guess. Right after Ivy's first birthday, he left for the last time."

"Leaving your mother to care for you alone?"

"Oh, he didn't vanish off the face of the earth, not right away. He sent money and short letters now and then. They got fewer and far between and finally stopped. I don't know where he ended up."

"Your mother never tried to find him?" Kieran scooped up the last bit of his own dessert.

Fern caught herself watching his tongue lap the spoon. Hoping her blush didn't show too clearly, she gathered up the bowls to put them in the sink. "No, why would she? She was getting along all right, and tracking him down would have violated her whole free love philosophy."

"That was an interesting food substance," he said, turning in his chair to follow her with his eyes.

"Don't tell me you've never eaten ice cream before."

"It isn't a part of our cuisine."

She leaned back against the sink with her arms folded. "Which cuisine is that?

Where do you come from?"

"A country you're not likely to have heard of."

She shook her head in exasperation. She should have known there'd be no use trying to pry a straight answer out of him. Still restless despite her fatigue, she opened the refrigerator, and her eyes lit on the bottle of Riesling. Well, why not? She took it out and rummaged in a drawer for a corkscrew. "Would you like a drink?"

He nodded. She found a pair of wineglasses and filled one for each of them. "Mom worked a lot of low-paying jobs, like Ivy, so she wouldn't get too distracted from her real calling. She was a poet instead of a musician, or that's how she thought of herself anyway." She drained half of her wine, flashing on a memory of her mother at the dining room table tapping away at a secondhand electric typewriter. "She spent a lot of evenings reading her work at open mike nights in coffee shops, and she had poems published in little magazines, the kind that pay in copies. Try paying the electric bill with copies of a chapbook," she said with a dry laugh.

Kieran took a thoughtful sip of the wine. "Acceptable." He drank a longer swallow, then said, "Our people hold poets and musicians in high regard."

"Ours claim to, but you wouldn't know it from what most of them get paid. Not that Mom wasn't a fun parent when she was home. She had a great time making crafts with us, holiday decorations and stuff like that, and she didn't care how much of a mess it made. She couldn't sew, but she whipped up fantastic Halloween costumes out of boxes and paper and yarn. Like the year she sent Ivy and me out as a pair of dice." Tears threatened to well up. Fern squelched them by finishing her drink and pouring another. "The down side was all the time she spent away from home. She worked irregular hours, because she usually had jobs at restaurants and bars. She liked the flexible schedules and the tips. Meanwhile, as soon as she thought I was old enough, she stopped hiring babysitters and put me in charge of Ivy. I had to learn to cook in self-defense when we got bored with sandwiches, canned soup, and frozen dinners."

"That's why you feel confident of being able to bring up a child."

"Yeah, I've had practice. And after Mom died in a stupid accident driving home from work at two a.m., I figured it was my job to take care of my little sister."

"How old were you then?" He sipped his wine thoughtfully, watching her face as if sincerely interested in her dreary life story.

"I was fourteen, and she was eight. We moved in with Mom's mother in Baltimore. Granddad had died a few years earlier. They'd had Mom when they were already in their forties, so they were pretty old. At least, they seemed ancient to me. I didn't want to cause any trouble for Grandmama, so I buckled down to make good grades in school and tried to keep Ivy out of trouble."

His lips quirked in a slight smile. "Did you succeed?"

"Mostly. She was spacey but never really wild, at least not until she hit college. Grandmama had been dead a few years by then." She knew she was talking more freely than normal, probably because of the wine, but what the heck. After they'd settled the current crisis, she would probably never see this man again.

"Your grandmother died and left the two of you alone?"

"She had a fatal heart attack when I was sixteen. We didn't have any other relatives on Mom's side, and we didn't have any contact with our dad or his family. Ivy and I went to a foster home. Homes, actually. We lived in two before I turned eighteen and moved out on my own to start college." Noticing that her glass was empty again, she refilled it and topped off Kieran's.

"That must have been difficult for you."

"Nobody beat us or fed us gruel like Oliver Twist." His expression of polite but blank attention suggested that Dickens, like ice cream, wasn't part of his background. "But we didn't get awfully attached to our foster parents, either. We still exchange Christmas cards with the last family who had Ivy before she aged out, and that's about it."

"So you felt responsible for your sister."

She nodded. "I wanted to see her make a secure life for herself. It was bad enough when she hooked her college classes and stayed up all night smoking pot." At his puzzled glance, she said, "Marijuana. Thank God she never got arrested. It was just a phase, I guess, because she gave it up. Then she decided she had to drop out of college to become a musician. Couldn't she have finished her degree and performed on the side? And when she moved in with your cousin and got pregnant--" Fern broke off, fumbled in the napkin holder for a napkin, and wiped her eyes with it. "I saw her ending up just like our mother, spending the rest of her life in rented apartments scrambling to make the money outlast the month."

"Adair would not have allowed that to happen."

"Yeah, well, he's not in a position to do anything about it now, is he?" She downed another swig of wine. Her head felt a bit swimmy. *Shouldn't have guzzled that quite so fast, I guess.* "What's your family like? Are your parents still around?"

He shook his head. "They have both passed away."

"Sorry." His expression didn't look particularly sad, just distant, so she speculated they must have died years ago. "At least you've got your uncle, Adair's father, right?"

At that remark, Kieran's face looked more like a marble sculpture than ever. "Not anymore. Since Adair's death, we have become estranged. I'm not welcome in the family home."

She recalled what he'd said earlier about his uncle's trusting Halwyn more than him. "But if you show up with Baird, your uncle might thaw, is that it?"

"Perhaps." He stared at the dark window, avoiding her eyes.

"Well, you'll have to think of some other way to win him over. I lost my sister. I'm not about to lose her son." She stood up, bumping her half empty wineglass. It toppled over and spilled on the table. "Oh, damn."

"It's all right." Kieran grabbed a wad of napkins and sopped up the liquid.

"No, nothing's all right. I shouldn't have drunk all that. How am I supposed to protect Baird this way?" Her eyes blurred with moisture. She started for the hallway and stumbled over a chair.

Kieran leaped up. His arms closed around her. His graceful strength kept her from falling, and her head somehow found itself leaning on his chest. She burrowed her face into his shirt, inhaling his spicy scent. "Don't be afraid," he said. "I'm here to protect him, too."

She had to swallow tears and gulp a deep breath before she could speak. "How can I not be afraid? I'm alone with a baby, and some maniac is trying to kill us, or so you say."

"Hush. You're safe for now." He stroked her hair until she stopped shaking with suppressed tears. She became aware of his arms encircling her and his muscles flexing against her breasts and abdomen. Tendrils of heat coiled in the pit of her stomach. She raised her head to gaze up at him. His eyes locked onto hers. His thumb wiped a trace of wetness from her cheek. The touch of his cool skin sent a shiver through her, followed by a trickle of warmth along her nerves.

I can't be feeling this, not with Ivy dead just a few hours. It doesn't mean anything. It's just an adrenaline reaction on top of ten years of celibacy.

It meant nothing that Kieran was the most beautiful man she'd ever seen, like a Greek statue brought to life, without a single flaw in his pale skin even at this close perspective. Or that, unlike marble, his flesh would feel warm and pliant to her fingertips. It meant nothing that he was bending close to her, his lips grazing her forehead, then her cheek, then nibbling along her jawline to her mouth. She parted her lips in a gasp at the instant his mouth reached hers. His tongue darted at hers, and she tasted his clove-and-nutmeg flavor. First ice, then fire spread from the point where their mouths joined. With one hand he continued to stroke her head, while the other massaged her back in slow spirals. She stretched on her toes and rubbed against him like a cat being petted.

Sudden awareness of a hard ridge pressing against her abdomen shocked her out of the warm haze. Her body's melting response shocked her even worse. *Good grief, what am I doing? Have I lost my mind?* She couldn't afford to melt, not now, maybe not for years.

She placed one hand on Kieran's chest and pushed, or tried to. The strength to shove him away eluded her. His fingers, splayed over the small of her back, kept the lower half of her body molded to his. That embrace anchored her while she closed her eyes and drifted, with trails of heat swirling through her body and pooling in the pit of her stomach. His spicy scent and flavor enveloped her in a warm mist. Behind her closed eyelids, she saw rainbow-hued sparks flashing within the mist.

While his mouth continued to taste hers and his hardness pressed against her, the multicolored fog coalesced into a bright oval standing upright between a pair of towering trees. A man was running toward the glow. Although she saw him only from behind, she recognized Kieran. She felt urgency pounding within him. He charged into the oval of light and vanished.

Her eyes snapped open. Staring up at Kieran, she found him staring at her with a stunned expression that reflected her own shock. When she stepped backward, he didn't try to restrain her. Her mouth opened and closed a couple of times before she could force out, "What was that?"

"What did you see?"

She shook her head. Visions belonged to Ivy's New Age realm, not the practical world Fern lived in. "Nothing worth mentioning. Too much wine, too fast, that's all. I'm falling asleep and dreaming on my feet."

"Fern, listen to me." He reached for her, but she flinched away. "Do you have the Sight?"

"Now you sound like Ivy. She believed in all that woo-woo. I don't." Her head was still reeling. She leaned on the wall and edged away from his touch again. "No more. We shouldn't have done that. I've got to get some sleep now. Goodnight."

"We need to talk about what just happened."

"No, we don't. Nothing happened." Her heart raced with fear of both her own arousal and the scene she had imagined. For a few seconds she had felt as if she were touching his mind, sharing his emotions. Even if she believed in such phenomena, she wouldn't choose to merge her thoughts with those of someone so alien to her formerly safe life.

Or maybe she was going crazy. She wasn't sure which would be worse. She did know that worse than anything would be letting him think she was out of her mind. She couldn't give him any legitimate excuse to claim Baird.

She worked her way to the bedroom with careful steps, to keep from stumbling and giving him a reason to touch her again. He didn't try to restrain her.

Kieran watched Fern disappear in the direction of the bedchambers. His muscles knotted with the effort of remaining still. He could hardly resist seizing her and forcing her to acknowledge what had just transpired. The passion that had sparked between them had awakened her inner vision. That couldn't have happened unless she possessed some inherent power. Adair had sworn Ivy had a portion of wild talent, but Kieran had half suspected that belief had arisen from infatuation. Perhaps Adair had perceived truly after all.

When Fern closed the door of the room she shared with the baby, Kieran considered casting another spell to deepen her sleep. He had tasks that he couldn't risk her interrupting. He decided not to use magic on her this time, though. The wine alone ought to make her sleep soundly. He didn't want her too deep under to awaken if Baird needed attention.

Lingering outside her door to listen for her breathing to sink into the rhythm of sleep, Kieran visualized her lying on the bed, with the nightgown clinging to her lush curves. The women of his own kind, almost as slender as the men, displayed nothing like the soft roundness of a human woman's body. Lovemaking with elven females felt like a leisurely dance with complex choreography and tasted like crisp, chilled cider. A mortal's headstrong passion had a flavor more like heated mead. His body tightened at the memory of Fern's sweet-scented flesh and wine-flavored mouth. He retreated from the closed door and clamped down on his unruly thoughts. Except in moments of weakness like the one she had just suffered, she wouldn't want him, and he had never been in the habit of seducing mortals in dreams as many of his people did. When he enjoyed the lush earthiness of a human woman, he wanted her fully aware of him. Nor was this the time for frivolous dalliance.

Again he entertained the notion of inviting Fern into the Hollow Hills. He imagined her lying in his bower, nibbling fruit from his hand, with juice trickling down her chin and over her breasts for him to lick off. *Stop that,* he chastised himself. Yet that choice would solve both their problems, ensuring Baird's safety without parting him from the only kin he knew or breaking her heart by depriving her of her sister's child. Kieran shook his head ruefully. His craving for her ripe body must be clouding his mind. What kind of life would a woman who so fiercely insisted on her independence have in the elven kingdom? Adair had wisely decided not to transport Ivy through the gate between worlds, and she would have adjusted to the change better than her sister possibly could.

Kieran walked out through the kitchen to the rear deck of the cottage. A short flight of wooden stairs descended to the beach. The sand felt cool on his bare feet. At this hour, traffic on the nearby roads had subsided to an occasional passing vehicle, their engines a background roar easily ignored, their machine odors overshadowed by the salty aroma of the bay. The stars of this strange world glinted overhead. He allowed himself a moment to savor their serene, distant glow. Shaking off the reverie that tempted him to relax into a waking dream, he strolled to the tide line, watching moonlight glint on the surf. His realm had no oceans, so the advancing and receding waves fascinated him. While crossing water caused him discomfort, he could still enjoy the beauty of it from the shore. It provided a practical advantage, too, one direction he didn't need to guard against Halwyn's attack. He knew his renegade kinsman would eventually pick up their trail and cross the bay in search of them. The confusion generated by tidal waters would cloud his perception for only a limited time.

Kieran clenched his fists and muttered a curse under his breath. If only Fern weren't so obstinate, he could have carried Baird through the portal to safety by now.

The woman had protection of a sort, but the iron cross would, at best, only hide her from the enemy's magical perception. In direct combat, she wouldn't last more than a minute, especially when she had no idea of what she was facing. How could he persuade her to yield the baby to his protection without telling her the truth about himself? Even if he did reveal his true nature, would she believe him? Probably not without a visible demonstration of his powers, which might frighten her into fleeing from him or perhaps make her think she had gone mad.

On the other hand, Ivy had accepted the truth about Adair. Would her sister be so different? A ridiculous question, as he'd already recognized. In their short acquaintance, Fern had made her differences from Ivy more than clear.

Enough. He'd come out here to set wards, not engage in futile arguments with himself. The invisible barrier he could build would delay Halwyn a minute or two at most, but it would warn Kieran, awake or asleep, of the enemy's approach, and he would feel more comfortable with the whole area, not just the house, fortified. He strode along the beach to the approximate boundary of the cottage's land and crouched at the water's edge, trailing his fingers in the foam. When he raised his hand and whispered a phrase in his own language, a spark of green light flashed in the air. He smiled. Despite the suffocating omnipresence of iron and its alloys, this world still possessed remnants of magic. He stood, chanted the spell of warding under his breath, and paced up the beach to the road, tracing runes of protection in the air with each step. Ghostly outlines of the symbols in violet light floated at eye level. At the street, he turned left and paced off the front border of the lot, then did the same for the remaining side. He finished at the tide line and turned back to survey his work. The cottage's yard was now shielded on three sides by a wall of energy invisible to human eyes.

He wanted sentient as well as inanimate protection, though. What chance did he have of finding an ally in this place? More so than in the heart of a city, he hoped. Here, human builders had not completely obliterated the natural world. He knelt beside the water again, letting the waves lap over his bare feet, and reached with his inner senses to seek whatever creatures of faerie kind might linger here. Far out to sea, the songs of the merfolk reverberated in the depths, too far to offer aid, even if those beings had any interest in the affairs of land folk. Kieran reined in his questing thoughts and focused on his immediate surroundings. Traces of pixies and brownies who sometimes visited these human dwellings tickled his brain. He didn't consider trying to track down one of them and attract its attention. They were too simple and flighty to rely on. Because of a pixie's misguided testimony, his uncle had believed him guilty of Adair's death and banished him.

Catching himself clenching his fists and baring his teeth, Kieran forced his muscles to relax. Nearby, he sensed the stray thoughts of a creature at home on the border between earth and water, able to function in both elements. He felt its eyes upon him, doubtless drawn by curiosity at seeing one of his kind standing on earthly soil. Rising to his full height, he called out a summons in his native tongue.

A black hulk, almost as large as Kieran, arose from the surf. Shaggy, with glowing red eyes, it had a body something like a horse's and a head vaguely like a dog's. Thanks to the creature's innate glamour, a human observer would see nothing stranger than a large dog.

"Greetings, pooka," he called. "Will you draw near and speak with me?"

The creature splashed forward and emerged onto the sand. "What brings a prince of the royal lineage to this world?" The question held a mocking edge.

"My lineage means nothing now. I need your help. My name is Kieran. May I know yours?"

The pooka shook water off itself and said with a harsh laugh, "I don't think so, Lord Kieran. You already have enough power to turn me into a crab if I displease you. I'd rather not give you my name, too."

"Very well, I'll simply call you pooka. And I have no intention of turning you into anything." He sat cross-legged on the sand, out of range of the waves, and wiped droplets of salt water off his face. "Unless you soak me again. I'm fleeing from an enemy, along with a young human female and a half-elven child."

"Ah, an amorous adventure!" The mouthful of wolfish fangs leered. "But I'm surprised you'd be so careless as to beget a child on a mortal playmate."

Unable to keep his voice from sharpening with impatience, Kieran said, "Nothing like that. The boy is my cousin Adair's son."

"The slain crown prince? Rumor has it you killed him in a duel."

He clenched his jaws and breathed deeply to tame the anger welling up in his chest. "That's a lie Halwyn concocted after he murdered Adair himself."

"Halwyn?" The pooka sat on its haunches and gazed at him with a more somber expression, as far as a canine-like muzzle and teeth could show such nuances. "I've heard about that one. They say he doesn't treat us lesser fey folk any better than the mortals he enslaves."

"True. I can't allow him to get his hands on Adair's child."

"What about the woman?" A sly tone crept into the creature's voice.

"She's the sister of Adair's lover, an innocent caught up in a fight she doesn't understand. The sooner her part in this ends, the better for her."

"I don't see you hurrying to run away from her."

Kieran thrust aside the memory of Fern's lips and body pressed against his. The sooner he got away from her, the better for both of them. He needed her just long enough to get the baby to the portal. After that, he would return to his own world with the infant prince, and she would stay here where she belonged. "Keep your opinions to yourself. Will you help or not?"

The pooka scratched its ear with a hind hoof. "If Halwyn's the enemy pursuing you, it would be a pleasure. My brother at home in the Hollow Hills lost a mate to Lord Halwyn's huntsmen. They have strange notions of sport in his domain."

"Excellent. If you sense any breaching of the wards, come to me at the back door of the house." He waved toward the cottage behind them. "I hope it won't become necessary to ask you to fight." He knew that commitment would be a bit much to expect from a wild creature that normally devoted itself entirely to its own survival and pleasures.

"I haven't had a good scrap in too long. Around here, we have to lie low so the mortals won't notice us. Not like the old days when they all believed. Anyway, I wouldn't mind the chance to take a bite out of Halwyn." The pooka shook its shaggy coat again and trotted into the surf. "Rest easy, Lord Kieran," it said over its shoulder. "I'll lurk about and keep an eye open for him."

Kieran waved an acknowledgment and got to his feet, brushing sand off the drab garments he'd bought in the vast indoor marketplace where he and Fern had shopped. Though he felt some comfort at gaining an ally, even a less than reliable one, he wouldn't rest easily until he knew Baird was safe from Halwyn.

Chapter Five

When Fern's eyes opened, for an instant she couldn't remember where she was, much less why. Rubbing her eyes, she strained to peer into the darkness. Of course, this was her bedroom in Bev's beach house. The next moment, she heard the drowsy whimper of a baby. Baird.

Then memory flooded her half-awake brain. Ivy had died a few hours before, leaving Baird in Fern's care. Tears blurred her vision and clogged her throat. No time for that, when her nephew needed her. She sat up and swung her legs over the edge of the mattress, clutching the bedpost to keep from swaying. After the dizziness faded, she felt almost normal. Her mouth felt dry and her head stuffed with cotton, but she suffered no other aftereffects from the wine.

She clicked on the bedside lamp and blinked until her eyes adjusted to the weak light. Scooping up Baird, she rocked him while he nuzzled her breast with snuffles and squeaks. "What woke you? Hungry already?"

She realized his whimpers weren't the only sound she heard. A low voice floated on the breeze from the bay. Though she couldn't understand the words, she recognized Kieran's musical tones. She tiptoed to the open window. At the edge of the water, she saw Kieran stand up and move one arm as if waving, then start walking toward the house. Whom could he have been talking to?

A blush spread over her face when she recalled the few moments before they'd separated. She had let herself get swept away in a passionate kiss with a man she hardly knew, and as she realized now, had no reason to trust. How did she know what he might have been doing in the middle of the night while she slept?

Lifting Baird to her shoulder, she patted him on the back while walking to the kitchen. She opened the back door to meet Kieran as he stepped onto the rear deck.

"What were you doing out there?" Her voice came out sounding more belligerent than she'd intended.

He froze, only his eyes moving as he scanned her up and down. She realized she'd forgotten to pull on the robe over the nightgown. Another annoying blush heated her cheeks.

"I was walking on the beach, enjoying the night air," he said. To her ears, his smooth tones almost shouted "lie".

"I heard you talking to somebody. Who?"

"No one. I was thinking aloud." When she glared at him in silence, he added, "Very well, if you must know, I was talking to a dog."

"What?" He took advantage of her confusion to try slipping past her into the house.

She automatically backed into the kitchen to let him by.

"I was collecting my thoughts by musing out loud to a stray dog that wandered onto the grounds. Haven't you ever carried on a conversation with an animal?"

"Not lately." Not since her first foster home, when she'd poured out her loneliness to the family cat, the only creature she had thought would listen to her. "Where's this dog now?"

He said with a vague wave toward the beach, "Gone home, I suppose, if it has a home."

She wasn't sure she believed him. He could have met with a co-conspirator, for all she knew. She had only his word that he'd come alone from, well, wherever he'd come from. As for the logistics of making contact, even though it wasn't likely he carried a cell phone hidden in a pocket of that silver-gray outfit, he could have borrowed hers while she slept. It was clear, though, that he wouldn't admit to any such meeting if it had happened. "Whatever. I have to give Baird a bottle and try to get him back to sleep."

When she returned to the kitchen from changing the baby and getting the formula, Kieran was still there, sitting at the table. "You don't trust me," he said while she warmed the bottle.

"Why should I? It's like pulling teeth to get any information out of you."

"Don't you trust your Sight? Doesn't it tell you I have Baird's welfare at heart?" She could almost see the capital S his intonation attached to the word.

"I told you, I don't believe in that stuff." After shaking up the bottle, she carried the baby into the living room and sat on the couch to feed him. Kieran followed.

"Is that why you aren't wearing the cross?" He lounged in the armchair opposite the sofa.

"In the middle of the night?"

"You need protection by night as much as by day, if not more."

"Protection?" She studied his face, wondering if he meant that claim seriously. "You've got to be kidding. Next you'll tell me to wear garlic around my neck to ward off vampires."

"Enough, you've made your skepticism abundantly clear. Yet you implied that your sister believed in otherworldly phenomena."

"She was into all that New Age rigmarole. Astrology, Tarot, precognition, channeling spirits, all that."

"Those things sound quite old to me." He flashed a smile and continued, "You disapproved of her interests."

"Not disapproved, exactly. I just wished she would have thought more about her future, and not the kind you see in a crystal ball." Fern sighed. "We used to hear stories from our grandfather about his own grandmother, who came over from Scotland in the nineteenth century. He said she claimed to have second sight."

"Oh, did your grandfather have the Sight?"

"Granddad? No way." She shook her head with a weak laugh. "He was just repeating what his grandmother told him, tales about seeing ghosts and predicting deaths. He made it clear they were only stories. But Ivy always wanted to believe that stuff was real. Sometimes she had what she thought were premonitions that came true, and she kept insisting I had the same gift."

"And you deny it."

"Even if it existed, it would be a damn useless gift. Why didn't it warn me about Ivy in time to save her, instead of kicking in when she'd already collapsed and stopped breathing? Big help that--" She snapped her mouth shut, suddenly realizing what she'd almost admitted. She never discussed those kinds of experiences with anyone, not even Bev. What hardworking businesswoman would want a freak for a partner?

"So you do experience foreknowledge sometimes."

She remembered painful episodes from her childhood, especially when she'd told people they were going to get hurt and they later had--warnings that adults had interpreted as threats. When she had started getting punished for saying things like that, she had at first hidden and then deliberately suppressed her premonitions. When both she and Ivy had felt something was wrong right before their mom's auto accident, Fern had dismissed their intuition as nervousness over the thunderstorm that had made staying home alone so scary that night. Later, after the police had knocked at the door with the terrible news, she'd done her best to forget those feelings. Again the worst occasion of all forced itself into her memory, the afternoon of her grandmother's death. She'd almost fainted on the school bus when that vision had eclipsed her outer sight, the image of her grandmother on the kitchen floor, as clear as a photo. Fern had run into the house, called for an ambulance, and collapsed onto her knees beside the unconscious woman. At that age, she hadn't even known how to perform CPR. She could only wait in helpless panic for adults to show up and prove themselves equally useless. After that day, she'd squashed any random forebodings like venomous spiders. *Maybe things like that used to happen to me*, she assured herself. *But not anymore. I'm cured.*

"Every example could be explained as coincidence. I'd need a lot more evidence than vague feelings. If that so-called gift were reliable, it would've shown Ivy how to avoid whatever killed her." Maybe a genuine premonition had driven Ivy to ask Fern for help and to check Baird into the day care center right before disaster struck. That idea brought no comfort. Instead, it ignited a spark of anger. What kind of half-baked supernatural power worked too erratically to do any good when you really needed it?

"Yet you sensed evidence of your own talent when our thoughts touched."

"I did not!" Baird started, let go of the bottle, and stared at her. "It's okay, I'm not mad at you." She jiggled him gently and inserted the nipple into his mouth. "It was a fragment of a dream. I must have fallen asleep for a second."

"Oh, do you usually lapse into sleep when a man kisses you?"

"It doesn't happen that often," she muttered, fixing her eyes on the baby to avoid Kieran's teasing smile. Since a romance in college, she'd had few dates and no relationships. Her fiancé back then had broken the engagement when she'd made it a non-negotiable condition that her kid sister would have to live with them. In the years since, Fern had been too busy for anything beyond friendship with the few men who'd wandered through her life.

"Aside from that," Kieran said, "if you had dreamed or imagined that vision, I wouldn't have sensed the brush of your thoughts."

"Are you saying you can read my mind?" she asked, alarmed.

"Not at all. I wouldn't want you to read mine, either. I didn't share your vision. I only sensed that you saw something. Would you care to tell me what?"

"No, thanks." Even if she'd trusted him fully, she wouldn't have wanted to confer reality on that experience by discussing it. Let it fade from her memory as quickly as possible.

"I see. You fear the supernatural realm."

Bristling at the smug note in his voice, she said, "Don't try to analyze me. I wouldn't call it fear. I don't like anything that's too fuzzy to hang onto, that's all. I like to get predictable results for my efforts."

"Really? Then you're probably doomed to frequent disappointment."

"Huh?"

"I understand children are far from predictable."

As if to confirm the statement, Baird squirmed, jerked his head away from the nipple, and wailed. She lifted him to her shoulder and patted his back, but he kept screeching. "There, you're upsetting him." Confronted by Kieran's cool gaze, she said, "Okay, we are, together. Babies pick up on tension around them."

"In that case, you should stop disagreeing with me." His eyes followed her as she dragged herself to her feet and paced across the living room, patting the baby more vigorously.

"Come on, honey, where's the burp? You need to go back to sleep." His screams pierced her head like a needle through her eardrums.

When she turned to cross the floor again, Kieran intercepted her. "Allow me." He pried the baby from her arms and cradled him in the curve of an elbow. Fern grudgingly acknowledged to herself that Kieran had learned baby-calming techniques faster than she'd expected. Baird stopped crying instantly and stared into Kieran's face with his mouth open, milk drooling from the corner. Kieran murmured a phrase in that unknown language he'd used before, then began to sing. The tune sounded familiar. Fern caught the syllables "shul-a-roo", which awoke the memory of a song on one of her mother's favorite folk albums.

She drooped onto the couch. "What's that, Gaelic?"

He nodded, still crooning the lullaby. She had to brace herself against the soothing rhythm, which tempted her to close her eyes and drift into sleep on the spot. Again his voice reminded her of harp music.

"So you come from Ireland."

He gazed down at the baby, now dozing in his arms. "Not recently."

With a moan of exasperation, she clutched her head, not sure whether she felt like tearing out her hair or bashing her skull against a wall.

With a soft laugh, he strolled toward the back rooms. "Shall I return him to his bed?"

"Sure." When she followed him down the hall, he'd already settled Baird in the padded drawer. The baby smacked his lips a couple of times without opening his eyes. Fern glanced at Kieran, then looked away quickly, conscious of the fact that this was her bedroom too, at least for now. The cotton gown clinging to her body and legs, although opaque, didn't feel like enough of a shield. "How do you do that, anyway? He wouldn't calm down for me."

"Perhaps we understand each other. After all, we are kin. Don't you believe in ancestral memories?"

She sniffed. "About as much as I believe in channeling." She swayed on legs that felt like jelly. Would every night for the next few months drain her as much as this one?

"Forgive me for provoking you. You need sleep, too." His fingers curved lightly around her elbow.

A shiver crept up her arm and down her spine. She imagined his hand following it, grazing those sensitive spots he'd touched earlier. She edged away. "Yes, and I'm not a baby. I'm fully capable of going to bed by myself." Heat blossomed in her breast when she heard her accidental double entendre. How would she react if he wanted to go to bed with her? "What about you? Don't you ever sleep? Or do you spend every night prowling around talking to stray dogs?"

He didn't rise to the taunt. "No, I spend part of it looking at the stars. That was what drew me outside to begin with. They shine so much clearer here than in cities, even small ones like your town."

The wistful tone crept under her skin despite her suspicions. "You don't care much for cities, do you?"

"No, I have never lived in one. I couldn't. Even in this short time away from home, the metal and concrete oppress me. And the choking fumes--how can you bear them? The night sky refreshes me, soothes the rawness in my throat. Gazing at the stars brings me peace, even though their patterns are different from the ones I'm used to."

Did that mean he came from south of the equator, someplace with different constellations? She smothered a yawn, too tired to press him for information he wouldn't give. "Peace. Sounds good." She caught herself sympathizing with that need and wondered when she, too, could hope to find that elusive blessing again. "Right now, I'll settle for an approximation of a decent night's sleep, which won't be easy to get if I know you're wandering around the property when normal people should be in bed."

"I may sleep later, when I'm sure you and the child are safe. Rest and rely on me for now."

Could she rely on him to protect them? Or was Kieran the one they needed protection from? Her feelings urged her to trust him, but accepting that impulse would mean putting faith in the irrational instincts she had always resisted. That weird vision she'd had when he'd kissed her suggested that her intuition had a real supernatural dimension, but it could also mean--if she hadn't been just dreaming on her feet--that she was losing her mind. She would almost rather believe the latter, because then she wouldn't have to rearrange her entire world view.

When the baby woke her at dawn, Fern lifted her head an inch off the pillow to look at him through bleary eyes. He wasn't crying yet, just babbling and waving his arms. The blanket she'd tucked around him had, at some point during the night, come loose. Instead of wrapping snugly around his chest, it hovered over him, anchored only at his feet.

Hovered? She blinked. *The blanket's floating.* She leaned on one elbow and rubbed her eyes. *No, it isn't!* Of course not. Now she plainly saw it lying loose on top of Baird's legs and stomach. Her brain had mixed a leftover scrap of dream with the visual input. Now that she was really awake, the blanket behaved exactly the way a piece of flannel should. She swung her legs over the side of the mattress and groped at the foot of her bed for the robe.

By the time she got back from the bathroom, Baird was crying. She changed him. Not wanting to face Kieran half-dressed again, she scrambled into her clothes before venturing across the hall once more to warm a bottle under hot water in the sink. Was he still asleep, if he'd slept at all? Sitting propped against the headboard of the bed to feed Baird, she reflected that they'd survived the night with no sign of Halwyn. Maybe they'd shaken him permanently. She still wasn't sure whether to put her faith in Halwyn, Kieran, or neither. She reminded herself again that Halwyn had been the man with the gun, reason enough to make at least a tentative alliance with Kieran.

When Baird finished his bottle, she laid him face down on a towel on the floor with the ring of plastic keys in front of him, while she switched on her cell phone to make a few calls. First, she left Bev a message about temporarily borrowing the cottage. Next, Fern called the hospital and got transferred to the morgue, from which she learned Ivy's body would probably be released the following day. After that conversation, she had to close her eyes and breathe deeply to compose her thoughts. What in the world was she supposed to do now? She didn't have any experience with arranging funerals.

Well, there's nobody else to do it, so pull yourself together. She did remember the name of the funeral home that had buried her grandmother. She got their number from directory assistance. A brief discussion, involving the transmission of a credit card number, settled that the mortuary would pick up Ivy's body and await further instructions. Fern then called the hospital again to inform them of the arrangements.

After turning off the phone, she stared numbly into her open wallet. Gnawing on a fingernail, she tried to estimate the balance on that account by now and shuddered at the total. If they spent any more time on the road, she would have to start using her backup credit card. I should go home, that's what. All that stopped her was the awareness that Halwyn, if he hadn't given up, knew where she lived. So did Kieran, for that matter. He didn't strike her as the type of man to shrug and forget about her if she abandoned him here and drove off with Baird.

She glanced at the baby, who had somehow snagged the key ring with a hand and worked it into his mouth. *Funny, I didn't think I left that toy within his reach.* Maybe he'd already grown strong enough to scoot forward on his tummy an inch or two. *Never mind that, time for breakfast.* Her stomach gurgled, and a headache was building behind her eyes. Scooping up the baby with his toy, she bundled him into the kangaroo-pouch carrier. As an afterthought, she looped the chain of the Celtic cross around her neck. Kieran had made such a big deal of advising her to wear the thing that she felt uneasy without it.

In the kitchen, she soon determined that there wasn't anything in the house fit for breakfast, aside from the granola bars in her bag. *Not unless we want canned tomato soup again.* They would have to settle for that if Kieran wouldn't let her go shopping. Well, why not? With no sign of the other man, leaving the cottage should be safe enough. And where was Kieran, anyway? She sensed that he wasn't in the house. *Wait a minute, how could I possibly know that?* True, she hadn't heard him moving around, but he might still be shut in the other bedroom, asleep. Yet she felt sure he wasn't. After wolfing down a couple of crackers to appease her hollow stomach, she stepped onto the back porch.

Kieran sat on the steps gazing at the waves that lapped the beach. A huge, black, shaggy mound crouched on the sand nearby. Kieran turned to look at her as she descended from the deck. "Good morning. Did you sleep well?"

"'Good' is a matter of opinion." Although inured to rising early for work, she didn't enjoy it any more than the next sane person, and Baird's idea of "morning" fell even earlier than her usual wake-up time. "We made it through the night, anyway. Did you sleep well? Or at all?"

"Enough." He looked annoyingly refreshed, actually. He stood up to lean against the stair railing. The black hulk stirred and lumbered over to him.

"Good grief, there really is a dog." She goggled at the beast, which vaguely resembled a Newfoundland, only bigger. "That is a dog, right?"

With a low laugh, Kieran ruffled the animal's ears. "What else would it be?"

"You have no idea where he belongs? Does he have a collar?"

The dog gave a short, sharp bark that sounded almost like an expression of contempt.

"No," Kieran said. "He must be masterless."

"It's not unusual for summer visitors to dump their pets, thinking local farmers will adopt them or something. It's awful. He's too friendly not to have lived with people before. He seems to like you, anyway."

Right on cue, the dog wagged his tail and leaned against Kieran, his jaws open in an exaggeratedly goofy grin.

No, that beast could not possibly understand what I'm saying. Shaking her head to dispel the silly notion, she said, "Listen, I'd like to pick up some food for breakfast. You have any problem with going to the grocery store?"

"I'm not sure whether it's safe to leave this property."

"Aren't you being a little too much of a worrywart? It's been peaceful ever since we got here last night."

"True, I don't sense Halwyn nearby." Kieran bent over to stare into the dog's eyes. The animal sat motionless, its gaze fixed on the man's face. After a moment of silence, Kieran said, "Yes, I believe it's safe to leave the grounds briefly. I shall go with you, of course."

"Of course. Heaven forbid I might decide to skip out while your back's turned. Wait here, I'll get my purse." *Okay, he makes decisions on the basis of occult feelings and communing with animals. Do I really want to hang around this crazy person?* On the other hand, he offered her only source of information about Halwyn, so she was more or less stuck with him. *And at least I don't have to worry so much that he'll think I'm crazy.*

A minute later, she emerged onto the front porch with her purse slung over one shoulder, the baby still bundled in the carrier on her chest, and car keys dangling from her hand. Kieran waited on the sidewalk with the dog next to him. When Fern headed for the car, he said, "Isn't there a shop close enough to walk? I would rather not get into your vehicle unnecessarily."

"What, you don't like my driving?"

"I say nothing against your driving. I would simply rather walk."

The tightness around his mouth reminded her of the tension he'd displayed during yesterday's drive. "Are you prone to carsickness?"

"Of a sort."

She sighed. "If I asked you whether the sun rose in the east, you'd probably say 'Sometimes'."

His lips quirked in a smile. "That's a matter of perspective, isn't it?"

"Anyway, it's only four blocks to the mini-mart, so we can walk, sure." The midday heat wouldn't descend on them for another couple of hours.

This early in the morning, the ocean breeze made the sunny day perfect for a stroll. She set out along the sidewalk.

Kieran reined in his long stride to her speed, and the dog kept pace on his other side. "He's coming with us?"

"As you mentioned, he seems to want companionship," Kieran said. "Perhaps we could buy him something to eat."

"Oh, Bev will love that, finding the Hound of the Baskervilles mooching around her yard next time she comes down for a weekend."

"Maybe he'll beg for food elsewhere after we leave."

The animal followed them all the way to the convenience store. "Sorry, you aren't allowed inside," she said at the entrance. The dog plopped down on the sidewalk. In the mini-mart, she snagged a cart and tossed cereal, milk, orange juice, and a bag of apples into it. "Anything else you think we need?" As soon as the words slipped from her mouth, she mentally scolded herself for letting the "we" creep in. Within a day or two, she would shake this strange man and never see him again. One mind-blowing kiss didn't change the temporary nature of their alliance.

"What about provisions for the dog?"

"You were serious about feeding him?" When Kieran responded only with a courteously blank gaze, she said, "Oh, all right," and added a small sack of dog chow. Since the shop didn't take credit cards, she had to use most of her remaining cash. She would have to find an ATM soon. This hunted fugitive lifestyle was turning out more inconvenient, not to mention expensive, than it looked in the movies.

When they emerged from the store, the dog waited beside the exit. Fern had half expected him to wander off. On the grounds that Kieran had insisted on buying the dog food, she assigned him to carry it, along with one of the plastic grocery bags, while she lugged the other bag. The temperature was climbing, though not yet to the point of discomfort, at least not for her. Kieran plucked the shirt away from his chest as if he felt overheated. "The sun is very bright here," he said when they walked up to the shade of the cottage's front porch.

"Well, yeah, that happens a lot in the summer. Not where you come from?"

"We seldom have cloudless days like this, no." Of course, he didn't volunteer any information about where that statement referred to.

"Don't count on it staying cloudless too long. As the saying goes, if you don't like the weather, wait a little while and it'll change. There're always thunderstorms to look forward to."

"I'm not accustomed to those, either."

When she opened the door, Kieran stepped inside with her, while the dog lingered on the threshold. "I hope you don't expect me to let him in the house," she said. "I draw the line there. This place doesn't belong to me, after all."

"I think he would rather stay outside anyway," Kieran said. "I'll serve his food out here."

"Whatever. As long as you don't expect me to cater to that beast." She put Baird, who'd fallen asleep on the homeward walk, into his temporary bed and returned to the kitchen to set out breakfast. While serving juice and whole-grain cereal, she said, "We have to talk about what to do next. There's been no sign of Halwyn since we left my apartment. I can't stay away from home forever on the basis of a few odd events."

Kieran took an apple from the bag. "You aren't convinced of the danger yet?"

"All I really know is that he's after me, and I can't even be sure of that, come to think of it. He could be chasing you, for all I know." She opened the milk carton and poured a splash onto her cereal.

"Powers of Light, woman, what will it take to persuade you that you and Baird need my protection?" Kieran bit into the apple, chewed and swallowed thoughtfully, and said, "Not completely fresh, but not bad." He picked an extra bowl from the dish cabinet and filled it with dog chow. "I'm not certain he will accept this, but I'll try." Carrying the bowl outside, he set it on the deck while Fern watched through the screen door. She couldn't resist the predicted spectacle of a stray dog acting finicky about food.

The dog had already circled the house to wait by the back door, as if he'd known where breakfast would be served. He sniffed the bowl, sat down, and pointedly turned his head away. "I don't believe it," Fern said. "I've seen cats act that way, but I thought dogs would eat anything."

"Perhaps this one is more discriminating in his diet. I think he'd prefer milk." "You've got to be kidding, right? Okay, go ahead."

She watched Kieran fill another bowl from the milk carton and set it on the deck. The dog didn't jump up but waited until Kieran had put down the bowl and stepped back. Only then did the animal shove his nose into the milk and slurp it up. Fern felt vaguely relieved to see him splash it in a one-foot radius around the bowl, like any other dog. When he'd emptied the dish, he licked the spilled milk off the boards.

Watching him pad down the steps and trot across the beach to sit facing the water, she shook her head. "That animal is weird. No wonder you and he get along so well."

When she returned to the table and picked up her spoon, she noticed Kieran staring at her with an unexpectedly serious expression. "Do you truly consider me...weird?" He sounded almost hurt.

She shrugged, shifting her gaze to her cereal bowl. "You're certainly not like any other man I know. You're obviously from a foreign country, but you won't say where. You pop up out of nowhere with dire warnings, but you won't give me a straight answer to any of my questions."

He didn't volunteer to do so now, either. Instead, he asked, "Did you think of Adair as weird? He and I weren't so different."

"I liked him, but I didn't know him well enough to agree or disagree with that. He kept secrets as well, come to think of it. Ivy might've known about his background, but neither of them ever told me." She thought over Kieran's last remark. Had her sister's lover actually resembled him, other than in physical appearance? "Adair seemed more carefree, more impulsive. He and Ivy suited each other that way. They always looked like they were having fun, enjoying life together. Maybe it was their artistic temperament or something." A lump clogged her throat. She washed it down with orange juice.

Kieran poured himself a glass of milk and drank half of it before answering. "Are you surprised that I don't appear to be enjoying life at the moment?" His bleak tone echoed her own grief.

"It's not just what we're going through right now. I get the impression you've always been on the serious side compared to him." Where did she get that idea? From a few brief conversations? Next she would start believing her imaginary second sight revealed his inner self to her.

"Naturally," Kieran said, "since Adair abandoned his hereditary duties and left me to deal with the results. Oh, I loved him as a blood brother, but I found what you call his carefree attitude infuriating."

"Then he did have a lot in common with Ivy. She'd do whatever she felt like, let the chips fall where they may."

"The chips?" Kieran took another sip of milk and said with a wry smile, "Like a man chopping down a tree? Yes, Adair also tended to charge through life without noticing the debris from what he knocked down on the way. It never occurred to him that when he fell in love with a woman and decided to run away from his family to live with her, his father's wrath would fall upon the nearest target."

"You."

He nodded. "My uncle sent me to persuade Adair to come home, but you know the outcome of that conversation."

"He wouldn't leave Ivy. Can you blame me for admiring him for that?" After a spoonful of her cereal, she said, "I understand your side of it, though. People like that can drive you crazy, like my mom. On the other hand, they'd probably say we worry too much and tell us to lighten up."

"Difficult advice to follow, when they generate most of the weight we carry," he said with a quiet laugh. "Not that I wouldn't welcome that burden restored."

"Me, neither. No matter how many times I had to raid my savings account to bail her out." She pushed aside the half empty bowl and wiped her eyes with a napkin.

Kieran reached across the table to cover her free hand with his. His cool fingers sent chills up her arm, followed by a trickle of heat. She knew she ought to pull away instantly, but she couldn't resist savoring the contact for just a few seconds. She had a long road ahead with little comfort to look forward to. She closed her eyes, wishing she could pretend his handclasp was more than a casual gesture.

A wave of sorrow swept over her, not hers alone, but his, too. Behind her eyelids flashed a green light. In that glow she caught a momentary glimpse of a grove of trees where a man lay face-up on the leaf-strewn ground. Blood seeped from a wound in his chest. *Adair*!

Chapter Six

Her eyes flew open. She snatched her hand away from Kieran's. He stared at her as if he'd been hit over the head. "It happened again," he whispered. "What did you see?"

"Nothing!" She jumped out of her chair and inched away from the table. Either she was having hallucinations, a theory she had trouble justifying unless Kieran had sneaked a drug into her glass, or she'd caught a genuine vision from his mind, a recollection of something he'd seen. No! She could not accept that she had shared Kieran's memories, especially a memory of looking down at Adair's dead body.

He, too, stood up. "Stop denying your own experience." His voice sounded hoarse and strained. "I felt the touch of your mind. You do have the Sight."

Fern shook her head. "Stop saying that. It's crap." She fled to the bedroom and slammed the door.

Baird twitched and let out a wail. She knelt beside the drawer to pick him up. "I'm sorry, I totally forgot you were in here. I need a lot more practice to be a good auntie, don't I?" She rocked him against her breast until he quieted. "Better change you now that you're awake." Placing him in the middle of the bed, she hooked the plastic key ring over one of his hands to keep him entertained while she got out wet wipes and a diaper.

When she rummaged in the diaper bag, her fingers brushed a small bottle. Curious, she picked up the vial and examined the label. *Oh, yeah, Ivy's magic eye drops.* She narrowed her eyes to read the fine print. "For clear sight, rub a few drops on each eyelid." Clear sight? She felt she could use some of that. Too bad the amber fluid was probably just tinted water. Ivy's note came to mind. *Use this when you think things aren't what they seem.* Fern opened the bottle, poured a few drops into her hand, and rubbed her fingers together. The stuff felt and smelled like rose-scented bath oil. With a mental shrug, she tucked the vial into a pocket of her shorts. After changing the baby, she packed both bags, in case another rushed departure became necessary. In the back of her mind, she admitted she also wanted to postpone facing Kieran.

She finally ran out of excuses to putter around the bedroom and had to venture into the hall. She left Baird on his back in the padded drawer, watching dust motes in a sunbeam shining through the window. Relieved to find the kitchen empty, she washed dishes and folded the laundry she'd done the night before. She absentmindedly took out the vial and read the label again. If nothing else, it made a pleasant-scented hand lotion. She massaged another dollop of it into her palms and over the backs of her hands. A glance out the window showed her Kieran strolling along the beach with the dog. If that moment of contact had shaken him as thoroughly as it had her, maybe he would stay out of her path for a while. She would welcome that distance between them.

Would I? Of course I would. His gestures of sympathy or passion probably meant only that he would do anything necessary to persuade her to surrender Baird.

Just as she walked into the bedroom with an armful of clothes, a bolt of lightning struck her, or so it seemed at first. Something zapped her from head to toe, as if she'd stuck her finger into an electrical socket. Dropping the laundry on the bed, she collapsed forward, braced her weight on her elbows, and waited for the shock to fade. When her head cleared, she felt a sizzle of static in the air. Without conscious effort, her brain translated the sensation into knowledge--*somebody's here, searching for me.* Not for her, actually, because finding her was only a side issue, if Kieran had told any part of the truth. They wanted the baby.

She grabbed her cell phone, rushed into the kitchen, and clattered down the back steps onto the beach. Again without thinking, she knew the danger came from this direction. She also had a feeling she'd better not let the intruder, whoever it was, see Baird.

Kieran, with the dog beside him, stood halfway between the house and the shore. With his arms flung wide, he seemed to be warning off the invader. Near the surf line, a brownish horse trotted on the packed sand parallel to the water. She recognized the man astride the horse as Halwyn. He rode bareback, using a rope as a halter.

That does it! The heck with Kieran's objections, I'm calling for help. She punched 911 on her phone. When the operator answered, she said, "I need protection against a man who's been harassing me. He just rode into my yard on a horse." She didn't want to get into technicalities about who the land belonged to. "I've got a baby with me, and I think this guy is dangerous." She rattled off the address, ended the call, and hooked the phone to the belt of her shorts.

Kieran gave no indication of noticing what she'd done. He shouted a challenge at the invader in what she assumed to be their native language. Halwyn yelled a retort, then cut it off mid-breath and angled the horse toward Fern.

"You again. Didn't I warn you that your sister and her child were in danger?" His voice sounded as musical as Kieran's.

Breathing hard, she planted her fists on her hips and glared at him. "Yeah, so?"

"I can imagine the kinds of things Kieran has been telling you. He expects you to turn over Adair's child to him, doesn't he?"

"What's that got to do with you? I'm not about to give you my nephew, either." Halwyn emitted a silvery laugh. "Believe me, I have no interest in taking him--unlike my cousin there. Do you know he murdered Adair?"

"Liar!" Kieran burst out.

"I don't know any such thing," Fern said, taking a few steps closer to the two men.

But I don't know he didn't, either, whispered an insidious voice inside her head. "Well, perhaps it wasn't technically murder, since it happened during a duel."

Duel? What kind of archaic society did these men belong to? Her head pounded as she remembered what she'd seen, no, *imagined*, a little while ago. Adair lying dead at Kieran's feet. "Why should I take your word, any more than his? What about the shot you took at Kieran yesterday?"

"Forgive me, I had no intention of harming you or the child. I was defending myself against a dangerous outlaw. I'm assigned to bring him to justice." The horse paced toward her.

Fern cast a glance at Kieran. She sensed anger pouring off him like steam. The beast beside him growled, its fur bristling. "So what now?" she asked Halwyn. "You're not just a detective but a bounty hunter, too?"

"Fern, don't listen to these lies!" Kieran shouted. With a roar of incomprehensible syllables, he flung his arm up, pointing at Halwyn. The dog lunged at the horse's forelegs.

Her head swimming with confusion, she rubbed her eyes with both hands. The viscous liquid still clinging to her fingertips spread over her closed lids. Blinking to clear away the oily substance, she remembered the label on the vial. *Clear sight.* Well, whatever Ivy had meant by her message, somebody here certainly wasn't what he seemed.

When Fern opened her eyes completely, the sunlight dazzled her at first. She could see nothing but a blaze of golden light. *Oh, no, have I blinded myself?* She hardly had time to panic, though, before the brightness vanished. She saw clearly again--just as the world turned inside out.

A violet glow flared on the edges of her vision. Whipping her head from side to side, she saw a shimmering, transparent curtain of light marking the boundaries of the cottage's beach. It made bright specks dance before her eyes. She forced them away from it to focus on the animal beside Kieran. The beast didn't look much like a dog now. It had a canine head, true, although with a slavering muzzle crammed with fangs fiercer than any domestic dog's. From the neck down, it resembled a shaggy pony, and it seemed to have grown bigger. Its eyes gleamed red. *It's still black, anyway.* Small comfort that remnant of consistency granted her.

Fern blinked and rubbed her eyes again, trying to scrub away the impossible sights. Her view of the beach and its occupants didn't change. She looked up at Halwyn. He had pointed ears. And his eyes had slitted pupils like a cat's.

When she glanced at Kieran for reassurance, the breath rushed out of her lungs. She opened her mouth to scream, but no sound came.

He had them, too.

The horse, at least, hadn't changed, as far as she could tell. Everything was a blur, though, for the dog-like creature charged forward and snapped at the horse's front legs. With a piercing whinny, the mount reared on its hind legs. The "dog" lunged again, leaped up, and slashed at Halwyn, who tumbled off the horse. He rolled as he hit the ground and sprang to his feet, apparently unhurt except for blood oozing through a rip in his trousers. Red blood. She'd half expected green or silver. *What are these people, some kind of aliens for real?*

Halwyn raised his arm. A ball of fire appeared from nowhere at the tip of his fingers. Kieran shoved Fern sideways, and she hit the sand with a painful thud. She glimpsed the fireball careening past them to extinguish itself in the earth at the foot of the porch steps. At the same moment, an approaching siren drowned out all other sounds. Conscious of Kieran's warm weight on top of her, she wiggled to turn her head toward Halwyn. The other man spoke, but she could only see his lips move, not hear him over the siren. His face contorted in rage. He wheeled around to run.

Kieran leaped up. The wail of the siren cut off. A second later, two police offers dashed around the house. Kieran looked after the fleeing man but didn't follow him. Instead, he grabbed the rope dangling from the horse's head and muttered to Fern, "What are these men doing here?"

She scrambled to her feet, brushing sand from her clothes, face, and hair. "I called 911 the minute I saw Halwyn." Her gaze shifted to his ears. She forced herself to focus on his eyes instead. *Cat eyes. That's even worse than pointed ears.* "And what in the world is going on? Who...*what* are you?"

"Later." He gritted his teeth as if he could barely keep himself from snarling at her.

The policemen, a young, beefy one and an older, wiry one, stopped a few yards away, hands on their gun belts. "You called about a guy on a horse threatening you?" said the older one. "This him?"

Fern shook her head. "This is the horse, but the man got away." She waved in the direction Halwyn had run. It took her a second to remember that the two officers couldn't see the wall of violet luminescence that was perfectly clear to her. They behaved with calm courtesy, as if everything except the fidgeting horse struck them as routine. She introduced herself and Kieran. After getting a description of the intruder, the younger policeman tethered the horse to the porch rail and hurried away to follow Halwyn's tracks in the sand, while the other officer came inside with Kieran and Fern to jot down their statements. The dog-like creature stayed on the beach.

With her head spinning, she gave as little information as she could manage. She had no trouble convincing the policeman she didn't know why Halwyn had ridden up the beach on horseback or what he'd wanted with her. In fact, she knew so little that it might as well be nothing. Following her lead, Kieran offered curt answers that duplicated her pretense of ignorance. In his case, it had to be only a pretense. She now realized he hadn't told her more than a fraction of the truth. She sneaked sidelong glances at his ears. They still looked pointed. His eyes still resembled a cat's. Either the eye drops contained a drug that made her hallucinate, or he wasn't a normal man.

Within a few minutes, the other officer returned with the news that Halwyn had vanished. "I've radioed the animal control folks to pick up the horse," he said. The two of them left after recording Fern's contact information. They scanned Kieran suspiciously when he volunteered nothing except his name, but a few murmured phrases in that unknown language sent them away with their curiosity quenched.

Kieran faced Fern across the kitchen table, his expression grim. She took a deep, tremulous breath. "Okay, here's where you tell me everything you've been holding back. And I mean everything. Starting with why your ears and eyes look that way."

He started and grabbed her wrist. "You can see? How?"

His tight grip sent chills up her arm. "What do you think I'm seeing?"

"My ears are pointed. My pupils are oval, not round like yours."

"Halwyn's, too," she whispered. The pulse throbbed in her temples.

"And I assume you could also see the wards around the property." At her baffled stare, he added, "A wall of violet light."

"Then it's real." She pulled against his grasp, and he released her arm. "Everything I saw is real." Kieran had confirmed her perceptions with no prompting. She hadn't hallucinated those impossible things.

"How could you? What changed?" he demanded.

She flinched at his harsh tone. "These eye drops. Ivy left them for me." She dug the vial out of her pocket and handed it to him.

He muttered what sounded like a curse. "True sight. Adair must have given her this. Damn inconvenient."

So the liquid had something to do with the bizarre change in her vision. She leaped up and hurried to the sink, where she splashed water in her eyes. While she dried them with a paper towel, Kieran said, "That's useless. You can't unsee what you've seen."

Staring at him, she confirmed that his eyes and ears still looked inhuman. She crumpled the paper, tossed it into the trashcan, and sank into the chair opposite him. "What am I seeing? What are you?"

"We have no time for this. Halwyn might return at any moment. We have to get Baird away from here now."

"You think I'm going anywhere with you when you might be some kind of monster, for all I know?"

A tinge of hurt flickered in his eyes before he said coolly, "So might Halwyn, isn't that so? Have I done anything to suggest I mean harm to you or the child?" He clasped her hand, and his tone softened. "I give you my word I'll reveal everything on the way. But we must leave immediately."

"All right, I admit I don't want to be here with Baird if Halwyn comes back. What was with the horse, anyway?"

"I suspect he simply got tired of riding in steel boxes on wheels and wanted something he could control. He could have stolen the horse from a field along the way. We passed many of those." He stood up and put on his gloves. "Get Baird, gather his things, and let's go. At least we have the advantage of your car, and the talisman you wear will cloud Halwyn's inner sight to some extent."

"Talisman?" Her fingers found the Celtic cross. "Oh, this. You mean it really does give some kind of protection?"

"As I said, I'll explain on the way. Move!"

She moved. Less than five minutes later, they'd piled their gear in the car and buckled Baird into his seat. Just before she slammed the door shut, the black animal jumped into the backseat, too.

"What makes that whatever-it-is think it's coming along?"

Kieran spoke a few non-English words to the creature, who emitted a gruff bark as if in reply. "Let him," Kieran said to Fern. "We may need him later."

"He better not hurt the baby!"

"No fear of that." He fastened his belt and watched Fern settle into the driver's seat. "Where do you think we should go, anyway? I'm out of ideas."

"Surely my plan of taking Baird to the shelter of his grandparents' home sounds more rational now?"

Her chest tightened. "Not to me. I'm not giving him up to people who might not even be human." She started the motor and backed out of the driveway.

"Will you consider meeting them, at least--ask their advice? Adair's parents have a right to see their only grandchild, don't they? Furthermore, they can offer temporary safety while you decide on your next step."

She couldn't deny they deserved that much consideration, with their son murdered. In their place, she would feel the same need. "Meet them? Okay, I can live with that. Where? I'm not taking him to their home, wherever it is, so you'd better have some neutral ground in mind."

"There's a place in the mountains of Virginia where I can get in touch with them and arrange a meeting."

"Fine, that's a few hours away. Plenty of time for you to tell me what the heck is going on." She pointed the car toward the southbound highway.

As soon as they'd merged into smoothly flowing traffic, she said, "Okay, let's hear it. What are you and Halwyn, and what is that monster in the backseat?"

"He's a pooka, a kind of shape-shifter."

She noticed he'd evaded the first question. She seized upon the only part of his answer that made a tiny amount of sense to her, a word she remembered hearing in a classic movie. "That beast is really a six-foot-tall rabbit?"

"I don't recall ever seeing a pooka take rabbit form, but I suppose it could." "Never mind. Does he have a name?"

"I don't know it. Magical creatures avoid giving their real names. Names hold power."

"Okay, I'll call him Harvey." She ignored Kieran's quizzical glance. Let him stay confused for a change. "Magical creatures? So you're not a space alien?"

"Certainly not, what gave you that idea?"

"The pointed ears were my first clue."

"I'm not human, but I'm not from outer space, either. My home belongs to this planet, but in another realm that can be reached only through enchanted portals, what you might call a different plane of existence. That is the label your sister gave it. Your people's legends have called it the Hollow Hills, Underhill, or Faerie. Halwyn and I are what you call elves."

Chapter Seven

"You're what?"

"Elves. So was Adair."

"No, don't say it again. My sanity won't take it." The words buzzed in her head like a swarm of wasps. She veered off the road and pulled to a stop in a supermarket parking lot. Her hands shook when she unclenched them from the wheel and dropped them to her lap. She left the engine running for what little coolness the air conditioner could supply.

"Fern, we can't linger here and wait for Halwyn to catch up."

"It's bound to take him a little while to regroup, isn't it? I can't drive right now." She drew a ragged breath. Okay, she could handle this revelation. She'd always known Adair was a little strange, probably from a foreign country. He had just turned out to be stranger than she could ever have suspected. "It does explain a lot. Adair acted like he came from someplace far away, even though he spoke almost perfect English, like you. How do you do that?"

"It's called a tongues spell. It enables us to speak any language until we gradually acquire the natural use of it."

"Okay, if you're what you say you are, why did you look normal--I mean, human--before?"

"We cast illusions upon ourselves. You can see through the glamour now because of the magic ointment."

"Well, I don't like seeing through it. How long before this stuff wears off?"

His eyebrows arched as if in surprise at the question. "Never. The effect is permanent."

"You mean all that freaky stuff Ivy believed in is real, and more? And I'll never be able to ignore it again?"

"Why would you want to?" His tone became unexpectedly gentle. "Wouldn't you prefer reality over illusion? Especially when it includes dangers you need to be aware of?"

"This isn't my idea of reality. It's a fairy tale. What I'd prefer is a normal life. So much for that, I guess." She glanced over her shoulder at the dozing baby. "Adair was an elf, too. That makes Baird only half human." Shaking her head, she covered her eyes for a few seconds. When she looked at Kieran once more, his oddly beautiful transformation hadn't reversed itself. "Tell me again, straight this time, why you're here."

"Exactly what I said. To bring Adair's child to his rightful home. I owe that to his family. My own parents withdrew to the shadowlands when I reached young manhood."

"Shadowlands? What's that?"

"Ancient elves don't become infirm like your people, and we don't die of old age. After many centuries, some of us become weary of life and simply...fade. Those who reach that stage retreat into what you might call an alternate dimension, out of phase with the rest of our world." He flashed a wry smile. "Adair learned those words from Ivy and passed them on to me. Your learned folk have such peculiar terms for things that seem natural to us."

"So your parents faded, or whatever. You didn't feel like they deserted you?"

"I was prepared for their departure. By then I had already been fostered to Adair's household for several seasons, and Adair and I pledged blood brotherhood. We cut our wrists and mingled our blood, as boys often do. His parents were like a second mother and father to me. That changed with Adair's murder." She heard bitterness in his voice.

"How? You said Halwyn killed him."

"He did. But he wore a glamour, a magical illusion, of my appearance. He lured Adair into the Hollow Hills with a message that purported to come from me. Of course, when Adair met Halwyn he saw through the disguise almost at once, but it was too late. Halwyn made sure a pixie witnessed the duel and testified that I had killed my cousin."

"Pixie? Twinkly little creature with butterfly wings?" She decided she didn't have to worry about giving Kieran the impression that she was crazy. The whole world was insane.

"You're thinking of wisps. Pixies have blue skin, red eyes, and a mischievous nature. However, they don't have very keen intelligence. They're easily fooled and too scatterbrained to lie. So Adair's parents accepted that I'd quarreled with him, possibly out of envy, and killed him. My grief at the sight of his body was misconstrued as guilt. Since his death was supposed to be the result of a duel, not cold-blooded murder, they only exiled me from their home."

"Only? You don't sound like exile is an 'only' kind of thing to you."

"No." He spoke so quietly she had to strain to hear him. "It is far from a small thing." Raising his voice to a normal level, he said, "I could hardly grasp how Adair would so carelessly abandon his family and native land."

She struggled to sort out the scraps of information Kieran had offered her the night before. How much truth did they hold? "So you really did try to convince him to leave Ivy and go home, but he wouldn't do it, right?"

"As I said, he could have brought her with him."

"He might've taken Ivy where you want to take Baird? Out of this world?"

"Yes, into the Hollow Hills. He invited her, but she declined. On reflection, he decided she was right. At first I thought they were a pair of fools."

"Why?" She bristled internally. While she might hold that opinion of Ivy, she didn't like hearing someone else express it.

"Living in our realm and eating elven food would have extended her life far beyond the normal human span, and she would never have suffered illness or pain."

"You said you thought that at first. You changed your mind?"

"I considered the situation more carefully, as Adair had, and acknowledged the disadvantages."

"There's a catch? I'm not surprised."

He hesitated, as if unwilling to reveal the drawbacks of what he'd just described as a paradise. "His kin would have seen her as his plaything. A human mistress would never have been honored as his true consort."

"Oh, yeah? Who do they think they are, anyway? Or do all elves feel that way about all humans?"

He glanced out the side windows, then over his shoulder. "Fern, we can't stay here. We have to keep moving to decrease the risk of Halwyn's finding us. The steel in the car fogs his perception, but that can only slow him down, not stop him altogether."

"Oh, all right. I guess I can drive now." Baird's safety mattered more than her mental stability. She pulled out of the parking lot and turned inland toward Route 13, which ran southbound to the Virginia end of the Eastern Shore. "Now, what about elf-human relations?"

"Many do look down upon your kind. Not all. But Adair and his family are a special case. He was the son and heir of King Oberon and Queen Titania."

"Oberon and Titania? Like in Shakespeare? Those are really their names?"

"They are hereditary titles assumed by every king and queen of the elven realm, not given names. Most elves make occasional visits to the mortal realm, and Adair followed that custom. He explored more of your world than most do, and he enjoyed it more than he expected. I joined him on some of his forays, though I didn't share his fascination with human society."

"What did his parents think of that?"

"They tolerated what they saw as a passing phase, sure he would get bored with the dirt and violence of your world, not to mention the unpleasant weather. Instead, he eventually met your sister and decided to stay with her."

"And his family wouldn't stand for it?"

"He forswore his heritage when they refused to allow him to bring his beloved into the Hollow Hills as his wife instead of a mere pet. They wouldn't accept the idea of a mortal woman as queen after them."

"I thought elves lived forever, so how could he ever inherit the throne?"

"We can be killed, as Adair was. More to the point, the king and queen wanted their heir ready to take his rightful place when it came time for them to fade into the shadows. They were bitterly disappointed when he renounced his birthright. Instead, he insisted on living in the human world, a choice they hold responsible for his death. They will be pleased to have his child to take his place."

"Whoa. It just hit me, you're saying Baird could become the crown prince."

"Well, yes, that is the point."

"Your king and queen would accept a grandson with human blood?"

"Considering he is all they have left of their only son, yes. It's true that halfbloods are generally considered less worthy than purebred elves. They are welcomed as breeding stock, since our kind bear fewer and fewer children every century, but they're looked upon with a sort of patronizing pity for their weaker magical abilities. The son of the royal prince wouldn't be treated that way, though."

Fern wasn't sure she believed the elven court would be so broad-minded. She didn't like the idea of Baird growing up among people, even nonhuman people, who despised him for his ancestry. "So they would've rejected my sister or treated her like some kind of lower animal, but they'd accept her son as their prince? What a bunch of hypocritical bigots."

"Yes, once they examine Baird, they will accept him. He possesses some magical power. I have already noticed signs of it. And he'll be safe from Halwyn under their protection."

"That'll be a happy ending for you, too, won't it? You'll get to go home."

"That's true. I don't deny how important that is for me. If I come back with Adair's child, their majesties will admit me to the court. King Oberon will test me with the truth spell his wrath kept him from considering before. They will recognize my loyalty."

"You get credit for saving Baird, Baird gets to grow up as a fairy prince, and the villain gets foiled. Meanwhile, I never see my nephew again. No, thanks."

"Do you seriously believe you can protect him here in the mortal world, with no weapons besides a few warding charms like that necklace, and the Sight you've denied all these years?"

"I'll do whatever it takes. Yes, I've been denying it, for some of the reasons I already told you. But if I have to use it, I will." Her voice trembled with a mixture of anger and fear. "Why don't you drag Halwyn back to--what did you call it--the Hollow Hills and turn him over to the king and queen to clear your name? Then it would be safe for Baird to live here with me, where he belongs."

"How long do you think his grandparents would allow that before sending another messenger to claim him? They would never yield him to you."

"Then I'll move away and keep running, as long as I have to." She would lose her home, friends, and all hope of material security, but at least she wouldn't lose her sister's baby. Her own baby, now. "Come to think of it, how did you know Halwyn was after Baird?"

"I have my sources of information. Pixies and most other lesser fairy folk have no love for Halwyn. He enjoys draining them of their magic through torture. Their fear and loathing made them eager to keep me aware of his actions. When I learned he'd gone through the portal, I knew he must be planning to capture Adair's son."

"Back up, what's this about torture?" A chill trickled down her spine at the thought of such a person getting his hands on Baird.

"Some of our kind have no scruples about stealing power from others. Any creature with magic can be milked of that energy through strong emotions, and some, like Halwyn, prefer the energy of dark emotions such as fear and pain. They sometimes kidnap human infants for that purpose."

"Then he might want Baird for that, not just to keep him from becoming king?" She glanced over at Kieran, who answered only with a tight-lipped nod. "You're just trying to scare me into giving him up."

"Yes, I'm trying to scare you, but only to shock sense into you. You've heard of changelings, children stolen and replaced by magically disguised substitutes? Many changelings fall into the clutches of Halwyn and others like him. Human bloodlines often carry a kind of magic, even though it's different from ours, like the gift that runs in your family. Human powers, unlike the elven kind, aren't blocked or weakened by cold iron. That difference intrigues some of us. Those who seize human children usually want them for such gifts or sometimes for musical or artistic talents."

"I don't want to hear any more." Her stomach churned with nausea. She turned up the air conditioner fan to its highest setting and tilted the vent to blow toward her face. "How could Ivy fall in love with a member of a species who can do things like that?"

"Surely you don't think we're all bloodthirsty predators? Not after knowing Adair for so long?" He touched her bare arm.

She flinched. "I didn't really know him at all. I just trusted Ivy's judgment that he was a good guy. She had to know all about his background, and she didn't tell me. How could she keep a secret that big? Why didn't she trust me?" Her voice cracked on a sob. She swallowed the tears.

Kieran withdrew his hand and sadness tinged his voice. "Would you have believed her?"

Fern sighed. "I would've thought she was losing her mind. She and Adair could have found a way to convince me, though. For one thing, they had those eye drops."

"Perhaps they wanted to protect you."

"From all those bloodthirsty predators that Adair was the exception to?"

"He wasn't the exception, Halwyn's kind are. They are a small minority. Many of those exchanges I mentioned have no evil motive. Often the children taken have been orphaned, neglected, or cruelly treated by their human families. There are other ways of drawing psychic energy besides torture. It can be freely shared if the human partner is willing. But that doesn't apply to a helpless infant, of course. Halwyn cares nothing for the wishes of his prey."

"The king and queen tolerate this stuff?"

"They might not approve, but for the most part they avoid interfering in the private affairs of the nobility."

So far, she didn't think she would like Adair's parents much more than the renegade elf. "If Halwyn kills Baird, how does he expect to get appointed the heir? Won't your aunt and uncle figure out the truth?"

"He might claim the child died in one of your motor accidents. Or he might cast the blame on me."

Almost as if he knew they were discussing him, Baird woke and started crying. Fern glanced into the backseat, where the pooka panted with his tongue out like the dog he pretended to be. Baird, with his cries subsiding to a whimper, patted the creature's shaggy fur and clutched a dangling ear.

"We have to stop," she said. "The car needs gas, and Baird needs changing and feeding. Will we be safe for a few minutes?"

"If we must. It will be good to get out of this vehicle for a while."

She pulled off the highway at the next town. At the gas station, after fueling the car she changed Baird on the backseat while Kieran walked the "dog". Before leaving, she dashed inside to buy a book of maps for the local region. Next she drove half a block away to the nearest drive-through fast food outlet. "Elves don't eat meat?" she said while they scanned the menu. "Adair was big on fruits and veggies, and I notice you are, too."

"We don't like the overprocessed, aged meats commonly available in your cities. Game we hunt for ourselves is another matter."

At his suggestion, she ordered fruit yogurt for Kieran and milk for both him and Harvey. Instead of eating in the parking lot, they drove to a shady playground they'd passed on the way in. She spread the food on a picnic table next to a pond where ducks waddled ashore to investigate scraps she crumbled from the edge of her egg and sausage sandwich and tossed on the ground. "Harvey will warn us if Halwyn gets close, won't he?"

"He should," Kieran said. The pooka bared a mouthful of fangs in an expression disturbingly like a smile.

"How long does he plan to hang around with us, anyway?"

"As long as we need him."

Fern scanned the pooka suspiciously. From what little she knew of fairy lore, creatures like that had tricky natures, not inclined to act out of sheer generosity. "Why is he being so helpful?"

"Because his kind, like most of the less powerful inhabitants of our world, have no love for Halwyn. He preys on them or enslaves them whenever he can. Few serve him willingly...except maybe for the redcaps."

"What's a redcap?"

"Just take my word that you don't want to meet one," he said in a cold voice that stifled any impulse she might have to pursue the topic.

While she opened a bottle to feed Baird, she watched Kieran peel off the gloves he'd worn for most of the drive.

"What's with those? It's awfully warm for them."

"To prevent accidentally touching the metal of the car. Iron burns our skin like acid."

"So that's why Ivy had this necklace made. What's the point of the four-leafed clover?"

"It helps to cloud elven sight. If not for the combination of iron and the clover, Halwyn would have caught up with us much sooner."

"And why a cross? Don't tell me I can scare Halwyn away by waving a cross at him like a vampire."

"That shape symbolizes the new order that drove us to the fringe of human lands. We find it unpleasant, but it doesn't hurt us. Your sister must have studied the traditional means of warding against our kind and wanted to take no chances. I noticed a metal tool beside her body. She must have tried to fight off Halwyn with it. Cold iron."

So that's why she had a wrench, Fern thought. She'd forgotten about that odd fact in all the confusion.

"How did he kill her without leaving a mark?" She had to force that question past a choking tightness in her throat. But she needed to learn as much and as quickly as possible.

"Elf-shot. Darts that dissolve within the body as they poison the victim. The result looks like what your healers call a stroke."

"She wore a bracelet custom-made to match the necklace. Why didn't it protect her?"

"I'm sure it did for a while, at least by hiding her from Halwyn when she left the shelter of her home. But she couldn't keep him from sensing Baird's aura entirely, and he had probably been in your world for at least a week by the time I arrived. I passed through the gate only a few hours after him by our world's reckoning, but time flows at different rates in the two realms."

"If he'd been here that short a time, where did he get a private detective's license?"

"A what?"

"In the store, he showed me his identification."

"He'd obviously questioned enough people, doubtless under a spell so they would forget afterward, to learn that such 'identification' would disarm your suspicions. He needn't have carried a real license or even a paper that looked like one. All he had to do was cast a glamour over whatever he showed you to compel your mind to see it as he wished."

"No wonder I couldn't make out the name on it. If I'd had these eye drops then, I'd have seen it was a fake, wouldn't I?"

"Yes, but I must warn you that the enchantment works only for ordinary illusions such as the ones that disguise Halwyn and me or keep most mortals from noticing the brownies, elementals, and other fey creatures who lurk in hiding in your world. You wouldn't be able to see through stronger spells cast by a powerful elven mage."

"Then let's hope I never have to face any. So when I didn't answer Halwyn's questions about Ivy, he tracked her through Baird's aura?" The occult term tasted strange on her tongue. This situation forced her to embrace everything she had rejected for most of her life.

"A half-elf's life-force shines like a beacon among the human throngs. That was how I also knew Ivy had visited you a short time before. Otherwise, I would have gone directly to her home instead of looking for her at the shop, just as Halwyn did. To remain completely safe, Ivy and the baby would have had to stay barricaded behind powerful shields every moment of the day and night, wards she wouldn't have been capable of creating. She certainly knew about running water and took full advantage of it. Didn't you mention that she wanted you to shelter Baird at your home? Your neighborhood is bounded on three sides by water."

"Oh...that's why you were in such a hurry to cross the river and then the bay?"

"Yes, that barrier also made it hard for Halwyn to follow us. But he eventually did find our trail, as you saw."

"Just like he tracked Ivy after she left the store."

"He would have picked up her traces with some difficulty because she crossed water. I believe he stayed a few steps behind her most of the way and caught up with her soon after she left the baby at the church. Her mortal magic, the gift of second sight, made her stand out from ordinary people, although not so brightly as a half-elf. Halwyn must have followed her home and killed her, first trying to force her to reveal her child's hiding place."

"And then he went after me, because he sensed I had Baird. How do you think he got around so fast before he snagged the horse?"

"The same way I did, most likely. By casting a spell on drivers to pick him up on the roadside and transport him wherever he needed to go."

"Magical hitchhiking. I guess that's no stranger than the rest of this craziness." She sighed. "I wonder how he knew about Baird in the first place. I can't imagine Adair would have told him."

"Halwyn didn't spend much time at court," Kieran said, "but he had ways of learning the news. Our people, like yours, sometimes gossip. And in all fairness to those who consorted with him, he never made his envy of Adair public."

"If he's in line for the throne, so are you." She reminded herself that everything she knew about elven politics, so far, depended on Kieran's word. She hadn't heard more than fragments of Halwyn's side of the story.

"True, and that explains why the tale of my murdering Adair sounded plausible. But I don't want his position. If I did, we wouldn't be here now." His somber tone chilled her.

"What do you mean?"

"I would have disabled you with a spell and seized the child the first moment I stepped into your home. That's what Halwyn would have done."

She suppressed a shiver. At a snuffling protest from the baby, she glanced down and realized she'd let the nipple slip out of his mouth. She repositioned the bottle and stared into Kieran's eyes. "I have to learn everything I can about protecting myself and Baird because I'm not giving him up."

"You insist on denying him his rightful heritage?"

"He has a human heritage, too. I've spent years trying to build a normal life, and I'm going to make sure he has one, too." Discovering that the supernatural world that had fascinated Ivy was real didn't bring Fern any comfort. It made matters worse. Now she had a whole new category of dangers and obstacles to overcome. "You said yourself that Adair decided not to take Ivy into the elven kingdom. And he already knew she was pregnant, so he must have wanted his son to grow up here."

"He might have changed his mind later. He was still young, as our kind measure age, so he was impulsive. Not that I'm much older, but trying to keep him out of trouble prematurely aged me." His face momentarily relaxed into a self-mocking smile.

"How old are you, anyway?"

"That's hard to answer because of the difference in time flow. I can tell you that when, as a child, I first viewed your world through an enchanted pool, this land was just beginning to be settled by people of your race."

"Almost four centuries?" The idea made her momentarily lightheaded. He looked little older than her own age.

"Remember, as I just said, time passes at a different rate in our realm. I have not literally experienced four hundred years. Exactly how long in your terms, I can't say, because we don't have seasons like yours."

"What's your home like, then? You have the same weather all the time?"

"No, we each control the climates of our own domains. We have mists or gentle, warm rains, or crystalline frosts and swirling snows that melt before the cold can become uncomfortable, all as our personal wishes decree. Bounteous varieties of flowers and fruits adorn the landscape at all times instead of being restricted to a fixed season. A diffuse glow through rainbow-hued clouds lights what you would call day. We don't have a sun, nor do we have night as you know it."

"Don't you sleep?"

He laughed. "Yes, though not as much as you do. We dim our chambers with draperies. Besides, each daily cycle includes a period of purple-hazed twilight, when the stars of our world shine. Our constellations differ from yours, and we have no moon. Again, the lengths of what you'd call our day and night vary. Nature shapes itself according to our will, not the reverse."

"It sounds very peaceful. Why did Adair want to hang around in our messy world?"

"He said its chaotic, fast-paced atmosphere appealed to him. He found it invigorating." He shook his head. "I must admit this place has some intriguing aspects. Your stars, for example, and the ocean. I've never seen waves before. And I can understand taking delight in the challenge of a world that resists one's will instead of conforming to it."

Did that mean he might learn to appreciate the human world enough to stay? Or was he commenting on its quaint attractions like a visitor touring an exotic but primitive country? *What do I care? I sure wouldn't want him to stick around, would I?*

They finished their brunch with a couple of apples from the bag they'd bought at the convenience store early that morning. "Okay, tell me where we're really going," she said as they got back in the car. "Can you show me on the map?" She opened the book to the page showing an overview of Maryland and Virginia.

"We need to reach the place where Halwyn and I crossed into this land, a gate between worlds. As I said, it's in the mountains. No, I can't find it on your map. Once we get near the spot, though, I'll be able to sense the portal's energy and guide you there."

"Then what? No way will I take Baird through that gate." Her stomach knotted at the very idea of stepping into another dimension.

"I don't expect you to. You can wait on this side, with the pooka to stand guard, while I enter the gate and send a messenger to my uncle and aunt. Be prepared for a long wait, though. A task that might take me less than an hour could consume most of a day by your time."

"How much Earth time does an hour over there use up?"

"There's no fixed ratio. The separation varies with the currents of magical energy."

She sniffed. "Typical vague answer."

"One more thing we must keep in mind. We have a limited time to reach the gate. It can be opened from inside the Hollow Hills at will, but on this side it phases in and out of existence. Sometime before sunset tonight, it will shut down until about two moon cycles from today, two months."

"When before sunset?" Anxiety sharpened her tone. She didn't entirely believe he wasn't inventing some of these "facts" to exert control over her.

He sighed. "Again, the gate, like most magical entities, remains constantly in flux. I can't predict the exact moment. Not until late afternoon, at least."

Almost four hours after leaving Bev's cottage, they reached the Chesapeake Bay Bridge-Tunnel, which crossed from Cape Charles on the Eastern Shore to Virginia Beach. Kieran shot nervous glances at the expanse of open water lying ahead of them. "Another bridge?"

"Well, you did say crossing water will make it harder for Halwyn to catch up. Anyhow, we can't get to the middle of Virginia without traveling back across the bay somewhere. I guess you'd better brace yourself, because the whole thing is seventeen miles long."

She almost felt sorry for Kieran when they merged onto the bridge. The brilliant blue of the sky and the aquamarine sparkle of the water were wasted on him. He clenched his fists on his lap and avoided looking out the window. With his lips pressed tightly together, he swallowed over and over as if fighting nausea. Paler than usual, his skin looked even more like blue-veined marble. His distress seemed to increase during the tunnel part of the span. When she asked how he was doing, he muttered, "I can feel the weight of the sea overhead." He let out a pent-up breath when they emerged from the tunnel onto another stretch of bridge.

She slowed at one of the artificial islands in the middle, where people parked to snap pictures or fish from the pier. "Want to stop for a few minutes? You might feel better if you got out of the car and breathed some fresh air."

He shook his head. "I prefer to get this over with as fast as possible."

When they finally reached the western end of the bridge and headed into Virginia Beach to pick up Interstate 64, he said with an apologetic smile, "It's so unlike anything I've experienced before. At home we don't have vast expanses of open water or unobstructed horizons of any kind.

The landscape consists of woodlands, meadows broken up by copses of trees, gardens, bowers, and sheltered hollows between the hills. The largest body of water would be a lake like the one where we fed the ducks this morning."

With Baird growing restless in his car seat, Fern proposed stopping for lunch at a convenience store. Kieran didn't try to hide his relief at getting out of the car.

"You might as well enjoy the break," she said, "because according to the map we have to go through another tunnel soon."

He gave her a hard stare, then laughed. "Woman, I suspect you're tormenting me on purpose."

"Check for yourself, if you don't believe me. There's a river coming up in less than half an hour."

In the store they picked up sandwiches, drinks, more supplies for later, a small cooler, and a bag of ice. At the checkout counter she fumbled in her purse for her wallet, while Baird squirmed in the sling on her chest. "Allow me," Kieran said. He dug into a pocket and gave the clerk a handful of green and yellow scraps of plant matter. Fern blinked. Dried flowers. The clerk just thanked him and gave him a few coins in change, as if she saw nothing odd.

Outside, Fern cast a furious glare at Kieran. "What was that?" she hissed. "Did you cast a spell on that woman?"

"Not on her," he said. "I placed a glamour on the flowers and leaves to make them look like your money. You saw through the illusion because of the ointment that changed your vision."

"Did you do the same thing at the store yesterday? Pay for your clothes with fake cash?"

"What would you expect me to do? I had no real money."

"You cheated people." She buckled Baird into his seat beside the waiting pooka and slammed the car door. "You see, that's one thing I can't stand about this whole magic deal. It's unreliable. It's all lies."

When they'd both taken their seats in the front, Kieran placed a hand gently on her arm. His cool fingers on her overheated flesh made her shiver. "Not all. Adair loved your sister, and I truly care for Baird. And everything I've told you since you became immune to my illusions has been true."

"Yeah, well, I'll reserve judgment on that." She drove a few blocks until she found a park where they could eat their veggie subs and she could change and feed the baby. Harvey dashed around on the grass, chasing squirrels. "I hope the police don't stop by and give us a hard time for violating the leash law."

"Don't worry about the pooka. No one can see him unless he chooses."

"With the magic eye drops, I guess that means not only can I see him the way he really looks, I'll start seeing pixies and who knows what flitting around."

"If they happen to be present, you'll see them."

"That's worse than the second sight Ivy insisted we had. I guess she was right about that." Admitting that truth felt like diving off a high board into a pool of unknown depth. "I've had it all along, but not like those two visions last night and this morning. If they were real."

"I'm sure they were. You shared my memories for an instant, didn't you?"

"How? Why?"

"When we kissed, our minds as well as our lips touched. The contact broke open the wall you had tried to build around your power."

She felt herself blush. "One more thing to thank you for--not! If psychic powers are real, you can keep them."

After changing Baird, she settled him in the curve of one arm with a bottle and juggled a sandwich with her other hand. Kieran poured milk for the pooka into a disposable bowl from a package of picnic supplies they'd bought. She watched the huge, shaggy beast lap the milk as sloppily as a real dog. She darted glances at Kieran's pointed ears and feline eyes, fighting to convince herself that if she looked away often enough, his appearance would return to normal.

"I can't believe I'm rushing all over two states with a couple of fairyland creatures and trying to escape from another one. You think your uncle and aunt, the king and queen--good grief, I'm still not sure I believe that, either--can get Halwyn off our backs?"

"You mean, can they force him to stop threatening you and the child? If you refuse to seek shelter with them, the only way you'll be safe is if Halwyn is captured or slain."

"I don't understand why he wants the throne so badly in the first place. Did he have something against Adair?"

"Not personally, only that Adair didn't agree with his attitude toward your kind."

"That we're toys or living energy batteries or whatever?"

"Halwyn regards human folk as inferiors, little more than talking animals. He also maintains an abiding bitterness against the human race for driving our people to the fringes of the earthly plane. Centuries ago, our realm and yours overlapped much more than they do now. Gradually, as the human population expanded, our domain grew smaller, until we found ourselves pushed out of this world altogether. Some creatures such as the brownies, pixies, pookas, and other lesser fairy folk adapted to living secretly among you. We elves became, as Halwyn and his faction see it, exiles from our rightful lands."

"So he plans to invade and reconquer the Earth?" She put down the ragged half of her sub, wiped her fingers on a napkin, and hoisted Baird to her shoulder for a burp. Unlike the revelations about kidnapping and torture, that scenario sounded so far-fetched it didn't stir any fear inside her.

Kieran said with a dry laugh, "He has no such unrealistic ambition. The time for reconquest is long past, if it could have ever happened. We've always been few and slow at reproducing compared to humans. Now we bear children very seldom, one reason why human changelings are valued and half-elves are desired for breeding partners. Another practice Halwyn disapproves of, naturally. He aims to become king mainly so that your race will be treated as he believes they deserve, as toys or prey. As part of that policy, he would end what he calls the contamination of our bloodlines with human spawn."

A lump of bread stuck in her throat. She choked it down. "But you claim you don't feel that way at all?"

He cast a bleak stare at her. "If I did, would I take these risks?"

She took another bite of her sub, and her stomach churned. She tossed the rest of the sandwich to Harvey. "Now I'm even less sure I want to meet any of your people. But if we have to do it, let's get moving."

Chapter Eight

When they entered the Hampton Roads Tunnel, Kieran asked in a strained voice, "This one is short, yes?"

She nodded. On the way, she noticed him flexing his fingers on his lap and drawing labored breaths. He didn't look quite as sick as before, though. Soon after emerging from the tunnel, they reached a less crowded section of the interstate, with traffic flowing at top speed and long stretches of woods and open fields between towns. They traveled steadily, making only brief pit stops to tend the baby. Fortunately, Baird was still young enough that the car's motion kept him lulled asleep through most of the trip. When they got hungry, they nibbled on the snacks they'd bought back in Virginia Beach. Kieran's claim that the portal would close by sunset gnawed at Fern's mind and urged her to hurry. The sky gradually turned overcast. By the time they got to the edge of the Shenandoah Mountains, on the fringe of the national park, a light drizzle was falling from the gray clouds. Fern glanced at her watch. Close to seven p.m.

"Lucky it's June," she said. "The sun won't set for almost another two hours. Do you know if that gate of yours is still open?"

She glanced sideways at Kieran, who closed his eyes and spread his fingers as if plucking invisible harp strings. "Yes," he said after a few seconds. "Still capable of being opened. Continue traveling northwest."

His directions guided her along the winding, uphill roads. They encountered only a few other vehicles. Once she had to brake for a doe and a fawn bounding across the car's route. The drizzle increased to a steady rain. Finally, Kieran asked her to slow down. "Very near," he murmured. "Stop as soon as you can."

Scanning the side of the road, she soon found a spot where the trees thinned enough to let her pull off the pavement. She drove under the trees and parked with the hood pointed into the woods. "Now what?" she said, switching off the motor and setting the hand brake.

"We can't get any closer to the portal this way. I'll have to walk. You had best wait in the car."

"How long?" Her stomach fluttered with anxiety at the thought of meeting elven royalty. If they would consent to meet her at all. *If I'm not dreaming all this weirdness. Actually, this would be a good time to wake up*. She blinked. Nothing changed.

"The walk will take ten or fifteen minutes each way. I'll stop just inside the gate, at the juncture of the two worlds, where the time difference doesn't apply. From there, I can send a message to Oberon and Titania. One of them will surely answer."

"Nice to hear you're so confident. Then what?"

"Then I return here, and we wait for one or both of them to come to us." "What's to stop them from just zapping me and taking Baird?"

"I will not let that happen." He leaned closer and put an arm around her shoulders. "You are his closest human kin. They must respect that."

"Oh, yeah? I sure hope they see it that way." She covered her eyes and released a shuddering sob. Kieran's one-arm embrace tightened. Warmth radiated from him down her spine and through her rib cage to the pit of her stomach. "All I want is to take Baird home and make a secure life for him, a normal life. All I ask from them is to get rid of Halwyn so my baby will be safe."

"I'll see what I can do." His breath ruffled her hair. "I promise I won't let either of you come to harm."

She almost believed him. She just wasn't sure she trusted his definition of "harm" to coincide with hers. When he released her with what felt like reluctance, she let out a trembling breath.

"Stay in the car," he said, exiting from the passenger side. "The steel will give you some protection." He opened the back door, and Harvey jumped out. "The pooka will watch over you from outside. If Halwyn does appear, don't hesitate. Run him down with the vehicle."

"I don't know if I could do that."

He slammed the back door, peeled off his gloves to tuck them into a pocket, and strode around to her side. Rain slicked his hair and trickled down his face. She rolled the window down a couple of inches. The fragrance of damp earth and honeysuckle vines drifted in on the wet breeze. "You may have to force yourself. Baird's safety may depend on disabling Halwyn. Enough. Time grows short." He turned away and started walking into the forest.

Fern switched on the ignition to take advantage of what little coolness the air conditioning offered. With a tissue from the box between the seats, she blotted clammy moisture from her forehead. The pooka paced up and down, crushing stalks of yellow wildflowers under his huge paws. Abruptly he halted and swiveled his muzzle toward a clump of trees right behind the car. Turning her head and squinting through the rain in the same direction, she thought she glimpsed movement in the underbrush. A second later, a branch stirred into motion. Clusters of twigs scrabbled in the soil and leaf mold like the legs of giant insects. Her heart leaped with alarm.

She blinked, and the scene snapped into focus. The tangles of branches became living things like stick puppets about two feet tall. They had goat hooves in place of feet and beards that resembled tufts of moss. They skittered into the open, dozens of them. Kieran, almost out of sight on the narrow path between the trees, whirled around and sprinted toward the clearing. The stick-things mobbed him. With her breath trapped in her throat, Fern watched their claws rip into his skin. Another figure lurched into her field of vision. This one looked human, in a grotesquely distorted way. Its arms and legs were twisted like gnarled tree limbs. The same height as the stick-things but squat and muscular, with fingers and bare feet ending in talons, it wore a tunic of red rags and a drooping, hood-like hat of the same color. A fierce grimace displayed rows of pointed teeth like a shark's. A second glance revealed that the creature's hat and clothes appeared soaked with darker stains than rainwater. Blood?

That must be a redcap! God, please help us! She clutched the Celtic cross. Too bad these monsters weren't movie demons that a cross really could vanquish. *Stay in the car*, Kieran had ordered. The last thing she wanted to do was charge into that battle, especially with Baird to worry about. Her heart raced with terror at the sight of the stick-mannequins tearing at Kieran. He knocked them away or broke them in half while Harvey crunched several between his jaws, but there were so many that the mob didn't seem to decrease. The redcap pounced on Kieran and sank its fangs into his leg. He tore the attacker loose and threw it to the ground. Blood trickled from the gash it left behind.

What could she do? Run over them with the car, the way he'd suggested? She might easily hit him, too.

A tap on the window made her heart leap. She looked sideways and faced Halwyn gazing in at her. She squeezed the cross again, until its points gouged her palm. "Stay away from me." According to what Kieran had told her, Halwyn must have used a spell to force some driver to bring him here.

Gloved hands resting on the side of the car, he said with a smile, "I don't mean you any harm. What lies has Kieran been telling you now?"

"Then why are you chasing us, especially with all those...things? And how did you find us?"

"You can see them?" For an instant his eyes blazed with anger. The glow vanished so quickly she thought she might have imagined it. "Interesting. Then there's no point in my lying, is there? I'm not chasing you personally, Miss MacGregor. As I said before, I'm after Kieran, to take him home to stand trial for our cousin's murder. Knowing what he's capable of, is it unreasonable that I'd collect a few allies to help capture him?" The reassuring tone might have convinced her right away if she hadn't heard Kieran's side of the story. "As for how I found you, whenever Kieran stepped out of this metal vehicle, I sensed his location. It wasn't hard to guess he'd be guiding you to the portal. What reason did he give you for that?"

"He's going to arrange for me to meet Adair's parents. They'll sort out who's on the right side."

Halwyn's smile widened. "So that's what he told you? Come, now, do you believe he'll give up his goals that easily? Didn't it occur to you that at the first opportunity he'll grab the baby and escape through the gate with him?"

That scenario sounded all too plausible. "I won't let him." The vow sounded feeble even to herself. How could she stop Kieran, if he resorted to force? "And I sure won't let you lay a hand on Baird, either."

"I haven't the slightest intention of hurting him. I suppose Kieran told you I plan to steal or kill the child?" He didn't wait for an answer. "Yes, I want to keep your nephew from inheriting the throne, but I mean him no harm. My goal is the same as yours, to have him stay in the human world and spend his life here."

"What are you saying? That you're just out to get Kieran, and Baird and I happened to stumble into the line of fire?"

"Well put. If you help me capture Kieran, both of our purposes will be achieved." Apparently sensing her hesitation, he added, "If he surrenders peacefully, he won't be injured any further. He will have a fair trial."

Although Fern didn't trust Halwyn, the more she thought about Kieran the more she felt sure he hadn't granted her the full truth. Once she let down her guard, he could easily snatch Baird, flee into the portal, and seal it against her. And for all she knew, he might have lied about his innocence of Adair's murder. The kiss and the mind-touch didn't guarantee his sincerity. How could she trust the intuition she'd denied for so long not to lead her astray? On the other hand, she couldn't stomach the idea of actively helping Halwyn, not with his bloodthirsty "allies" swarming in front of her.

This is my chance, she thought. *To hell with both of them.* She revved the engine, threw the transmission into reverse, and backed out of the clearing onto the road. On the pavement, she spun the car around and sped eastward. Now that she knew the danger threatening Baird, she would have warning if the king and queen sent any other agents in search of him. If she had to abandon her home and become a fugitive for the next twenty years, she would keep the baby out of their clutches. She wasn't ignorant and helpless any longer. She knew a little about guarding against elven magic, and she would learn more. One last glimpse of Kieran haunted her, the sight of his arms and legs bleeding from multiple scratches and bites while the twig-things and the redcap swarmed over him. And the shock on his face when he glanced her way, a wave of pain and anger surging from his mind into hers. *No, I must have imagined that part.* She couldn't do anything for him. Her nephew's safety came first.

Kieran wrenched yet another spriggan off his leg and tore it limb from limb, then kicked the redcap in the head and stomped on its hand as it groped for his ankle. From the corner of his eye, he saw the car backing up. Momentarily distracted, he stared through the windshield at Fern. *No! Dark Powers, what is she doing?* Why didn't she use the vehicle's steel as a weapon against Halwyn and his minions, as she'd been told? Instead, she was running away.

He forced his attention back to the fight. A few feet away, the pooka struggled against three spriggans at once. The thick fur offered some protection, but the pooka, like Kieran, had suffered wounds. One spriggan wrapped its arms around the pooka's neck, scratched dangerously close to an eye with its thornlike claws, and with the claws of the other hand dug into the pooka's fur. It was trying to gouge out his throat.

Kieran kicked the redcap aside yet again and dashed to the pooka's side, his feet sliding on the wet leaves. He grabbed the spriggan, lifted it in the air, and ripped its head off. The beasts broke as easily as the dry twigs they resembled, but their numbers made up for their weakness. The other two that had menaced the pooka fastened onto Kieran's legs, and the rest of the gang crawled over him, stinging like a nest of hornets. He slipped in the mud and stumbled to one knee. Halwyn charged toward him.

Kieran saw a flash of polished stone in his enemy's right hand. The dart flew toward him, at too close a range to dodge. It pierced his shirt and penetrated the flesh of his shoulder. The point burned with poison. Agony blazed through his veins. Collapsing onto his side, he gritted his teeth to suppress a groan. *Fern, why couldn't you trust me?* Now, not only would he be unable to protect her and Baird, he would never have a chance to conquer that mistrust.

Baird emitted a siren-like shriek, a scream like nothing Fern had ever heard from him. At the same moment, pain stabbed through her collarbone. She slammed on the brakes and stopped on the roadside with a squeal of tires. Her head pounded. *Kieran*! He was writhing in torment and despair. For all she could tell, he might be dying.

Halwyn lied! That line about arresting Kieran peacefully had been a load of bull. She realized she had listened only because she wanted to escape from the whole mess. Halwyn planned to kill Kieran. She couldn't let him.

Before this thought completely formed, she'd already turned the car around and started back to the clearing. She didn't stop to think what she could do against Halwyn and his monsters. Kieran was in danger because of her, and she had to help him. She raced up the road with his agony screaming in her brain. In the seat behind her, Baird still cried, now in normal infant tones.

She took in the scene at a glance--Kieran curled on the ground, Halwyn looming over him, the pooka snarling at the redcap that barred him from attacking Halwyn. Twig creatures clustered around the two elves.

She gunned the engine and drove straight into the clump of monsters. Although she thought she heard branch-like arms and legs crunching under the wheels, she couldn't be sure over the pain that still reverberated in her head. Whatever creatures she didn't crush scattered for the trees. She swerved to avoid running into Kieran, and Halwyn dodged at the same instant. With a hard right turn of the wheel, she rammed into Halwyn and hit the brakes. When she opened her door and leaped out with the car keys in one hand, she saw the redcap flat in the dirt. The pooka sprang on it and bit through its neck.

The pain and noise in her skull faded. She hastily locked the car and took a step toward Kieran, who lay with his eyes fixed in a stare and his arms wrapped around himself, shuddering. A warning itch at the nape of her neck made her glance at Halwyn. He stirred and shoved his arms under his body, trying to lever himself upright. Fern rushed at him, whipped the necklace off, and lashed him in the face with the cross. To her astonishment, he let out a high-pitched scream and fell backward, stunned. A black scorch mark scarred his cheek where she'd hit him. "It must be the iron," she said aloud.

A groan from Kieran redirected her attention. "Bind him," he said through clenched teeth.

"With what?" The rest of the stick monsters had disappeared, the pooka snarling after the last of them as they fled into the woods. Harvey then trotted over to Halwyn and crouched over him, jaws gaping above his neck.

"No," Kieran whispered. "No murder. Bind with iron before he wakes up."

"But you need help!"

Kieran glowered at her. "Listen, for once." He forced out each word as if it cut his mouth like a razor blade.

"Chain," she said. "I do have a chain in the trunk." She'd borrowed it to fasten a secondhand bookcase to the car's roof months earlier and never gotten around to returning it. After getting the chain from the car, she bent Halwyn's arms behind his back and wound the links around them and his waist, then dragged his inert body a few yards to the nearest tree. After one accidental glimpse, she kept her eyes averted from the redcap's mangled corpse. Nausea welled in her throat at the welts that appeared on Halwyn's forearms where his sleeves crept up to expose bare skin. After wrapping the chain around the tree trunk, she knotted it as tightly as she could. The pooka, its lips curled in a silent snarl, stood guard beside the unconscious elf. "That won't last long if he comes to and starts struggling."

"Doesn't have to," Kieran rasped. "I'll bring help through the gate. They'll take him back for judgment. Meanwhile, the metal cripples him." He pushed against the wet ground and managed to raise himself onto his knees.

After cramming the iron cross into the side pocket of her shorts, she hurried to him and reached under his arm to wrap hers around his back for support. He shook his head. "Go away. Don't want your help."

Her heart stuttered at his harsh tone. *If I'd trusted my instincts, this wouldn't have happened.* She could hardly blame him, but they didn't have time to argue. "Well, you need it. You can't even stand, much less walk ten or fifteen minutes into the woods."

After a few seconds of cold silence, he nodded and draped his arm over her shoulders. She stood, hauling him upright with her. She noticed several oozing slashes on his arms and legs. "You're bleeding."

"Least of my troubles."

"Your blood's red."

"What did you expect?"

"Green, maybe, considering the pointed ears." She sensed his puzzlement but decided it would take too long to explain the remark.

He staggered when they started walking. "You're right," he said hoarsely. "Weaker than I thought. May I borrow energy from you?"

"What? How?"

"Strong emotion." With one arm, he pulled her body tightly against his. The fingers of his other hand cupped the back of her head and tangled in her wet hair. She stared into his moss-green, feline eyes while his mouth descended upon hers. Her lips parted in a gasp of surprise. She felt as if he were stealing her breath, making her heart race to circulate the little air she had left.

When his tongue darted between her lips, she involuntarily licked out to meet it. His spicy flavor and the contrast between his cool, damp skin and the heat of his mouth sent sparks dancing through her nerves. His long fingers caressed the nape of her neck, stirring heat that radiated along her spine and out to every extremity. The arm encircling her swept down her back to mold her curves and hollows to his lean form.

The kiss became harsher, crushing her lips against his teeth while his fingers massaged her neck and her lower back with insistent force. She made a halfhearted move to pull away, but he only tightened his embrace. He flexed his legs to align their bodies more intimately. Feeling his hardness made the heat within her rush to pool in that spot. She wrapped her arms around him and closed her eyes to savor the pressure of his body against her breasts and the vee of her thighs, the tingling in her nipples, the melting inside her that made her yearn to open and draw him in. If only his embrace meant affection and desire instead of raw need.

Abruptly he broke off the kiss and held her at arm's length. "Enough. We can't linger here."

Her head reeled. She clutched his forearms until the dizziness faded. "What happened?" she whispered, quivering with embarrassment at her reaction to him.

"I told you. I drew upon your energy."

"Like Halwyn with his slaves?" She flushed with indignation.

"No, not like him. I did you no harm, and I did nothing against your will. Now perhaps I can fight off the poison."

Had her will actually consented to that moment of ravishing? She postponed that question. "Poison? What did Halwyn do to you?"

"Elf-shot. An envenomed dart that dissolved within the wound. It would have killed a human victim, as it did your sister. Since it did not strike me in a vital spot, I won't die." He released her arms and glared at her. "But I might have, if Halwyn had been a bit more skillful or fortunate."

She flushed between shame and anger. "I'm sorry. I shouldn't have left, all right? I panicked."

"Why didn't you do as I told you? If you had run him down to begin with, this would not have happened." His pain, anger, and sense of betrayal crashed over her in waves.

How can I be feeling his emotions? She drew a labored breath and said, "Because I was thinking mainly of Baird, and I wasn't sure what to believe. You weren't totally honest with me. Don't try to claim you were."

"I'll answer your charges after we open the gate." He took one unsteady step up the narrow path.

"Hang on, I can't leave Baird alone in the car for half an hour or more. Stay here while I get him." Despite his partial recovery, Kieran didn't look strong enough for any unnecessary effort.

He seized her wrist in a painful grip. "Wait." He froze, with his head tilted as if listening.

The ground rocked under her feet. She closed her eyes as a vision flashed into her mind--a vee-shaped cleft in a stony hillside. An elongated shimmer of prismatic light. Through the rainbow veil, she caught glimpses of blue-green grass, trees with feathery leaves, and the multicolored wings of exotic birds, or possibly giant butterflies. The perfume of roses blotted out the scents of honeysuckle and wet leaves. She heard chimes like silver on crystal and yearned to race toward them. Tears welled in her eyes.

Suddenly the images vanished like a bubble bursting. She blinked and stared at Kieran. "What was that?"

"You saw the portal through my eyes, didn't you?" His voice sounded flat with despair as well as exhaustion. "It's sealed. We're too late."

"What do we do now?"

"I can't risk another confrontation with Halwyn until I've recovered. We must find a safer place."

"Didn't you say he couldn't get loose?"

"Not by his own strength, but he would have no compunctions about summoning a few spriggans or other creatures to break the chains."

"Spriggans? That's what the walking tree branches are called?"

He nodded. "Halwyn wouldn't care how badly they got hurt in freeing him. I don't like leaving him here, but I can't slay him and become the murderer he called me. There are other ways to make contact with the elven realm. If I can manage to get a message to the king and queen, he can still be brought to justice."

On the way to the car he stumbled a couple of times. Even though he'd regained some of his strength, he was still obviously far from healed. Fern opened the passenger door for him so he wouldn't have to put the gloves back on. A light rain kept falling, and thunder rumbled faintly in the distance. The pooka jumped into the backseat, where Baird squirmed in his seat with hiccuping sobs. He stopped crying when Harvey nuzzled him. Thank goodness the creature didn't smell like a wet dog, she reflected. He barked a series of syllables at Kieran.

"Is he talking to you?"

"Yes, thanking me for saving him from the spriggans. That is why he decided to continue traveling with us, even though our chances don't look good at the moment."

"You were right," she said while backing out of the clearing and turning onto the road. "I shouldn't have doubted Halwyn was trying to kill you. But I think one thing he said was true. You were planning to carry Baird through the portal no matter what, weren't you?"

Kieran's expression of guilt answered that question. "You lied to me!"

"Can't you see I was right? The only place Baird can be safe is inside the Hollow Hills. Would you rather I have used magic to stun you and snatch him out of your arms?"

"Never mind that now. What are we going to do?"

"Shelter first, until the poison wears off." Fatigue slurred his voice. "I know a man who might be able to help us send a message to Adair's parents, but he lives quite a distance south of here."

She waited for more detailed instructions. When Kieran didn't volunteer any, she said, "Okay, we head south."

After a few minutes of driving, while he leaned back against the headrest with his eyes shut, he asked, "You had obviously decided to abandon me. Why did you change your mind and return?"

The word "abandon" stung, but she couldn't deny its accuracy. "I felt your pain. I sensed you were in danger. Baird reacted, too, which must be because he's half-elf and related to you. But how did I know?"

"You have the Sight, whether you like it or not. You've managed to block it, for the most part, but this incident confirms that the kiss we shared yesterday must have opened up your power."

"Then when I thought I imagined you standing over Adair's body, it was a vision of something that really happened? Now I'm sure I don't want this power!"

"You saw me discovering his body after Halwyn killed him, magically disguised as me. And as for your wanting the ability to sense my condition, I didn't ask for it, either." He shot her a reproachful look before shutting his eyes again. "Do you think I want my mind touched by someone who suspects me of murder?"

A whirlwind of guilt and anger raged in her head. The lines of strain around Kieran's mouth and eyes didn't do anything to mitigate her self-reproach. "You aren't getting any better, are you?"

Eyes still closed, he shook his head. "The steel of the car augments the effect of the poison. I can't stand it much longer."

"Then we won't even try to get to wherever you're planning to take us next, not tonight." Twilight was closing in. "You need to rest until the dart wears off. It will wear off, won't it?"

He sighed. "I have never been wounded this way before. It should heal, I think.

Eventually."

"I'll find us a place for the night." Although she had never vacationed in this area, she knew there had to be plenty of tourist accommodations this close to the national park. A short drive led to the nearest town, and after passing antique shops, roadside produce stands, and the local post office, she stopped at a combination gas station and convenience store. Kieran waited in the car, his arms folded as if warding off a chill, while she refilled the tank, changed the baby, and asked for directions.

When she rejoined him, she said, "The guy told me about a place a few miles away with cabins for rent. He says they don't allow pets, though." She glanced at Harvey, who panted at her with a cartoon animal grin.

"Don't worry," Kieran said, his voice low and strained. "As I said before, the pooka can make himself invisible to mundane sight."

"Meaning everybody except other fairy creatures and lucky people like me who use magic eye drops?"

He didn't react to her sarcasm, only closed his eyes again and huddled in his seat, shrinking from contact with the door.

Chapter Nine

Fifteen minutes later, she found the tourist cabins the store cashier had told her about. Parking in front of the office at the entrance to the complex, she left Kieran and Harvey in the car with Baird while she went inside. By now, she knew Kieran well enough to believe his claim that he couldn't drive off with her car and the baby, even if he weren't too sick to try. Fortunately, the manager had a vacant unit available, which she rented for one night. She frowned at the bill before stuffing it into her purse. At this rate, she would have to resort to her backup emergency credit card soon. On the other hand, having nothing worse than money to worry about sounded idyllic at this point.

In the gathering dark she drove slowly along the winding road through a corridor of overhanging trees, while she tried to read the manager's hand-printed directions by the car's dome light. Rain slicked the pavement and splintered the glow of the headlight beams. She discovered their cabin, built of gray-brown, weathered wood, set back from the road and shielded from the units on either side by clumps of trees. She turned up the gravel driveway with a sigh of relief at the prospect of a night's rest. Baird babbled to the pooka in the backseat. Kieran shivered as if racked by a fever. Whatever burst of energy he'd siphoned from her must have worn off. A blush heated her cheeks at the thought of how he'd drawn it. *He used me.* But did she really wish he'd kissed her from any other motive? Surely the last thing she wanted was a lover from another species and world. Even Ivy, who'd had the temperament for that kind of adventure, had run into disaster by welcoming it into her life.

Fern shook off the memories of her sister before they could overwhelm her and opened the back car door for the pooka to jump out. Lightning flashed, followed a few seconds later by a sullen peal of thunder. Unbuckling the baby, she asked Kieran, "What are the chances we'll be safe here overnight?"

He made a visible effort to collect himself for a reply. "That depends on how fast Halwyn becomes conscious and how soon he can compel a minion to free him. After that, he must use his powers to sense where we've gone and then force some unsuspecting human to transport him. If he is weakened enough by the touch of iron, that might take quite a while." He opened the door, swung his legs out, and heaved himself upright. "The pooka will stand guard out here through the night, and I'll set wards to alert us of any danger, as well."

While she unlocked the cabin and carried Baird and their supplies inside, Kieran paced the perimeter of the small cleared space that surrounded the building. Between trips to and from the car in the rain, she watched him wave his arms as if weaving threads of light and chant words she couldn't understand. A shimmering, violet veil appeared in his wake. When he finished his circuit of the lot, the wall of light encircled it completely. He stepped onto the low porch and leaned against a post, drawing labored breaths. "That will also mask us from Halwyn's magical perception, at least for a while. It is more substantial than the wards I created at your friend's home."

"And it took more out of you, too, didn't it? Not that you had much left to work with, anyway. Get inside before you fall down."

He forced a faint smile. "You speak wisely."

Trying to shake off the guilty awareness that his condition was at least half her fault, she slipped her arm around his waist and hooked his over her shoulders. Better that than have to try hauling him upright if he did fall, regardless of the maddening way her pulse quickened when their bodies touched. The cabin comprised a bedroom, bath, and living room with fireplace. She walked him into the bedroom and lowered him onto the bed, where he sat with his head in his hands.

"You're getting the spread wet," she murmured, hastily retreating into the bathroom. She came back with a pair of towels, one of which she handed to him before heading into the front room to tend to Baird.

She'd left the baby lying face-up on a blanket on the rug in front of the hearth. She'd hooked a teething ring of soft plastic around his hand to keep him content until she'd finished helping Kieran inside. Now the toy floated a couple of inches above Baird's chest, while he batted at it with random swipes of his arms.

"I don't believe it," she whispered. She sank onto her knees, plucked the toy out of the air, and gaped at it. Nothing remarkable, just the same old ring of squishy, gel-filled material with multicolored plastic fish suspended inside it. "You really do have magic, little guy. Oh, Lord, what am I going to do with you?" If his powers grew stronger with nobody around competent to teach or control him, how could she handle any dangers they might present? "I'll just have to learn to deal," she whispered. "I'm not giving you up." Dropping the toy, she wrapped him in the other towel to rub him dry.

After filling a bottle and warming it under running hot tap water, she sat in an armchair to feed him. He gulped down the milk, then fell into a doze immediately after his final burp. "You've had a hard day, sweetie. Haven't we all?" She tiptoed into the bedroom with him and cradled him in one arm while lining a drawer to substitute for a bed. She didn't want to call the manager's office for a crib. Though she had no evidence that letting an outsider through the enchanted barrier would weaken it, she had no concrete reason to be sure it wouldn't. Nor did she completely trust Harvey's supposed invisibility, despite Kieran's assurances, and she didn't want to get into an argument over her "dog".

Kieran, lying on his side with the towel under his head, watched her. The sensation of his eyes on the back of her neck made her breathing rapid and shallow. Once finished with the baby, she turned to look at him. Blood still seeped from the scratches on his arms and legs. "You need those cleaned up," she said, detesting the thready sound of her own voice. "I'll take care of it."

She got a wet washcloth and another towel from the bathroom, along with antiseptic wet wipes and a package of Band-Aids from the baby bag. "Better take off your shirt so I won't miss anything." She blushed at the accidental innuendo. She had no interest in his bare chest, she insisted to herself. She just needed to make sure none of those wounds got infected. He might have immunity to standard earthly diseases, but who knew what filth spriggans and redcaps carried on their claws and teeth?

"This really isn't necessary," he said, though he compliantly stripped off his soaked shirt and stretched out on the towel. He had already taken off his shoes while she'd been out of the room. He was still shivering.

"I'll be the judge of that," she said, "and the quicker I get done, the sooner you can wrap up in the covers and get warm." She laid an open palm on his shoulder. The skin, though as pale as ever, felt scorching hot.

She scanned his upper torso in the lamplight. His lean, milk-white chest was smooth except for a sprinkling of downy, silver hair. On one shoulder a purple patch like a swollen bruise surrounded a dull red puncture. "Oh...that's where the dart went in?"

He nodded.

"You're sure it's dissolved?"

"Yes, that is how it works. The dart is gone. Only the venom remains."

When she dabbed at the entry wound with antiseptic, he clenched his teeth with a hissing intake of breath. "Sorry. This may not help, but it can't hurt." She followed up with the cool washcloth and patted the spot dry with the towel. Next she did the same for each of the gashes, bandaging the ones that wouldn't stop bleeding. She decided to leave the dart wound exposed to air. Cleaning the scratches on his arms didn't bother her much, except when he flinched in silent pain at the sting of the medicine on the wet wipes. Tending his legs, though, made her face flush with heat again. She could only be grateful he hadn't been clawed above the knees. When she got to the bite on one calf, the semicircle of fang marks distracted her from the inappropriate fluttering in her diaphragm that brushing against him provoked. "That looks awful."

"Redcap," he whispered.

"Monster. Did it help Halwyn from pure meanness or what?"

"Redcaps crave human and elven flesh and blood, and folk such as Halwyn give them ample opportunity to feed. Other creatures, such as the spriggans, obey his kind out of fear or because they loathe humanity. Some, like boggarts, delight in mischief and cruelty for their own sake."

She gulped. "Sorry I asked."

After she rinsed out the cloth, she came back into the room and found him under the covers. She turned off the lamp. "I'll let you get some sleep." From the fading of the thunder, she guessed the worst of the storm was moving out of the area.

He reached out to clasp her wrist. "Wait. Sit with me."

"Why?"

"To ward off nightmares. From the venom." She had to strain to hear the whispered reply.

"Okay, just for a minute." Her heart raced. She sat on the edge of the mattress, careful to keep her hip from touching his side. His thumb brushed back and forth over the pulse point on her wrist. Shivers coursed up the inside of her arm. Her nipples hardened, an effect she told herself resulted from a damp shirt and bra in the cool night air.

"You owe me that much," he said, his voice slurred. His catlike eyes gleamed in the dark. "You deserted me."

"Haven't I apologized for that enough? Besides, you got us into that mess by heading for the portal in the first place without telling me your whole plan." That counter-accusation might not be quite fair, but she couldn't endure his reproachful tone without defending herself.

"Why couldn't you trust my word? Your sister trusted Adair. She had faith he would not have left her voluntarily."

"Well, he didn't keep secrets from her, did he? You lied to me several times."

"What should I have said?" He squeezed her fingers. "Would you have believed in elves or in Halwyn's threat, if I had told you those things to begin with?" He shifted restlessly, as if the dart wound pained him. "King Oberon didn't trust me, either. And I told him the truth. I am innocent of Adair's murder."

"Yes, I know. I believe that now."

"He knew me from birth. He knew I loved Adair and valued my own honor. Yet he believed lies and slander instead of my word." The sadness that emanated from him spread to envelop her like a gray fog. "He sent two of his beast-men guards to drag me into his court like a fugitive. When he sentenced me to exile and they cast me out at spear point, pixies and sprites nipped at my ankles, and sylphs and undines whispered taunts in my ears as I passed."

"Didn't you try to defend yourself? To prove the real facts of the crime?"

"Why should I have to?" Kieran said in a hoarse whisper. "He should have believed me from the first. But now..." His voice trailed off. After a few seconds of silence, he drew a deep breath and said, "Pride isn't enough. Now I will submit to proof. Truth spell. Your witness will help."

"Me? How?"

"You can testify to Halwyn's vileness. That should be enough. Enough for them to give me a fresh chance to vindicate myself." His thumb traced circles on her palm. She wondered if he was aware of her trembling. She sensed the hurt behind his words when he continued, "May not want to live at court now. Not if they could believe I murdered Adair."

"But you still want that reconciliation, don't you? Vindication."

"Yes. Only family I have. At least to know they accept me. I don't want to live in exile the rest of my life." His voice sounded thick with unshed tears.

"You're lucky to have a family to go back to. Mine's all gone. I loved them even if they drove me nuts."

"Nuts?" he murmured.

"Out of my mind. Mom and Ivy understood each other. I had to be the normal, practical one. I tried so hard to keep my friends from finding out I had a hippy mother and an airhead sister."

"Did your mother have the Sight, too?"

"I don't think so. She wouldn't have hidden that kind of thing if she'd had it. She'd have trusted people to accept her even with a touch of weirdness." Something she hadn't thought of in years popped into her head. "Once in a while she read Tarot cards at the coffeehouses where she recited her poems. So maybe she had a little bit of psychic power and didn't realize it." *What if I'd made more of an effort to confide in her about my intuitions, instead of hiding them? What if she'd believed me?* The thought made Fern's breath catch in her throat. *Too late, I'll never know.* "Other than that, I think the power skipped a couple of generations."

"To you and Ivy."

"Yeah, and what did it get us? She fell in love with an elf prince and got herself killed, and I inherited her enemies. Adair probably would never have noticed her if she hadn't had this so-called gift on top of the musical talent, would he?"

"Perhaps not," Kieran sighed. "But perhaps so. She was headstrong and vibrant. Knew what she wanted from life. Like you..." His grip on her hand went slack, and his breathing slowed and deepened. Fern carefully stood up. He didn't move. She hoped this lapse into sleep meant natural healing, not a residual effect of the poison.

Vibrant? Me? Shaken by the implied compliment, not to mention the comparison with Ivy, she laughed under her breath. *He must be getting delirious.* In the living room she turned on both lamps and listened to the rain drumming on the roof. Hunger that had lurked in the background for the past few hours crept into her awareness. She made a cheese sandwich and ate it on the couch with a diet cola and another apple. Everything tasted flat, but she knew she had to get proper nourishment and rest for Baird's sake. Curled on the couch with her feet tucked under her, she read a chapter of the paperback mystery she carried in her purse. Her ears insisted on straining for noises underneath the rain. No sound from Kieran, Baird, or the pooka. She resisted the impulse to go to the window and peer into the darkness. As the night wore on, the temperature fell. The breeze sifting through the window, not airtight even after she closed it, felt downright chilly. Her eyes wandered to a pile of firewood on the hearth. Why not? A fire might make the cabin feel safer and less lonely, even if the feeling was only an illusion. She stacked logs in the fireplace, along with kindling and shredded paper from a box in the corner. After using up three matches, she coaxed the wood into flame.

A few more pages into the mystery novel, Baird woke up and cried. She managed to get him changed, fed, and settled down without disturbing Kieran. As she tiptoed out of the bedroom with a blanket and pillow from the closet, she wondered whether his overly sound sleep was a good or bad symptom. Her eyes began to ache in the firelight. Abandoning the book, she turned off the closer of the two lamps and stretched out on the couch. Although she usually didn't sleep well with a light on, tonight she didn't want to relax her guard in total darkness. *I'm not afraid of the dark*, she assured herself. *I just need some light in a strange place.* With rain still pattering on the roof, she slipped into unconsciousness.

She opened her eyes to an unsettling quiet. It took her a second to realize she didn't hear the rain anymore. Next she heard stumbling footsteps from the other room. She sat up, listening, with the blanket over her lap. Should she offer Kieran any help? If he resembled human males in that way, he wouldn't appreciate the humiliation of a hint that he couldn't cross a room by himself. Noises of knocking pipes and running water emanated from the bathroom, followed by the sounds of a lurching gait and a body colliding with a wall.

Instead of lying down, he appeared in the doorway between the two rooms. He'd pulled the cover off the bed and wrapped it around his shoulders. "Fern." He spoke quietly, with a tremor in his voice. "Cold." He staggered toward her. "Warm me."

She stood up and grabbed his elbow to steady him. His body shook with chills. In the dim lamplight, his eyes looked unfocused. If he hadn't said her name, she would have suspected he didn't know who she was. She guided him to the couch and wrapped her blanket around him over the bedspread. She added a log to the fire, then sat beside him. To her surprise, he slid an arm around her waist and drew her close, her hip and side touching his. His shivers coursed through her, too, although his skin felt scorching hot. Fumbling with the blankets, she got the double layer draped over both of them.

"You have a fever," she said. "Really bad."

"Need you," he muttered. "Warm me."

"I'm trying." She thought of the aspirin in her purse. Should she persuade him to swallow a couple of tablets? Or would the drug be toxic to his nonhuman system? She decided not to take the risk. Inside the blanket tent, the heat radiating from him made his bare chest feel like a miniature furnace. It seemed to suck her breath away. His fingers traced circles on her rib cage through her shirt. She wanted that touch on her skin instead. No, she wanted him to go away and leave her in peace before she melted into him and lost herself.

"I need your strength." Capturing her free hand with his, he bent to nuzzle the side of her neck. His lips seared her. "Can't fight off the venom."

Her head tilted back of its own accord. His cheek rubbed against hers. His skin felt perfectly smooth, without a trace of beard stubble. He nibbled up to her ear and along her jawline. Now she trembled almost as violently as he did.

"You smell like the freshness of earth." His hot breath made her skin quiver. She gasped at the sensation. "Is that supposed to be a compliment?"

"Like green growing things. You taste like wood smoke and salt."

"But you can't stand salt." She fought to keep the tremors out of her voice.

"A little adds sharpness. Keen flavor." His thumb caressed her palm, while his other hand continued to spiral over her ribs, creeping closer to the curve of her breast. "Please. Let me borrow your energy. For healing." His lips brushed hers.

Her mouth opened in an involuntary sigh. His tongue probed, and hers met it eagerly. His flavor of nutmeg and cloves teased her senses. Sparks flashed behind her closed eyelids. He sipped from her like a chalice, with delicate licks and nibbles between devouring kisses.

She drew back. "You're doing it again. Drinking my power." She could hardly believe she heard herself admitting she had that kind of power.

In the dimness his eyes gleamed like a cat's. "Please. For healing."

"You want more than a kiss this time, don't you?"

"Yes." The plea in his whispered reply melted her. "Much more." His hand roamed to her breast, with his palm grazing the nipple. Lightning zapped from there to the pit of her stomach and lower.

"If we made love, would it heal you completely?"

"Perhaps," he sighed into her hair. He let go of her hand to wrap both arms around her. Turning sideways, he tried to pull her body against his, while his lips and tongue explored her neck and throat. She twined her arms around his neck and laced her fingers through the silken fall of his shoulder-length hair. Her fingertips traced the outlines of his pointed ears. A shudder convulsed him.

"All right." Twisting free of his embrace, she slipped from the couch onto the rug and tugged him down with her. After so many years of celibacy, why was she willing to abandon her self-containment for this man, who wasn't even human? Just because he needed her energy to throw off the poison, and she needed him to save Baird? Or did she want him just for himself? *I'll think about that later.* His mouth captured hers again, and she was drowning in his ravenous passion. They reclined against the front of the sofa, twisting sideways to lean toward each other. The way he stroked her hair made her want to purr. She spread her fingers over his chest, not to fend him off but to feel his heartbeat. Or did she only imagine she could feel it? Maybe it was only reverberating inside her mind, a bass note underlying the harp music of his need. *I'm picking up his emotions again.* She resisted the impulse to repel him and bar the gates of her mind. She could no longer deny the reality of this power to sense his feelings, and he required that sharing to draw energy from her.

When her fingers brushed one of his pebble-hard nipples, he groaned into her open mouth. The sound pierced her to the core. The ache in her breasts radiated lower. Without breaking off the kiss, she slid down onto the floor, and he flowed with her. She yearned for the pressure of his burning flesh, even if the heat came from a poison- induced fever. She sensed he craved the same thing. They turned toward each other and tightened the embrace, so that their bodies touched at every point. The friction of her clothes tormented her. Wiggling out of his arms for a few seconds, she stripped off her shirt and bra. She couldn't suppress a moan of satisfaction when her nipples brushed his bare chest. She rolled onto her back, spontaneously spreading her legs to cradle him in the vee of her thighs.

Sensations, both hers and his, cascaded over her. She felt his hardness from inside as well as outside, his driving urgency, as well as the dryness of his throat, the persistent twinges of pain from the dart wound, the heat and chills coursing through him. Underneath all these feelings, a silent cry of loneliness wove through the harp song of his passion. His heat flowed to her center, and she sensed how he responded to her yielding softness with a sharper pang of need.

His mouth abandoned hers to explore her throat and breasts, wandering toward the firm, tingling tips with excruciating slowness. She emitted a low moan of dismay when he no longer pressed against the aching spot between her legs. When his tongue flicked one of her nipples, she involuntarily arched her hips at the surge of electricity that shot through her nerves to make her internal muscles clench. His hands roamed everywhere at once, one of them toying with her other breast, while the other finally settled in the place she needed it most. She felt the pressure building inside him in harmony with the expanding waves of pleasure his stroking and licking produced in her. When the final delirium swept over her, he captured her mouth and drank her passion.

His hands shook as he peeled her shorts and underpants off her trembling legs. Somehow he'd already shed the rest of his clothes. She was still melting and burning in answer to the need that radiated from him. A cry of ecstasy burst from her when he plunged into her depths. With her eyes closed, she found herself enveloped in a cloud of swirling colors. She was floating--no, drowning--no, soaring with him through those clouds that sparkled with the incandescence of rainbow-hued lightning bolts.

Sinking back into her body, she clasped him tightly, holding him deep inside her.

What the heck was that? I've never felt anything like it before.

His response surged through her, almost as clearly as words--*Nor have I.*

He still pulsed with hunger for her, and her body echoed his sensations. Again she felt his passion rising and saw those colors scintillating inside her head. His shaft hardened within her channel. Again they soared to the peak together.

For a few seconds a warm darkness wrapped her. The rainbow lights were gone. When she opened her eyes again, he leaned on an elbow to gaze at her. His green eyes glowed. "Thank you," he murmured, bending down to nuzzle her throat, then her hair. She felt him stiffening against her inner thighs yet again.

"Impossible," she said. "Ordinary men can't do it that often."

He said with a soft laugh that made the skin of her neck prickle, "We aren't subject to mortal limitations. Elven ladies, I've heard, have to keep their mortal lovers suspended on the brink for hours to get full satisfaction."

"Does this mean you're healed?"

He rested his head on her shoulder, and her arms automatically wrapped around him. Now he felt only warm instead of feverish.

"Only temporarily refreshed. Don't know whether the poison will fade away yet. Have to rest." He spoke with his voice muffled against her throat. The vibrations sent delicious tingles through her.

"On the floor? Not too restful." She didn't want to get up, though. She wanted to lie here forever and not have to face the dangers and complications ready to pounce on her with sunrise.

"You could rest if you came home with me. No fear, no hurt. Safe." The words and the emotion behind them enfolded her like a woolen cloak.

"Home? Elfland? You've got to be kidding."

"Why would you not want to dwell in the Hollow Hills? If you could see my world, you would desire nothing else."

"Yeah, I've heard about that." Ivy had been a fan of fairy tales and ballads, like the song of Thomas the Rhymer, seduced by the Fairy Queen and trapped in Elfland for seven years. "I wouldn't want anything else because the magic would make me forget my real life. No, thanks."

"Don't have to forget any parts you want to remember. I'd present you to Oberon and Titania. They would be grateful to you. Good caretaker for their little prince." His voice grew firmer, although still faintly slurred, as if he were drunk. "We'll enter the king and queen's domain through a waterfall rippling between walls of stone lined with mosaics of precious gems. The royal palace is shaped from a living tree, several times larger than this house. It's surrounded by an orchard perpetually both in bloom and in fruit. The throne room gleams with polished wood, and flowering vines adorn the walls and perfume the air. In the chamber where Adair and I used to sleep as boys, silver and golden fish as long as my arm swim in a crystalline pool."

"It sounds beautiful. No wonder you miss it."

"My own home domain is exquisite, too. My ancestors carved it by magic from opalescent stone. I wish I could show you my grove where rainbow-winged birds nest and fly or my sleeping bower cushioned with living moss. But those delights can't make up for the scorn of my foster father and mother."

"I know." Tears welled in her eyes, echoing the sadness he projected. "Even if my mom was a space case, at least I knew she loved me."

"When we deliver Baird safely to my aunt and uncle, they will welcome both of us with joy. You can share the beauty of my world with me. You will live far past the mortal span, with no illness or weakness, no drudgery, dirt, or labor."

"I happen to like working, thank you. And who says we're taking Baird into the Hollow Hills? I haven't changed my mind about that."

"You would never have to be separated from him, and both of you would be safe. I would keep you by my side. You wouldn't be a target for treacherous attack the way Adair was." Mental caresses that seemed to stroke her like a kitten underscored the pleading in his voice. "You would soon forget the burdens of your mortal life."

"I don't want to forget. All that is part of what makes me...me."

"One more thing--I would not have to part from you."

Her breath caught in her throat. "Since when would you care about that?" He couldn't mean that last statement. Either the poison was talking, or he was deliberately trying to manipulate her.

"I've known all along that human lovers fascinate some of our people because your kind live hot and fast. I've never fully understood that allure. Now I do. Come home with me, if only for a visit."

"Sorry, there's just no way." If he wasn't babbling in the aftermath of his fever, he was probably trying another ploy to get her to surrender Baird to the elven rulers. "Never mind, I don't want to argue with you when you're sick. It wouldn't be fair." With any luck, he would forget half of this conversation by morning, and she wouldn't have to face the question of how seriously he meant that ridiculous invitation. "I know it's out of character for me, but let's enjoy right now while we can." She wiggled under him and reveled in the instant stiffening of his shaft.

"I agree. Let me taste you, sip your nectar." His tongue flickered over her throat and breasts, then teased her lips until she parted them. "Let me show you the fullest delights of elven lovemaking." He explored and sampled every inch of her body, until pleasure sparkled in her veins like champagne. She opened up to draw him in. Sensation submerged thought, and again they floated through the rainbow-hued mist together. She didn't care whether that image was real or illusion, whether it came from his mind or her own. She wanted nothing at this moment but release and oblivion.

She fell asleep to the ringing of wind chimes inside her head. She dreamed of crystalline caverns, singing flowers, butterflies the size of hawks, emerald-skinned women with vines for hair, dew-spangled webs guarded by spiders with ruby eyes, and men with the heads of bears and foxes. Kieran stretched out a hand to draw her through a dim, green tunnel into a grove of ancient trees. She glided after him, and the darkness swallowed her.

Chapter Ten

Fern woke briefly in the middle of the night, with her back warmed by the smoldering fire and her front chilled. She watched Kieran in the faint glow from the hearth. He showed no sign of consciousness, even when Baird started whimpering. After hastily putting her clothes on, she fed the baby and put him back to bed. Once she had him settled, she covered Kieran with the blanket and lay down on the couch, where she told herself she would notice immediately if he got sick again.

The next time she opened her eyes, sunlight seeped through the window curtains, and she was alone in the living room. Her inner thighs felt sore, and her back ached from a night on the sofa. The smoky residue from the ashes tickled her nose. While opening the window for fresh air, she heard the shower running in the bathroom. Idly she wondered how he managed the metal fixtures. Maybe he wrapped a washcloth around the faucet handles. *Good, I won't have to face him right away.* A blush warmed her cheeks. He must have been half delirious the night before, judging from his incoherent speech. Did he remember inviting her to join him in the Hollow Hills? Would he regret what they'd done? *Do I regret it?* Her body still tingled from the stimulation, and again she felt like purring when the tactile memories of his caresses flowed over her. Yet she hardly knew him. She'd never made a habit of falling into bed with men, and last night's fall had even skipped the bed part.

Awareness of Kieran fizzed along her nerves--something deeper than the physical aftereffects of lovemaking. She shared the sting of hot water on his bare skin, the weakness in his limbs, the persistent soreness of the dart wound. She'd assumed the melding they'd experienced the night before, if it was real at all, would vanish by daylight. Why did it linger this way? When she walked into the bedroom, she felt the distance between them lessening. They gravitated to each other like magnets of opposite poles.

When he stepped out of the bathroom, with a hand on the door jamb to steady himself, their eyes met. She blushed again and averted her gaze from his level stare. She felt a barrier slam into place within his mind. Though his nearness made her skin prickle like a cool breeze wafting over her, she couldn't sense his emotions. That suited her fine. She didn't want him rummaging through hers, either. Naked except for a towel draped around his waist, he collapsed onto the bed. In the second before she averted her eyes, she noticed he'd removed the Band-Aids, revealing the scratches as almost healed. The flesh around the dart wound, in contrast, still looked swollen and painful. She scurried into the bathroom for her own shower, glad for a reason to shut a door between them. After dressing in the clothes she'd laundered at the beach cottage, she came out to find him dressed, too. He wore the silver-gray outfit in which she'd first seen him. Seated on the bed, he stared up and down her body. She flushed. "How are you feeling today? Any better?"

"The energy you replenished for me is slowly fading." He dropped what felt like the thin top layer of his barrier. "As you should be able to sense."

"Why should I?" She clenched her fist as if that gesture could ward off the threat of his words.

He sighed. "Don't waste time denying the new link we created between us. If a kiss or two could weaken the barrier caging your Sight, we shouldn't be surprised that a total coupling could shatter it."

"What are you saying? What do you think happened?"

"The physical union created a psychic bond between us." She sensed his reluctance to make that bond a concrete reality by putting it into words. His thoughts, like her own, felt tightly coiled in resistance to the idea.

"How do we get rid of it?"

"I don't know if we can." She sensed a tangle of conflicting emotions within him. "Do you truly want to?" His eyes captured and held hers.

"Why wouldn't I?" To avoid looking at him, she dug into the baby bag for a clean outfit and took a bottle into the bathroom to warm it under the hot water. Baird would probably wake up at any moment, with all the noise. "I value my independence too much to want some kind of magical bond chaining me to a man. Anyway, I'm not the first, am I? I'll bet you've had flings with other human females."

"That's true. Sometimes human visitors enter our realm for brief interludes."

"You mean elves capture them as pets or slaves, right?"

"Not always. Men and women with musical or poetic gifts come as guests and are sent home safely after--"

"After they lose their entertainment value?"

"I wouldn't put it that way, precisely. There are also permanent residents, the changelings I told you of, the ones who've been rescued from hopeless plights here in your world. Are you surprised that amorous encounters sometimes happen between elves and mortals?"

"I guess that makes me one more encounter." She stood in the doorway glaring at him, her hands on her hips.

"I have never experienced this merging with any other woman, elf or human."

"You do want it canceled, don't you?" He must. He couldn't have meant it when he asked her to live with him in his own world. Not that she would ever consider such a move.

He bowed his head onto his hands. "I'm honestly not sure."

Baird picked that minute to kick off his blanket and make snuffly waking-up noises. Fern changed him, then stripped off the rest of his clothes and carried him into the bathroom for a quick once over with a washcloth and towel. His gurgles had turned to wails by the time she got him dressed. When she sat on the edge of the mattress to feed him, an alarming thought popped into her mind. "What about pregnancy? I didn't even think!" Kieran's poison-induced mental confusion must have been contagious.

"Little fear of that," he said from his spot at the other end of the bed. "The low fertility of our kind makes conception rare even with mortals, although less rare than among ourselves."

"Oh, I guess Ivy and Adair found Baird under a cabbage leaf."

"Fortune blessed them. In general, the odds are against it."

"Thank heaven." A single baby under a year old was all she could imagine handling at once. Counting days in her own cycle, she decided with relief that the odds were low because of that factor alone.

After Baird finished his bottle, she left him in the middle of the bed, babbling at Kieran and grasping his index finger. She ate a granola bar, then poured a glass of juice for herself and milk for Kieran. "You still don't look good. You have to take some nourishment."

He sipped the milk with clear lack of enthusiasm. "I don't think the fever will return, but you can see I'm still weak. I'm afraid I can't recover completely without more help than you can give."

She flushed at the memory of her "help". "Then what could cure you?"

"The venom's effects are magical. Its traces have to be eliminated by magical means."

"Where can you get that, if the portal won't open for two months?"

"There are other gates on this continent," he said. "Each one has a different cycle, but none is located nearby. There's another possibility, though." He drank the rest of the milk with an appearance of grim determination. "I think I mentioned that I had another source of help in mind. It's a man who lives only a few hours' travel from here, a half-elf."

"Really? A half-elf living in our world?"

"He chose a human way of life rather than remaining in the Hollow Hills. That does happen occasionally, strange as that choice seems to me." A faint smile played on Kieran's lips. "I accompanied Adair on one of his pleasure trips into your world, before he met Ivy. We visited this man, Donal O'Connor. I remember the name of the town nearest his home. You should be able to find it on your map."

"So he can help you, how?"

"He specializes in potions. He should easily be able to supply me with a healing elixir. Also, he maintains a relationship with his full-blooded sister in the elven realm. If he agrees to contact her for us, she may be willing to deliver a message to Oberon and Titania."

"Just like that? Well, the sooner we get started, the sooner we'll get there. No telling when Halwyn might catch up, right?" She began stuffing Baird's scattered paraphernalia into the baby bag. "But what makes you think your friend Donal will help you? Suppose he's heard about your alleged crime and believes you're guilty of murder?"

"Unlikely. He doesn't have much use for the royal court. You remember what I told you about the prevailing attitude toward elves of mixed blood?"

"Yeah, which is one more reason I wouldn't want Baird living there."

"And I told you he would be an exception. The point is, though, that Donal has no royal or noble blood. By the time he reached adulthood, he'd grown tired of being treated as inferior, an object of pity or contempt except as a potential breeder."

"Who wouldn't? So he decided to live on Earth instead?" She slung the bag and her purse over her shoulder and picked up Baird.

"He has lived here for many decades. Even if he learned about Adair's murder from his sister, he would not necessarily accept the prevailing judgment about my villainy. I'm sure he will at least hear us out."

"Okay, sounds like the best option. Let's get going."

Outside they found Harvey lying at the bottom of the porch steps and keeping watch in the direction of the road. The curtain of energy, though less visible in daylight, remained intact around the property. Kieran said, "I don't sense Halwyn anywhere nearby."

"Then maybe we still have a good head start on him."

"We can hope so." With a wave of his hand, he made the warding barrier vanish. They piled themselves and their gear into the car, drove to the manager's office to drop off the key, and headed for the nearest freeway interchange. A quick search of the regional map gave Fern the location of the small town in North Carolina near Donal O'Connor's home. She calculated that the trip would take about four hours. She hoped Kieran's strength would hold up that long.

On the drive down the interstate, Fern kept a worried eye on Kieran. The surge of energy he'd drawn from her faded within an hour of waking. He looked even paler than normal and acted as if every move pained him. Thanks to the unwanted psychic link, her own muscles echoed the aches in his. He sat hunched on his side of the car, careful to avoid touching the door. "The steel in the car bothers you more than normal, doesn't it?" she said after a while.

Tight-lipped, he nodded.

"Then we should stop more often so you can get a break."

"Each time we get out of the car," he said, "Halwyn has a chance to pinpoint our location."

"If he's free, and if he's close enough to locate your aura or Baird's. We don't know that either of those things is true."

"We don't know they aren't. I do know that if he did get free, he'd have no compunctions about enchanting human victims to transport him at maximum speed."

She thought of suggesting that Kieran use his own magic to scan for Halwyn's proximity, the way he had back at the cabin. That aura thing seemed to work both ways. She decided not to mention it. Kieran didn't need any more stress on top of fighting the poison.

In spite of the risk, they had to make frequent stops anyway to tend the baby. Last night's storm had brought some relief from the heat and humidity. She would have enjoyed the bright summer day in other circumstances. Kieran obviously gained some benefit from breathing fresh air, even in freeway rest area parking lots. He continued to grow weaker, though. She felt the strain any physical effort cost him. He refused to eat or drink anything except water. Annoyed with herself for fretting about him, she focused on the map and the highway to fend off the question gnawing at her mind--did she worry only because she needed him to protect Baird or because she cared about him more than she wanted to?

Around midday she turned off Interstate 77 onto secondary roads that wound through a hilly region not far from the Virginia-North Carolina border. Half an hour later, they reached the town Kieran remembered from his one previous visit.

"Now it's up to you," she said while waiting for the one stoplight on the two-lane main street to turn green. "I hope you know the way from here."

He roused himself from a half doze. "Go through the town and out the other side."

She followed his directions, and a few minutes later they turned onto a sparsely traveled county road. "Yes, we're getting close," he said. "Slower, please."

She complied, pulling to the shoulder to let an impatient truck zip past. Soon Kieran directed her to turn into a tree-lined, one-lane private drive. "I recognize this place," he said. "And I feel Donal's presence."

"He isn't hiding, shielding, whatever you call it?"

"Why should he? I haven't heard that he has enemies among our kind, and it's no crime to choose a human lifestyle. Merely eccentric." Through his fatigue, he projected a trace of wry humor.

She followed the curvy, gravel-surfaced lane through the woods to its end, a circular driveway next to a modest-sized, two-story house with dark wood siding. A faint, violet aura that reminded her of Kieran's wards hovered around the building. She parked beside a pond where a flock of mallard ducks swam. Under a huge oak tree, a trellis overgrown with honeysuckle vines shaded a bench next to the water. Kieran opened his door and stumbled out as soon as she shifted into park. He staggered over to the bench and sank onto it, waiting for her. When she opened the back door, Harvey leaped onto the grass and bounded toward the pond, barking at the ducks. They scattered in a flurry of quacking and splashing. Fern transferred Baird from the car seat to the baby sling on her chest, rather than carrying him in her arms. "Well, here goes. I hope your friend doesn't throw us out at first sight."

"To call him a friend is a bit of an exaggeration. We met only once." Kieran heaved himself off the bench and led the way across the lawn.

More trees clustered around the house and shaded the roof. A porch, weathered brown like the siding, ran the full width of the front. The instant Kieran stepped onto it, the door opened. A lean man with glossy black hair, gray-streaked at the temples, frowned at them. His gray eyes looked normal, but he had pointed ears. "Whatever it is, I don't want-- Kieran? Is that you?"

He opened the door farther. The frown relaxed, though he surveyed both of them with lingering suspicion. "You look like hell. Adair's not with you this time?"

Kieran peeled off his gloves, stuffed them into a pocket, and leaned on the nearest post. "Adair is dead."

"Oh, damn," Donal said softly. "I'll probably regret this, but come on in." Kieran introduced Fern. "She's the sister of Adair's lover. And this is his son."

After a curt nod to her, Donal ushered them inside. "I won't ask who that pooka chasing my ducks is." An aroma like incense tickled her nose. A wood-paneled entry hall led past several doors to a living room crammed with furniture and lined with bookshelves on every wall except the one dominated by a fireplace large enough for a half-grown child to stand in. Kieran collapsed onto a claw-footed couch and closed his eyes. Fern curled one arm around Baird and cast nervous glances into the corners of the room. Pale, translucent female figures, like women molded from wisps of fog, flitted around, their white hair undulating like smoke. "What are those? Ghosts?" If elves and pixies existed, why not ghosts? Her capacity for astonishment had reached its limit.

Donal scowled. "No, sylphs--air elementals. You can see them? How?"

"Magic eye drops," she said.

At the same time, Kieran said, "Unguent of true sight. Her sister Ivy gave it to her. I think Ivy and Adair must have planned to use it to convince Fern of the truth about him, when the time was right."

"So. Adair's son." Donal stroked Baird's hand. The baby gave him a round-eyed stare and clasped his index finger. "Hello, there, little prince. Where's your mother?"

Fern blinked away unexpected tears and swallowed to steady her voice. "Ivy's dead, too."

"Which must have something do to with the shape Kieran's in and why you're here. At least we don't have to talk around the subject of magic in front of you, since you can see through illusions."

"I almost wish I couldn't. I'm just thankful Baird looks the same as he always did." A dismaying thought occurred to her. "Will he develop pointed ears eventually?"

"Not likely, but not impossible. The genes combine differently in every case. One thing you can expect, no matter what, is that he'll live longer than the average human lifespan. How old do you think I am?"

With his graying hair but almost unwrinkled face, he looked like anything from a mature fifty to a well-preserved sixty-five. She ventured a midrange guess. "Fifty-five, maybe."

He said with a dry chuckle, "I'm almost ninety, and I expect to keep going strong well past a hundred." He waved a hand, and one of the sylphs swirled down from the ceiling. After he said something to her in a trill like birdsong, she vanished. "I sent her for refreshments. Now, you'd better tell me what's going on."

Kieran said in a voice heavy with weariness, "Halwyn murdered Adair."

"And framed Kieran for it," Fern put in. "Then he came after Baird and killed Ivy."

"I'm gratified that you've finally decided to believe in my innocence," Kieran said.

Fern winced at the sting in his tone. Speaking alternately, the two of them filled in the recent events for Donal, without mentioning the details of their night together, of course. A few minutes into the conversation, a sylph popped out of thin air and set a tray on the coffee table. Pewter mugs held herbal tea. Fern sipped the minty brew and nibbled one of the small cakes that came with it.

Too late, she remembered the legends about being trapped in Elfland by eating fairy food. Catching her expression of alarm, Donal said, "Don't worry, my home has a touch of magic, but it's completely in this world."

"I wasn't worried, not really," she said, annoyed with herself for entertaining such a far-fetched idea. They continued with their story.

When they'd finished, Donal said, "So you need a cure for elf-shot. No problem. I always keep a few healing potions on hand." He sang a command to another sylph, who obediently vanished.

"What do we owe you?" Fern asked. Another thing she remembered from Ivy's folktales and ballads was that magical aid didn't come free.

Donal waved away the question. "Forget it. Healing potions aren't that much trouble. Wait 'til you ask me for something hard." He grinned. "I don't normally give a damn about elven politics, but I'll make an exception for that bastard Halwyn. If he had his way, my type would be slaves or prey, until he got around to exterminating us."

"Your type? You mean half-elves?" She wrapped both arms around Baird, who had fallen asleep in the sling.

Donal nodded. "Like your nephew there."

"Is that why you decided to live in this world? Because of people like Halwyn?"

"I had enough of pureblood snobbery as a kid. My mother was an elf who took a human lover, so I grew up Underhill. As soon as I got old enough to leave home, I crossed over to this side." He shook his head. "Mother thought I was out of my mind, but she made sure I had a financial stake, or a reasonable facsimile thereof."

"Enchanted money. Fairy gold. Cheating."

The sylph reappeared, bearing a silver goblet, which she handed to Kieran. Scents of nutmeg and vanilla wafted from it. When he took a sip, the taut lines of pain around his mouth and eyes began to fade.

"Survival," Donal said, apparently not fazed by the accusation. "I used illusionary funds only to get started. I hired a brewmaster and went into the beer-making business, what they call a microbrewery nowadays. I infused a little bit of magic into the malt, perfectly harmless flavor enhancement. Made a bundle and invested it wisely, with a touch of clairvoyance, so now I can relax and experiment with my potions. I bought a few acres up here in the woods and had this house built. You could say I'm retired or I'm a hermit, whichever way you want to put it."

"And you expect to live to be over a hundred?" She had trouble imagining her nephew growing up the same way, outliving her by such a long time.

"Easily, thanks to the elven blood. Living on Earth dilutes the effect, though. If I'd chosen to stay inside the Hollow Hills, I'd have centuries to look forward to."

"Do you ever miss it?"

"That's a pretty personal question from a new acquaintance."

She flushed. "Sorry. I was thinking of Baird's future."

"Okay, so sometimes I miss it. The air tastes like champagne. The plants and animals sing to you. What's not to like? But perfection gets old quickly, and I enjoy my independence. I got tired of being treated like a half-witted pet. Anyway, it's not as if I'm ostracized. I keep in touch with my purebred half-sister, Fenella, and now and then I even go back for a visit. There's no law against it."

"Well, I'm not about to have that choice made for Baird while he's less than a year old. He belongs with me, right here."

Kieran set the empty goblet on the table. The washed-out, strained look had vanished. "Thank you. And if you decide you want any kind of repayment later, don't hesitate to ask." He glanced down at the cup. Fern sensed his reluctance to state the request they'd come there to make. "The truth is, we need another favor."

"What kind?" Donal asked, suspicion creeping into his voice. "I haven't heard anything good about Halwyn. But if you expect me to fight him, forget it."

"Nothing that drastic," Kieran said. "I need a way to get in touch with the king and queen. The only gate anywhere near here is presently locked, and I'm betting you have a means of instant communication with your sister."

"What if I do?"

"I'm asking you to let me use that device. I'm ready to humble myself and submit to a truth spell, if that's what it will take to convince Oberon and Titania I didn't kill Adair. The fact that I'm guarding Baird, and Halwyn is trying to kill us, should be enough to get me a fair hearing."

"I don't see any harm in that." Donal slammed a fist on the arm of his chair and stood up. "What the hell, I'll do it. I'll give Fenella a call and let her decide whether to pass on your message."

Donal escorted them upstairs to a bedroom where Fern laid the baby down to sleep in yet another blanket-padded drawer. She noticed that Kieran now walked with his normal energy and grace. They descended a separate flight of steps to the first floor. Corridors branched and made more right-angle turns than she could keep track of. They ended up in an office with more bookshelves, a computer, a printer, and a fax machine. Taking the swivel chair Donal offered, she scanned the room and peered through the window at the surrounding woods.

Their host gave her a sly smile. "What's bothering you now?"

"Nothing, really, except that the house didn't look this spacious from the front."

"It's not. Right after the builders left, Fenella paid me a visit to help with a magical touch-up. The place is bigger on the inside than the outside." He booted up the computer. "Are you surprised I've got modern conveniences? I may be a hermit, but that doesn't mean I want to be cut off from the outside world completely. When I retired, I switched from beer to perfumed massage oils. I run a mail-order business. Now, let's see if I can get Fenella's attention."

Watching him manipulate the mouse, Fern said, "You're instant messaging your sister in fairyland?"

Donal chuckled. "Got to keep up with the times."

"Actually, it seems a little strange to me, too," Kieran said. "Surely Fenella doesn't own one of these machines. I can't imagine it would even function inside the Hollow Hills."

"No, on her side she has a reflecting pool that shows images the way the computer does over here." A click filled the screen with a sparkling mist.

Another problem occurred to Fern. "Kieran told me about the time difference. How can you talk directly to anybody this way if seconds here use up hours there?"

Donal shrugged. "The magic built into the mirror pool compensates for the time flow discrepancy. Don't ask me how. I'm just an ignorant half breed. Nevertheless, if the message takes Fenella only a few minutes to deliver within the Hollow Hills, we may not hear her answer for several hours." The screen gradually cleared, revealing lush, green shrubbery and turquoise-tinted grass. "Fenella's garden. Now we wait. One of her pixies should let her know the pool's been activated. I've set the program to translate into English so you can understand," he said to Fern.

Over the next ten minutes, she checked her watch repeatedly and forced herself not to drum on the arm of the chair. Kieran, in a similar chair across the room, sat in silence. Finally a woman appeared on the screen. Her hair, black with silver highlights, cascaded to her waist. Her gown rippled with shifting colors, turning momentarily translucent to reveal the curves of her body. On her wrist she wore a miniature dragon, with aquamarine scales and opal eyes. At first glance Fern mistook it for an elaborate bracelet, until the creature licked the air with a forked tongue.

"Greetings, brother." The woman's amber eyes shifted to Kieran. "Well. This is a surprise."

"Greetings, Fenella. I've come to seek your aid." Longing burned in his eyes as he gazed into the other world displayed in the monitor.

"Indeed? How could I help you? And why should I?" She spoke with cool serenity and an echo of the wind chimes Fern had dreamed or imagined the night before.

"I'm innocent of Adair's death. Halwyn murdered him and cast the blame on me." Kieran's voice quivered with outrage.

"Donal, you must have some cause to believe this claim, or you would not have summoned me."

"I've heard his story, and it makes sense," Donal said. "This woman backs him up. She's Fern MacGregor, sister of Adair's human consort."

Fenella stared at Fern, who struggled not to squirm under that scrutiny. "So you know what your sister's lover was?"

"I do now, and I know Halwyn killed both of them. He's been chasing us. He's trying to capture Ivy and Adair's baby son, maybe kill him, too."

"How can you be sure of Halwyn's guilt?"

"Kieran told me, and I believe him."

Fenella arched her eyebrows and said in a tone of faint scorn, "Elven seduction can induce a mortal woman to believe any tale."

"Dammit, listen to me!" Fern's cheeks flushed at the word "seduction". She clenched her fists to still the tremor in her hands. "I'm not helpless. I have the Sight."

Kieran nodded. "She does."

"Not only that, I've used--what's it called?--unguent of true sight. I saw Halwyn order his creatures to attack Kieran. They tried to rip him apart, and Halwyn shot him with one of those poison darts. Doesn't that sound like Kieran's the injured party here?"

"What do you think of this story, Donal?" Fenella asked.

"She's reporting the truth as she sees it, and I'll swear she's not under magical compulsion."

The elven woman examined all three of them in turn, then fixed her eyes on Kieran. "What would you have me do for you?"

"Nothing hard or dangerous. I need to speak with Oberon or Titania. Can you persuade one of them to come to your pool and talk to me?"

"Do you think they will listen? I've heard about Oberon's rage whenever anyone dares to mention you."

Kieran sighed. "I must make the attempt. Assure them I'll gladly submit to a truth spell."

Fern broke in, "Tell them what I just told you. Halwyn tried to kill Kieran. That's got to mean something to them." Reluctantly, she added, "And tell them Adair's son is here, and I'll let them see him."

"Let them?" Fenella's voice tinkled with amusement. "Very well, I'll do my best. I must confess that Halwyn makes a more likely traitor than you, Kieran." She vanished, along with the garden, leaving a silver-gray fog.

Donal clicked the mouse to restore the computer to a mundane screen saver. "As I said, it may take hours of earthly time for her to bring a reply. I'll whip up some lunch, and then you can rest while you're waiting."

Fern's eyes and limbs, aching from hours of driving, welcomed the idea of rest. The buzzing in her brain, though, made relaxation feel impossible. While Donal disappeared into another part of the house to arrange the meal, she and Kieran retraced their steps through the labyrinth of halls and strolled out front. The pooka bounded up to Kieran, who laid his hand on the animal's head and concentrated for a minute. "Halwyn isn't within sensing range for either of us."

While acknowledging the "no news is good news" status, she didn't feel especially reassured. She retrieved the baby bag from the car and went back inside with Kieran. This time Harvey trotted in with them. One of Donal's sylphs floating in the foyer beckoned to them, and they followed her to the kitchen. Fern sighed in envy at the spacious room with dozens of cabinets, granite-topped counters, a freestanding island in the center, and a large redwood table by a bay window with a view of the pond. Sylphs served homemade vegetable soup and loaves of whole-grain bread, still warm. After a brief internal debate over calories and cholesterol, Fern succumbed to the temptation of real butter, not margarine. Chilled cider completed the meal. When guilt over daring to enjoy food in the middle of a dire crisis nibbled at the edge of her mind, she slapped it down. "What do elves eat back home in the Hollow Hills?" she asked.

"Fruits, nuts, and honey," Kieran said. "Milk from our cattle, which are silver-white and more delicately framed than your breeds. Sometimes meat from the beasts we hunt."

A scratching sounded at the back door. When Donal opened it, Harvey padded in. "I guess your pooka friend wants a snack, too." He poured the creature a bowl of milk laced with Scotch.

"You're feeding him liquor? At this time of day?" Fern said, mildly shocked. She couldn't get over thinking of the pooka as a dog, and no responsible pet owner would serve a dog whiskey.

Donal laughed. "He's a lot older than you are, old enough to know what's good for him. Anyway, if leprechauns like the hard stuff, why are you surprised other magical beings do?"

"Leprechauns exist, too?" She sighed. "I give up. Go ahead and tell me anything. I'll believe it." In the same what-the-heck spirit, she buttered herself another slice of bread.

"Speaking of magic, how safe are we here? I caught a glimpse of your wards on the way in."

Donal exchanged a glance with Kieran. "Learns fast, does she?"

"Of course. It is in her blood."

"I don't have the power to create a very strong barrier," Donal said. "Never expected to need one, anyway. The wards will give a few minutes' warning if Halwyn shows up. That's about all. I've also sent a few sylphs into the woods to watch for intruders."

She turned to Kieran. "What about you? Can't you set up something that would keep him out?"

"You saw the extent of my power at the other places we stopped. Halwyn's gifts equal mine. My wards, at most, would delay him a minute or two."

Donal looked puzzled. "Your magic should be a lot stronger than mine. You come of royal blood."

"So does Halwyn, remember."

"What's this royal blood stuff about?" Fern asked.

"The noble bloodlines earned that status through the strength of their magic," Donal said, "so magic and high birth go together. Me, I'm just a commoner in elven terms. My mother wasn't nobility. So I'm pretty limited in what I could do against Halwyn, even if I wanted to join the fight."

"I have Ivy's iron cross," she said, patting the pocket where she carried the necklace, "but I can't count on getting another chance to hit him with it. Too bad I don't own a gun. Steel bullets would hurt him, wouldn't they?"

Kieran nodded. "Possibly kill him, but it's idle to speculate when we don't have such a weapon."

"Those are all just stopgaps, anyway. We can't keep running and hiding forever. Don't you have a plan for getting rid of Halwyn? That looks like the only way Baird will be safe."

Kieran's eyes captured hers. "He would be safe in the Hollow Hills, under the protection of the king and queen." Sincerity radiated from him like heat from an open fire. She could no longer doubt his caring.

She leveled a defiant stare at him. "What if Halwyn found a way to steal him from the royal court? You said Halwyn has connections there."

"Oberon and Titania can certainly guard the child better than you can, running loose in the human world."

"Not going to happen. I won't have him raised in a gilded cage." A tiny voice in the back of her mind asked whether she had a right to deprive Baird of the beauty she'd glimpsed in her visions and in Fenella's bower. And when he grew up, would he resent her for that decision? "We need to get rid of the threat once and for all."

"Oh, do you have a plan?"

She suppressed her irritation at his sardonic tone and tried to speak rationally. "Maybe you can't kill Halwyn, but could you catch him and hand him over to your authorities? You keep mentioning truth spells. Could the king and queen use one on Halwyn against his will? Then they'd know he's guilty, and they'd punish him, not to mention making sure he never gets his hands on Baird."

"It's a sound idea, in theory, but how to you propose we capture him?" After a moment's thought, Kieran said, "Donal would you cooperate in setting a trap?"

Donal left the table to let Harvey out the back door, then faced Kieran with his arms folded. "I said at the beginning that I wouldn't fight Halwyn. I'm not suicidal. I like my life just the way it is."

Kieran waved away the objection. "I'm not asking you to engage in combat, only put on a show for Halwyn's benefit, if he finds us here."

Donal sat down again. "What do you have in mind?"

"Let him think you despise the sight of me. Let him see you throwing an exiled murderer out of your house."

"I could manage that," Donal said with a feral grin.

"What's the point?" Fern asked.

"I hope to deceive Halwyn into chasing a decoy. I can create an illusion of you fleeing toward the car with Baird while in fact you're still inside."

Donal broke in, "Hold on, that's not part of the deal. If your ploy doesn't fool Halwyn, I won't let him find her in here."

Kieran frowned. "Why not?"

"Because then it would be obvious I gave you shelter. Like I said, I'm not looking to get myself killed along with you."

"Very well. Fern, you follow me out and walk in the opposite direction while I try to keep Halwyn's attention on the decoy. Remember, the iron cross clouds his perception of you."

"Won't he be able to see through your illusion, though?"

"I think I can confuse him at least temporarily, keep him guessing which is the real woman and which the double. The fact that he'll expect you to run for the car should help to give him the impression that the illusion is the reality. All I want is to throw him off guard long enough to capture and disable him."

"Good plan so far, but that leaves the question of how we're supposed to catch him."

Kieran turned to Donal. "Do you have a potion that might help with that part?"

"Supplying you with a weapon comes pretty close to combat, in my book. Oh, hell, I'll see what I can dig up."

After ordering the sylphs to clear the table, Donal showed them upstairs. At the door of the room assigned to him, Kieran paused to clasp Fern's hands between his. "Try to rest. All will be well, I vow."

Shivering at his touch, she wanted to believe him. That belief would have come easier if she hadn't sensed his continuing doubts. She went into the bedroom where Baird lay on his blanket, weaving a web of sunbeams between his aimlessly wiggling fingers. When she picked him up, the pattern instantly vanished. If she hadn't witnessed so many other impossible things over the past few days, she would have thought she'd imagined it.

"Oh, honey, what if you really do belong over there, with your magic grandparents? I can't stand the thought of letting you go." She nuzzled his neck, and his babbling morphed into a giggle. "Wow, the baby book says you're not supposed to laugh yet. But then I guess you're not exactly an ordinary kid."

She changed and fed him, then put him back in the padded drawer with his teething ring. Lying on her back and contemplating the cracks in the ceiling plaster, she tried to relax her tight muscles and invite sleep. The presence of Kieran, resting just across the hall, weighed upon her. With effort, she could bar her mind against the full force of his emotions, but she couldn't mute her constant awareness of him. Did she want to break that link? *Of course I do.* The more she sensed his loneliness for his family, the guiltier she felt for blocking his goal of winning their forgiveness. *Does Kieran want to break it?* He had never answered that question.

Fern's nearness enveloped Kieran like tendrils of fog swirling around him. They crept into the tiniest crevices in his psychic shields. He hated to admit to himself how much comfort that sense of her presence bestowed. Among his vague memories of the night he'd spent racked by the venom, one remained vivid, the close fit between their bodies. He longed to experience that closeness again, unwise thought it might be. He almost envied Adair and Ivy, sharing a love so intense they'd been willing to die for it. By contrast with that love and Fern's ardor, casual dalliance with cool-blooded elven lovers held no appeal. Yet the bond would have to be severed, if not deliberately, then by distance. Separation was inevitable. He would return to his home, and she would continue her human life.

Meanwhile, he allowed himself to enjoy the touch of her consciousness like a warm handclasp. When he sensed her drifting into a doze, he yielded to sleep, too. The previous night, which he only half remembered aside from the dazzling brightness of the passion he'd shared with Fern, had left him unrested.

A knock at the bedroom door woke him. Donal said through the panel, "Fenella's ready with your answer. Come down as soon as you can."

Kieran met Fern in the corridor, and they walked to the office on the first floor together. Donal slipped out of the room to let them carry on the conversation in privacy. A close-up of Fenella's face showed on the screen. She spoke up as soon as Kieran approached the computer. "Titania has agreed to speak with you. She will come to the pool when I inform her you are ready to meet her condition."

"Which is?" With a sinking feeling, he thought he knew what that condition would be.

"That you are prepared to return to the court with Adair's son. If you wish to bring the human female along as your pet, you may, with the understanding that she will have no part in the boy's upbringing. He must learn to live as the heir of King Oberon, not a half-human child with mortal ideas about his place in the world."

The anger simmering within Fern scalded him. Grasping her hand, he projected calm and felt her resisting it. "Fenella, that condition is unacceptable. Fern is his nearest living kin."

"Do you actually expect me to carry that reply to Titania? She accused you of ingratitude and betrayal. She says you rebelled against them after they treated you as their own son. This insolence is unlikely to change her mind. Hand over the child, and she might show mercy."

"The king and queen don't know the full story. Now that I've met Fern, I cannot support them in taking her sister's babe from her." Fern's indignation lashed him like a gale-force wind, the kind of storm unknown in the elven realm. The passions of his people seldom became as violent as human emotions. Battered by the full force of her rage and grief, he realized he couldn't take Baird from her against her will. Yet the boy would never be completely safe on Earth, and he deserved to grow up with his true heritage. "I might be able to persuade the lady to live within the Hollow Hills and cooperate with Baird's royal destiny if she is allowed her rightful role in his life."

Fern broke in, "The hell with that! We're both staying right here."

Kieran silenced her with a gesture and continued speaking to Fenella. "I shall try to persuade her to change her mind, but I can't accomplish anything without a guarantee from their majesties. They must respect the child's human blood ties."

"You are in no position to make demands. I doubt Oberon and Titania will agree to accept this woman as anything other than your concubine."

He noticed Fern's fists clenched at her sides and heard the agitation in her rapid breathing. "That is not enough." Unless they could reach a compromise, Baird would lose either his elven family or his only human relative. Also, Kieran would never see Fern again, a prospect that, he was astonished to realize, saddened him almost as much. "Fenella, I'm grateful for your attempt, but I must speak with Titania directly. If she wishes to see her grandson at all, ask her to visit the pool. Then we'll discuss terms."

Fenella shook her head. "Their majesties will not be pleased with defiance from an outlaw. But I will do what I can."

As soon as the screen turned blank, Fern slapped his chest with the flat of her hand. Her voice husky with unshed tears, she said, "What the hell was that about? Concubine? Forget it!"

He staggered backward, caught by surprise at the force of her blow. "That was Fenella's word, not mine."

"Right, you wouldn't even want me for that, would you? Last night was just a medical procedure to you."

His pulse pounded in his head. Perhaps this human tendency to emotional excess was infecting him. "It may have begun that way. Surely our bond proves it became more."

"A bond neither of us wants. I sure don't, not with a man who's trying to take Baird somewhere I'll never see him again."

"It doesn't have to be that way." He clasped her hands lightly, and she snatched them away. "Not if I can convince Titania to let you live with Baird and care for him."

"And I told you I have no intention of spending the rest of my life in fairyland!"

He muttered a curse in his own language. "Why can't you be reasonable? Don't you grasp the necessity of compromise? I'm certain Titania will become more flexible when she sees Baird face-to-face. You must be ready to yield ground, too."

Fern said with an emphatic shake of her head. "Are you still delirious from that poison? Do you seriously expect me to bring Baird in here and let that queen of yours look at him, if she shows up at all?"

Kieran sighed. "Now you're being completely irrational. Do you think she can reach through the screen and snatch him out of your arms?"

"Irrational!" she cried. Lowering her voice to a normal level, but with a tremor of suppressed rage, she said, "Answer me straight. You're still determined to take him into the Hollow Hills, aren't you?"

"I have no choice," Kieran said quietly.

She wheeled around and stalked out of the room.

Fern raced blindly through the halls until she ended up in the living room. With her hand pressed to her stomach, she gulped spasmodic breaths. Kieran had planned all along to surrender Baird to his grandparents in Elfland. He'd never intended anything else. She sensed him catching up with her, then looming over her. He grabbed her arm. She jerked away from him and folded her arms across her chest. "Go away. I've said everything I have to say to you."

"Fern, please listen." She hardened herself against the sadness in his voice. "I won't allow them to separate you from Baird."

"No? That agenda isn't working out too well so far, is it?"

"We will find another way. But first we must dispose of Halwyn."

She rubbed the tears from her eyes and ran her fingers through her hair. Kieran was right about that point, at least. "Where's Donal? Think he has some ideas for us?"

The distant wail of the baby interrupted her. When she stepped into the hall, she paused in bewilderment, not quite sure how to get to the stairs. Donal walked around a corner with a sylph hovering over his head. "She'll guide you to the bedroom. When you're done, follow her down to my workshop."

Upstairs, she changed and fed Baird while the sylph floated in languid circles around them. The baby's eyes constantly shifted to track the gossamer shape. When he finished the bottle, the creature drifted closer to skim his hair with an insubstantial finger. Fern shivered. "So that's the kind of thing you're supposed to grow up with? Doesn't seem to bother you any, does it?" In fact, Baird smiled with obvious delight at the sylph's airy dance.

When she wafted toward the door, Fern remembered Donal's instructions and got up to follow, leaving Baird on his blanket in the drawer. Donal might brew his potions with chemicals hazardous to a baby, for all she knew.

The workshop turned out to be in the cellar, down another flight of steps she hadn't seen before. A high window let in the afternoon light, supplemented by commonplace fluorescent tubes. A stove, sink, and counter lined whatever wall space wasn't covered with shelves, which held beakers and jars, some glass, others metal. With no caged owls or stuffed lizards hanging from the ceiling, the place didn't look especially magical. Aromas of sandalwood and jasmine permeating the air, though, partly made up for the mundane decor. Standing at a long, broad table with Kieran beside him, Donal showed them four miniature silver flasks. "These should do the trick, along with careful strategy. Remember the color coding on the seals." He handed a blue-corked flask to Kieran. "When Halwyn gets close, drink this."

Kieran accepted the container. "What does it do?"

"Makes you invulnerable to weapons, non-iron ones at least, for a couple of hours. This one is activated by contact." He gave Kieran a flask sealed with red. "It's to use on Halwyn, but you have to get close to do it. Splash it in his face. It'll knock him out. Sorry I can give you only one of each of these. They're harder to concoct than healing elixirs. When he's unconscious, you can tie him up. I've got some old tire chains you can use."

"They don't hurt you?" Fern asked.

"Most half-elves are immune to iron. Baird is, right?"

"Oh, yeah. I've seen him touch the iron cross my sister gave me. How long will Halwyn stay unconscious?"

"Four or five hours, easy. That'll give me time to cook up something to incapacitate him over a longer period. Last, here's something for you to hang onto." He passed Fern a pair of flasks with green tops. "Healing potions, one dose per container."

She turned one of them over in her hands. She could hardly believe how she'd already started to take magic for granted. "You don't normally give this stuff away, I bet. We really should pay you. Real money, not enchanted, if you'll take a check."

Donal emitted a dry laugh. "I don't need money. Don't worry, if I think of a favor I want later, I'll let you know."

The open-ended nature of this transaction made her uneasy. She'd read too many fairy tales about dangerous bargains. What choice did they have but to accept, though? "Okay, fair enough."

"All I ask right now is that you not drag me into your fight. I don't have the power to stand up to a renegade elf of royal blood."

"This whole plan," Kieran said, "depends on getting within arm's reach of Halwyn without his catching one of us."

"That's your department," Donal said. "You're going to make an illusionary decoy, aren't you?"

"I can't think of any better idea." With a sigh, Kieran slouched against the table and stashed the red-topped flask in the pocket of his silver-gray trousers.

A pair of sylphs flitted into the workroom and darted from one wall to the other. Donal sang to them, and they whirled in front of him in agitated spirals. "Bad news," he said.

"What is it?" Kieran asked, straightening up. "They've sighted Halwyn?"

"He's in the woods, hasn't reached the wards yet."

"Doubtless he tracked us through Baird's aura or more likely mine. He would have sensed a full-blooded elf's energy from a greater distance," Kieran said.

Donal listened while the sylphs poured out a stream of liquid syllables. "Damn it. He captured one of my sylphs, tortured her to death."

Fern curled her fingers around the necklace in her pocket. "How?" she whispered. "Dark magic. I've heard he's an expert with pain." After listening to another burst of sylph language, Donal said, "Halwyn's on his way here with a gang of spriggans and a couple of redcaps."

"Where does he get them all?" Fern asked. "Those can't be the same ones he used in Virginia, could they?"

Kieran shook his head. "They lurk within the shadows of the earth, what you might call another dimensional plane only a half-step away, ready to be called forth by anyone who promises to feed them with fresh blood."

"Enough talk." Donal slammed his fist on the table. "Here's where I throw you out of the house, remember? Get your stuff together, and let's move."

"When I have him occupied," Kieran said, "double back and get into the car, where you and Baird will be safe from his minions." He drank the contents of the blue-sealed flask.

With a frantically fluttering sylph as a guide, Fern hurried upstairs to collect her bags and the baby. Her heart hammered as she picked him up. He rooted against her breast and crumpled a fold of her shirt in his fist. "Don't worry, sweetie, I won't let a thing happen to you," she whispered while securing him in the sling on her chest. She hung the cross around her neck and rejoined the two men in the foyer. When he saw her, Kieran's eyes darkened with sadness. Underneath that, she felt tension vibrating within him. He clasped both of her hands and leaned toward her, avoiding the necklace. His lips brushed hers. A shiver convulsed her.

"It will all end soon. Be strong," he whispered.

"Come on," Donal said, his hand on the doorknob. "Time to put on the show."

Kieran said, "According to the sylphs, Halwyn is lurking among the trees in that direction." He gestured to the left. "The moment the door opens, I'll cast an illusion of you running toward the car. Actually, I want you to walk straight forward--not run, because you might attract attention that way--while I stage the argument with Donal and then head for Halwyn's position."

She nodded. Donal flung the door open and shoved Kieran onto the porch. At the same time, Kieran waved a hand, and a shadowy figure popped into existence next to her. She couldn't help cringing from the ghostly shape at first sight. When it coalesced into a mirror image of herself carrying Baird, she wasn't sure whether it became less creepy or more. She stepped backward, hoping to fix Halwyn's attention on the decoy instead of herself. *Be invisible*, she told herself.

"What the hell did you think you were doing, barging in here?" Donal shouted. "You've got some gall, trying to drag me into your fight."

"I thought you might feel a duty to intervene on the side of justice. I should have known better from someone who deserted his own kind to live among mortals." Kieran's tone of aristocratic disdain chilled her even though she knew it was an act.

"As far as I'm concerned, you got more than enough justice when they didn't execute you for killing your cousin. I don't want to get involved in a traitor's plot. Now leave me alone and get the hell off my land."

From the corner of her eye, Fern noticed branches rustling with no breeze and clots of darkness stirring in the shadows of the woods. Her pulse raced. She breathed deeply to dispel the lightheadedness that momentarily dimmed her vision. She saw no sign of the pooka. She could hardly blame him, considering how he'd already risked his life in a battle that didn't really concern him.

"Very well," Kieran said to Donal. "It was a mistake to expect courage from your kind." He stepped off the porch and marched in Halwyn's direction.

She caught sight of the renegade elf now, standing just under the trees while spriggans and a pair of redcaps crept into view. A flick of Kieran's hand sent the decoy running toward the parked car. Fern strode down the path directly in front of the house. With one arm wrapped around

Baird and the baby bag and purse bumping against her sides, she forced herself to maintain a steady pace. Kieran's warning that Halwyn's attention might shift to her if she ran made sense. Yet she trembled with fear at having to restrain herself to one deliberate step after another with those creatures swarming around her. If their random circling switched to concentrated focus, Halwyn would surely notice her. She felt like a rabbit under the eyes of a hawk.

A cluster of spriggans, with one redcap, passed her racing doppelgänger and headed for the house. Why didn't they try to capture the illusion? Wasn't it working? Halwyn conjured a gleaming crescent from somewhere. A bow, she realized when he aimed it. An arrow flew toward Kieran. Holding her breath, she wondered whether it bore poison like the dart. It didn't matter. The arrow bounced, as if an invisible shield surrounded Kieran. The bow ejected another missile, which did the same. Kieran kept advancing. A sphere of fire appeared in Halwyn's hand. He flung it at Kieran. Instead of rebounding like the arrows, it simply vaporized. Kieran cast a similar fireball in return. The other elf deflected it with a wave, and it, too, vanished.

Beside her, oily smoke seeped out of the ground. It rose and spread into a curtain of undulating darkness. She froze, terrified that the stuff would envelop and smother her, yet too paralyzed with fear to flee from it. Baird started crying. Through the dark gray fog, she felt Kieran's distress. He couldn't see her. The smoke or whatever it was cut them off from each other. The next moment, a sickly, greenish glow appeared around her. It made her skin creep like the stickiness of cobwebs. Shuddering, she brushed at it, but of course it didn't rub off. "Kieran!" she cried. "What's going on?" Only a wordless burst of alarm responded.

Two spriggans sprang at her. She dropped her bags and slapped at them with no effect. Their claws dug into her bare legs. Kicking didn't begin to dislodge them. Another one leaped on her back, and her stomach roiled with nausea at the scrape of its filthy claws. Others poured through the smoke curtain to join the attack. She took off the necklace, looped one end of the chain around her fingers, and swung it in a wild arc. The cross lashed two of the beasts, which crumpled into tangles of twig-like limbs. One of them emitted a screech that hurt her ears. She whipped the chain around to strike the one on her back, which fell off. In that second of distraction, another wave of the things charged at her legs. With a scream of pain when their claws ripped her skin, she stumbled. She fell onto her side, rolling to protect Baird from the impact. His cries turned into a siren-like wail.

The spriggans mobbed her. She had to cover her eyes to protect them from the thorn-like fingers. A smell like withered leaves in late autumn almost choked her. The things grabbed her arms and pulled them wide apart, pinning her to the grassy earth. How could such spindly creatures have so much strength, or was it just because there were so many of them? She felt them scrabbling at the sling on her chest.

"No!" She bucked and flailed, struggling to throw them off. Useless. "Kieran! Where are you?" His helpless agony washed over her. The heavy cloth ripped. Her eyes flew open just in time to see a spriggan snatch Baird. The baby's cry escalated to an ear-splitting pitch. Black spots swam in front of her eyes. "No!" Her arms free now, she staggered to her feet and lurched toward the creature.

The oily fog vanished. Halwyn stood between her and Kieran, who grasped a squirming redcap by its neck. The spriggan scuttled to Halwyn and handed Baird to him. The elf supported the wiggling baby in the curve of his left arm.

Kieran lunged forward. Halwyn hissed and wrapped his fingers like claws around Baird's neck. Kieran froze.

"No...please." Fern stumbled toward Halwyn.

"Stay back. I'd rather keep the babe alive for now, but I don't have to, you know."

She halted. Her heartbeat hammered so hard it almost deafened her. "Give him back. I'll do anything."

He bared his teeth in a wolfish grin. "You don't have anything I want that much."

Tears blinded her until she wiped them away. She had to think straight, had to use all her senses. She looked past Halwyn at Kieran, who gazed at her with bleak eyes. His sorrow buffeted her like an icy wind. "Why didn't the illusion fool them?" she asked.

Halwyn laughed. "You didn't really think that trick would work, did you? Not when the half-breed's servants are so fragile they're hardly worth the trouble of ripping to shreds." He lifted his right hand to display the tattered, gray remains of a sylph. "It had overheard your plan and told me the essentials before I'd barely touched it. I knew your pathetic illusion wasn't the real woman and child, so it was easy enough to guess where I needed to cast my vision-enhancing spell." He dropped the sylph's corpse. Kieran took a single stride in his direction. "You know what I'll do to the infant if you come any closer."

Baird's cries pierced Fern over and over. A shuddering sob burst from her. In the background of her mind, Kieran's pain echoed hers. He shook the redcap like a rat in a dog's jaws. "And I can break your minion in half if you refuse to deal with us."

From the desperation in Kieran's tone, Fern sensed the futility of that threat. Halwyn only shrugged. "Try it, and I'll kill the woman. I wasn't going to bother with that, but I don't need her alive. If you cause trouble, she's dead."

With an audible snarl, Kieran flung the redcap to the ground. Halwyn said, "I can't hurt you at the moment, but that hardly matters. Your life won't be worth anything after I transport the infant into the Hollow Hills, slay him, and make sure our royal kinfolk blame you for it."

Kieran folded his arms. "Surely you aren't that much of a fool, Halwyn. You must know that won't work."

"What do you mean?"

"Didn't that sylph you tortured mention that I've sent a message to Oberon and Titania? They might not yet believe you murdered Adair, but they are considering the possibility. What will they think if you bring them such a tale? They'll force a truth spell upon you and sentence you to a painful death. Give up this mad scheme to inherit the throne. It's a lost cause." He exhaled a deep breath. "Surrender the child. You have no use for him now."

"Certainly I do." He flashed a smile at the screaming baby. "I need some compensation for all the trouble I've gone through. If I siphon off his power little by little, I can make it last a long time. It should have a very intriguing flavor. I'll feast on him for many months of human time before he finally wastes away and dies." Fern clenched her fists, her nails digging into her palms. "Or maybe I'll stop before he's completely drained. Perhaps I'll bring him up as my devoted servant."

"You--" She stumbled forward, brandishing the cross.

"Stop." Halwyn punctuated the quiet command by wrapping his hand around Baird's neck again.

She obeyed, flinging a desperate glance at Kieran.

"Don't worry, cousin," Halwyn continued. "Now that I've got what I need, I won't bother you anymore. You can even keep the woman. My creatures will let both of you leave after I'm safely inside the half-breed's home. It looks like as good a place as any to wait out the time until the portal opens again. It'll be tedious spending that much time in this world, but less of a nuisance than transporting a soggy, squalling infant cross-country to another gate. The half-elf didn't have the power to fortify this place adequately, but I have, so don't waste energy trying to break in." He gestured toward the house.

When Fern looked around, a redcap appeared at the front door. It dragged Donal's battered, unconscious body by one arm. "He's alive," Halwyn said, "and I don't plan to have him killed yet. He may be useful later. If nothing else, I can suck power from him. These half-breeds are good for something." Carrying Baird, he started to walk across the lawn. The spriggans clustered at the bottom of the porch steps.

Fern collapsed to her knees on the grass with her arms wrapped around herself. Blood trickled from multiple scratches, but she hardly noticed the minor pain compared to the pounding in her head and the nausea churning in her stomach. Tears flowed down her cheeks. *Oh, God, please save my sister's baby.*

Kieran shouted, "Wait!" Halwyn turned to face him with a cool stare. "You don't have to do this. You know this woman wants nothing to do with the elven realm. If you return her nephew, she will take him home and never trouble you again."

"Why would I consider making such a doubtful bargain?" Halwyn glanced at Fern as if he equated her with a mosquito buzzing around him. "She won't trouble me as it is. Nor will you. I have nothing to gain by yielding the child."

"You gain one thing, the chance of avoiding the vengeance of the king and queen. They may never be sure you killed Adair. If you slaughter their grandson, though, they will certainly find out in due time. In that case, you'll never survive their wrath. Better to cut your losses and salvage what profit you can from this situation."

Halwyn scowled. "What kind of profit?"

Kieran drew a deep breath. Fern sensed him fortifying himself for his next words. "I'll surrender myself in Baird's place. The energy of a full-blooded elf at the height of his powers will feed you better than a half-elf infant's. You know your plan to trick Oberon and Titania into thinking I killed him won't work. You won't get a better offer than this. I'm sure you're too clever to refuse it."

"Kieran, no!" When he whirled around to face her, she said, "We can't trust him."

"There are ways of ensuring he keeps the bargain," Kieran said quietly. "It's the only way to save Baird."

Chapter Twelve

She climbed to her feet, gnawing on her lip to keep from protesting again. If Kieran's sacrifice would get Baird out of Halwyn's clutches, she couldn't argue against it. She knew the trade meant a painful death for Kieran, though. Her mind wouldn't wrap around the ghastly image of his dead body. Fresh waves of faintness swept over her at the mere thought.

Halwyn ignored her and stared at Kieran. "You'll give your word to yield freely to me and let me drain your magic without resistance?"

"Provided you swear to let Fern and Baird go unharmed and never seek to capture or injure them in any way ever again, neither you nor any ally of yours nor any creature under your command or compulsion."

Under Kieran's calm façade, Fern sensed fear coiling like a snake in his guts. She knew Halwyn would drag out the draining process as long and agonizingly as possible. "You said you can make sure he'll keep that promise. How?" she asked.

"No elf can break an oath given in the proper form. We'll perform a mutual truth spell. Isn't that so, Halwyn?"

Ravenous greed emanated from the other elf. She wasn't sure whether the crisis had made her Sight temporarily so acute she felt this on her own or whether she picked up Kieran's awareness. Either way, Halwyn craved the power he could absorb from his cousin. She swallowed the protest that welled up inside her again. Tormenting Kieran with her anguish wouldn't help. He had no choice but to offer this sacrifice. She mustn't make it harder for him.

"I agree," Halwyn said. "Mutual truth spell to seal our vows."

Kieran strode up to him, within arm's length. Each raised a hand, and their fingertips touched. "Now. Swear as we agreed."

"I so swear."

"And I." Kieran began chanting in the musical rhythms of the elven language, and Halwyn's voice joined his. A golden light pulsed between their hands. It expanded to a globe that surrounded both of them. Chimes resonated in the air. Baird fell silent and stopped fighting Halwyn's grip. A fragrance like jasmine emanated from the shining bubble.

Halwyn broke contact first. The light, music, and perfume vanished. "It is done." He beckoned to the spriggans. One of them scurried over, took the baby, and scuttled toward Fern. She knelt on the grass with her arms outstretched. The spriggan handed Baird to her and retreated to its waiting comrades. She stood up, hugging the baby to her breast. His breath came in hiccupping gasps. She struggled to breathe, too, through the constriction in her chest. Fresh tears gushed from her eyes. She rubbed them with the back of one hand and gazed over Baird's head at Kieran.

"Go," he said. "Now, quickly. He can't break his promise. But you can't necessarily trust his creatures quite so implicitly."

She rushed to the car, opened the back door, and buckled Baird into his seat, flinging her bags in after him. Then she hesitated, watching the two elves from her position partly shielded by the vehicle.

"Well, keep your side of the bargain," Halwyn said. "Get in the house."

"One more thing," Kieran said. "Allow me to say goodbye to Fern."

Halwyn's scornful laugh grated on her ears and roused anger that she thought the last few minutes had exhausted. "Unbelievable. Consorting with mortals this short a time, and already you're infected with their sickening sentimentality. Very well, go ahead, but make it fast."

Kieran held her gaze while he walked toward her. She stashed the necklace in the pocket that held the healing potions. He circled the car to reach her. Leaning against the driver's door, she opened her arms to him. His fear and sorrow flooded her mind, along with a wave of yearning she didn't dare to name. His lips, cool and dry, touched her forehead as his arms encircled her shoulders and hers wrapped around his waist. She couldn't hold back her tears. He sipped them from each cheek in turn. "Don't," he whispered. "You know this is the only way."

She trembled with the effort of choking back her cry of protest. His hands released her for a second, then skimmed down her sides. One hand slipped into her empty pocket and inserted an object. The flask containing the potion meant to disable Halwyn. She gasped.

Kieran silenced her with a kiss. She closed her eyes and allowed herself to drown in his warmth for a timeless instant. Brushing her hair back from her forehead, he murmured against her lips, "You may need that. Halwyn's vow binds him, but you may face other enemies." He released her and stepped out of reach. "Take Baird home and guard him well."

She felt the touch of his mind like the tight grasp of a desperate hand while he marched between two rows of spriggans to the door where Halwyn waited. Getting into the car, she slammed and locked the door. The steel barrier didn't weaken her awareness of Kieran. He'd said, she recalled, that this bond arose from her Sight, not elven magic. Even after he walked inside and the front porch door closed behind him, she continued to feel his presence. Only a minute or two later did it abruptly vanish. She guessed Halwyn must have strengthened the wards or performed some other spell to sever the link.

Wiping away the tears that blinded her, she glanced over her shoulder at Baird, who had stopped crying. "No point in hanging around here now. There's nothing we can do. Like he said, the important thing is getting you home."

After driving from Donal's place to the main road, she took refuge in a fast food restaurant's parking lot and scanned the map. She calculated that the most direct route home, sticking to the interstates, would take about seven hours. She didn't consider stopping at a motel, even though she would end up reaching Annapolis very late that night. She needed the shelter of home more than she wanted rest. She fueled up at the drive-through window and headed for the freeway. Heedless of the speed limits she usually observed as closely as possible without getting run over, she raced as if hungry dragons roared at her back.

For all she knew, dragons might exist, on top of everything else. The world's mundane surface had cracked open, and strangeness poured out like molten lava from a volcanic crater. Yet the farther she fled from Donal's house, the less probable the past few days seemed. Could she have suffered a freakish nervous breakdown from the shock of Ivy's death? Might those eye drops have contained a hallucinogenic drug, after all? If only she could embrace either of those theories. In the depths of her mind, though, she had to admit that the only credible alternative to magic was raving madness. And a sudden lapse into schizophrenia would make her unfit for custody of her nephew.

As the last glimmer of twilight faded into night, she happened to cross a narrow river. A human-sized, quicksilver shape, faceless except for glittering blue eyes, rose out of the water. Liquid rippled down its sides. It hovered next to the bridge as if it wanted to flow onto the pavement but couldn't leave its stream bed. She averted her gaze and fixed her eyes on the road. *It's not real.* But it was. The whole invisible realm of magic was real, and she couldn't blindfold herself to it. She heard Baird, in his car seat, gurgling with delight at the water thing. *He doesn't need magic eye drops. He's probably been able to see them all along.*

After nightfall, she caught sight of glittering silhouettes that danced amid the trees by the side of the road. Lightning bugs? Too large. Pixies? No, she remembered Kieran had called the miniature, twinkling fairies--"wisps". *Magic is everywhere!* It would follow her home, slink around her yard, peek in her windows. Her idea of abandoning her job and living on the run with Baird now seemed pathetically naïve. Nowhere was really safe. She could only pray no other envious elven kinfolk ever came in search of the baby. Even if she studied all the fairy lore she could unearth, she might not have enough knowledge or power to protect him. Nor could she expect to guard him behind locked doors for the rest of his life. Eventually he would grow up and want to leave home like a normal young man. Suppose he fell victim to an attack because she'd cut him off from his father's family and kept him ignorant of magic?

A headache throbbed inside her skull. Thank goodness it wasn't raining anymore. Headlights and street lamps hurt her eyes even without the sheen of water to scatter the glare. More afraid of her own driving than of hypothetical hounds on her trail, she stopped once an hour for coffee refills. With liquid soap and damp paper towels in the restroom of the first place, she cleaned the marks left by the spriggans' claws. The cuts had stopped oozing blood and looked no worse than cat scratches. She decided if a market opened up for an atlas listing all the convenience stores off I-77, I-81, and I-95, she could write that guidebook and make her fortune. At one gas station she caught a glimpse of a foot-tall man dressed in earth-brown rags, who seemed to be arguing with a scruffy tomcat in the weeds beside the parking lot. She waved the necklace at him and took grim pleasure in watching him fade into the darkness. Back in the car, she sighed to herself, unable to forget that the charm so effective against such petty creatures would have little impact on another foe as powerful as Halwyn.

What had Kieran meant, anyway, by referring to other enemies? Wasn't it bad enough that he'd sacrificed himself? The only way she could bear that fact was to trust that his action had saved Baird once and for all. She was still silently cursing Kieran while she drove eastward on Route 50 toward Annapolis. By the time she pulled into downtown, the Sunday night tourist traffic had long since diminished from a torrent to a trickle. The ordinary appearance of her house struck her as surreal, with everything else in her world turned inside out. She noted with relief that no lights shone in her landlady's part of the building. The last thing Fern wanted was casual conversation.

After a final diaper change and bottle, Baird settled in his bassinet with no complaints. She gazed at him in the dim glow of the night light for a few minutes. "We're home now," she whispered. "Nothing bad is going to happen to you." She stroked his clenched fist, which opened to wrap around her finger. Her chest tightened with an ache that almost cut off her breath.

A few minutes later, she stood in the shower with her head against the cool tiles, while the water pounded over her. Her brain whirled with grief and confusion. She ought to feel better, now that she had Baird home and out of danger. Yet something more than her sorrow for Ivy haunted her. She couldn't shake the image of Kieran's eyes and the last, lingering touch of his mind. Toweling herself dry, she flushed at the memory of his hands and mouth on her body. Had those caresses meant more to him than a simple sharing of energy? She touched her parted lips as the realization flooded her. That night she had given him more than the healing gift he'd begged for. Regardless of whether he placed any greater importance on their union, she did. She didn't want to. She didn't need the added pain of caring for a man she would never see again, a man who'd surrendered himself to death by torture for her sake and her nephew's.

She dropped the towel on the bathroom floor, staggered into her room, and threw herself face down on the bed. Pillowing her face on her arms, she yielded to the tears she'd been resisting. Sobs racked her until exhaustion stopped them. Her throat sore and her stomach aching, she rolled over and stared into the dark. Time to stop fooling herself. She didn't just care for Kieran. She felt more than sensual desire or gratitude or admiration for his courage and nobility or even guilt for letting him make that sacrifice. She loved him. No way could she leave him in Halwyn's clutches.

The moment the thought popped into her mind, its absurdity forced her to choke down a fit of hysterical giggles. She'd barely escaped with her life and Baird's, and only because of Kieran's self-offering. How could she expect to free him from dark elven magic? Aside from her second sight, a couple of potions, and an iron cross with a clover in the middle, she had only one asset, the knowledge of his location. If Halwyn hadn't lied about his plans--and why would he bother?--he and his captive would remain at Donal's house for the next two months. So if she wanted to try rescuing Kieran, at least she would know where to find him. Now all she needed was a plan.

She turned on her side and thumped the mattress. *Right, and if I had a magic wand, I could wave it, zap him out of Halwyn's dungeon and teleport him here.* With Donal and Kieran imprisoned, she no longer even had a magical ally. The pooka had shown good sense by bailing out before the firestorm hit.

She couldn't do the same, though. Even if she knew of an antidote to the unguent of true sight, she couldn't revert to her old blindness. The veil of the world had ripped apart to reveal what lived behind the scenes. She could never settle for a merely human lover, after what she'd seen and suffered with Kieran. She had to get him back. But how? The question howled around her like a cyclone and swept her into a whirlwind of chaotic dreams.

Baird's gurgles woke her to sunlight seeping through the curtains and birds chirping in the oak tree outside her bedroom. *It's Monday morning. I should be getting ready for work.* Except that Bev wouldn't expect her today, and anyway she had a rescue mission to plan. Ideas swarmed in her head, spinning too quickly to grasp. After dressing, she fed the baby, laid him on a blanket on the living room rug, and sat on the couch with her coffee and breakfast yogurt to mull over the problem. What harmed elves, other than iron? From Kieran, she had learned plenty of discouraging facts about their powers but little about weaknesses. She didn't have any fairy tale books in the house, if they could be relied on for accuracy at all. She might have to resort to the Internet, with a margin of error squared or cubed and thousands of pages to search. Sipping her coffee and watching Baird weave sun motes between his fingers, she indulged in a fantasy of asking him for advice. She laughed aloud. Assuming he possessed an instinctive knowledge of elven traits, she'd have to wait a few years before he'd get old enough to answer questions on the subject. Too bad she couldn't ask Ivy and Adair, but if they were alive, she wouldn't find herself in this predicament to begin with.

Ivy. Yes. She carefully set her mug on a coaster on the coffee table, her eyes fixed on the opposite wall. Ivy could answer questions, in a way. She had left her songs.

Fern opened the cabinet under the stereo and rummaged among the CDs and tapes. She had several performance tracks recorded by Ivy. Maybe those traditional ballads were no more reliable than fairy tales or Web pages, but they were probably no less so. She found the cassette she'd been thinking of, inserted it in the tape player, and fast forwarded to the song she wanted to hear. The fairy ballad "Tam Lin".

It started, "I forbid you maidens all, who wear gold in your hair, to come and go by Carterhaugh, for young Tam Lin is there." The strong-willed heroine, Janet, naturally sneaked off to Carterhaugh--"as quick as go could she". After she met Tam Lin and became pregnant by him, she learned that he was in thrall to the fairy queen. He was also doomed to become a human sacrifice on All Hallow's Eve. Feisty chick that she was, Janet rejected her father's attempt to marry her off to one of his retainers. Instead, she vowed to rescue Tam Lin. She first had to pick him out of a troop of elven knights, then hold onto him while the evil queen transformed him into a succession of terrifying shapes.

Wiping away the tears her sister's voice provoked, Fern sat on the floor next to Baird and contemplated the lyrics. So there was a precedent for reclaiming a captive, if the song had a basis in real-life traditions. Could she challenge Halwyn to a contest for Kieran's freedom?

What could she offer that would induce him to take the challenge, though? Kieran had enticed Halwyn with the power of an elf from the royal bloodline. Fern, a mere mortal, couldn't hope to match that prize. According to Kieran, some elves did enjoy draining the energy of some mortals, those who possessed the Sight. It didn't seem likely, though, that Halwyn would consider her purely human power a fair trade for the magic he planned to leech from Kieran. Yet, as she began to recall from the dozens of times she'd reluctantly listened to Ivy's repertoire, fey creatures did like gambling. Suppose she offered double or nothing? Would Halwyn's arrogance and delight in tormenting her with what he would regard as vain hope lure him to accept the terms?

The full impact of what she was considering rushed over her. She covered her face with trembling hands. She would have to offer herself as the prize if she lost the bet. And she could make the gambit work only by opening herself completely to the psychic gifts she had suppressed for most of her life. No dark elf worth his charter membership in the arch-villain club would bother sucking energy from a mortal who'd locked her talent behind cold iron and thrown away the key.

She put her hands down and sat cross-legged next to the baby. "What do you think, sweetie? Am I magical enough to make decent bait?" She offered him a finger to grip. He babbled a string of vowels. "If I hadn't blindfolded myself on purpose all this time, I probably would have figured out there was something supernatural about Adair. If your dumb Aunt Fern hadn't acted like such a jerk about that whole subject, your mommy might've told me the truth, and maybe we could've found a way to protect her." Baird kicked his bare feet in the air and gave her a broad smile. "Yeah, right, too late for beating myself up. I wonder what else I've been ignoring that I should have seen." She gulped. "Here goes nothing."

She took a deep breath, stood up, and scanned the room in a slow circle. "Anybody there? Show yourself."

Movement flickered on the fringe of her vision. Even more slowly, she swiveled in the opposite direction. There, something fluttered outside the window. "I see you," she whispered. A triangular face peeked over the sill. "Stay right there!"

Scooping up the baby, she hustled outside. A little man, smaller than human but taller than the one she'd glimpsed at the gas station the night before, crouched under the window. He had chestnut skin and round, green eyes that filled half his face. Pointed ears showed under the rim of a hat apparently made of leaves. His tunic looked like green and brown leaves stitched together.

"If I can trust those legends Ivy collected," she said, forcing her voice to stay level, "you must be a brownie." She hoped her landlady didn't overhear that insane-sounding remark. At least Baird's eyes tracked the creature, confirming it was really there. "Have you been hanging around all along, or did you just show up because Baird's here?" No answer, of course. *When I set Kieran free, maybe I should ask him for one of those tongues spells.* She comforted herself by silently repeating that "when". "Does this mean I can leave out a bowl of milk every night and get my housework done? I could use the help."

She took one step toward the tiny man, with the Celtic cross dangling on her chest. The brownie hissed and darted into the bushes. "I think that went well for a first meeting," she said to Baird. A tingle on the nape of her neck made her glance up. A sylph perched in the huge oak tree. When it noticed her looking at it, the misty elemental flitted to a higher branch in a swirl of gossamer robes.

"You're welcome to stay, too," Fern said. "If you see anything evil coming, let me know." *Now, how do I expect her to do that? We don't speak the same language.* Shaking her head, she went into the house.

Inside, she huddled on the couch with Baird on her lap. "I'm going to have to go away for a day or so. Don't worry, I'll be back. I wouldn't leave you all alone." Fortunately, he couldn't understand the words and call her a liar. The truth was, she could lose. She had no idea how hard Halwyn could make the challenge. His vow might prevent him from hurting her without her consent, but he surely had plenty of indirect ways to block her from claiming Kieran. Assuming he accepted her offer at all, instead of laughing in her face. And if she lost? Kieran had given a pretty vague description of what having one's power drained involuntarily felt like. The word "torture" had figured in the explanation, though, and the gaps left all too much space for her imagination to fill with gruesome details.

She hugged Baird until he squeaked in protest. With a shuddering sigh, she kissed him on the forehead, put him on his blanket, and went to the phone to dial the bookstore. She noticed the message light blinking but didn't bother with it.

Bev's voice projected relief when Fern identified herself. "Oh, hon, how are you doing? I phoned and left a few messages, but you didn't call back."

"I'm sorry, I wasn't home much. I had a lot of stuff to do." She spoke faster before Bev could say anything else, afraid she might crumple into a useless heap if she listened to her friend's sympathetic words. "I have to ask you for a big favor."

"Name it."

"I've got to go someplace at least until tomorrow, and I don't want to take Baird this time. Could you watch him?"

"Sure, if you don't mind him spending the day in the shop. He's portable enough that it shouldn't be a problem, and Monday's never very busy."

"Thanks, you're the best." Fern let out a pent-up breath. She hadn't expected Bev to refuse, but she still felt relieved to have the matter settled. "We'll be over there in a little while."

She repacked the baby bag and her own overnight bag. Kieran might not want to face a drive all the way back from North Carolina right away. After getting the supplies ready, she booted up her computer. First, before she could lose her nerve, she typed a summary of everything she knew about Baird's ancestry and abilities. She finished with a warning that he might need protection again someday, in case Halwyn wasn't the only distant royal relative who resented Adair's half-breed child. Next, she logged onto the Internet and downloaded two legal forms, a standard will and a guardianship order. She filled out both, naming Bev as her sole heir and Baird's guardian. What about witnesses? Much as she hated the idea of any delay, neither did she want to risk having her wishes ignored by the courts, if she didn't return. With the baby in her arms, she marched around to the front of the house and knocked on Mrs. Perez's door. After a painful few minutes of discussion about Ivy's sudden death, Fern presented the forms for the older woman's signature.

"Don't you need two witnesses, dear?"

"Yes, but I don't have time to find anybody else right now. I'll have to do it later." Hurrying back to her apartment with the signed papers, she assured herself that "later" would come, and she'd have plenty of time to make more formal arrangements. If the worst happened, she could only hope the authorities would accept the documents as legitimate. After all, she didn't have any living relatives to contest the will. Last, she wrote a handwritten note to go with the typed material.

Dear Bev,

If anything happens to me, I've named you Baird's guardian. Please take care of him. I'm counting on you to handle everything with Ivy's funeral and what little property she had, too, but especially the baby. Ivy was right, he might be in danger. I know some of the things I've written may sound crazy, but I swear it's all true. Baird is very special. I know I can trust you to protect him.

Love, Fern

She folded the documents and stuffed them into a large envelope, inserting the note last where it would get read first. Before leaving the house, she put the three small potion flasks into the pockets of her cargo shorts. Along with the necklace, those comprised her only material weapons.

Less than ten minutes later, she parked in front of the bookstore. She lugged Baird, his car seat, her purse, and the baby bag the few steps through the humid heat into the cool air of the shop. She found her friend alone, with no customers at the moment. Bev hurried from behind the counter to greet Fern with a hug. "God, I don't know what to say. I'm so sorry."

Fern deposited the baby seat on the floor to return the hug with an awkward, one- armed embrace. "You don't have to say anything. I'm just grateful you're here. I know it's a lot to ask, dumping Baird on you for a whole day and night."

"Don't be silly, we'll have a nice time, won't we, little guy?" She tickled Baird's chin and took him from Fern. "I'll put his seat next to the counter, and he can watch the action from there until we close at five." He batted at her glasses. Smiling, she caught his flailing arm.

Tilly, the Maine Coon, uncurled from her basket and walked over to rub Fern's ankles. She bent to pet the cat. "The bottles in the bag should be enough to tide him over until I get back tomorrow afternoon. And there's another thing in there, an envelope. It's for you, but I don't want you to read it yet."

"So what is it?"

Fern straightened up, her stomach churning. "Some stuff you'll need if anything happens to me." Speaking the possibility aloud made it seem more real.

"Come on! What are you talking about?"

She winced, and Baird let out a startled cry. "It's just a precaution. After Ivy died with no warning, I want to be prepared, that's all."

Bev patted the baby on the back. "Shush, I'm sorry I yelled in your ear. Girlfriend, I don't want to hear anything like that out of your mouth again. Nothing is going to happen to you."

"Of course not." Fern conjured up a weak smile. "So you won't have to open the envelope, and I'll take it home with me tomorrow."

"Right." Bev glared at her. A second later, her frown dissolved, and she hugged Fern. "You take care of yourself. This kid needs you."

"I know. I'll be careful." She felt like a liar. Whether or not she came home to Baird had little to do with how careful she was. The success of her mission depended on other factors entirely. She kissed him, inhaling the familiar aromas of milk and powder. She murmured a quick goodbye to both of them and hurried out, afraid if she stayed a minute longer she would break down. Then she would face a worried cross-examination from Bev and would have to tell even worse lies.

Like needles of ice, shards of dark magic pierced Kieran's brain and heart. They spun his power into threads as fine as spider silk and absorbed it through hundreds of tiny holes in his aura. His life-force bled out with it, draining his body heat. He felt himself withering into a dried husk, as if his skull were being cracked open and scraped clean. He would become an empty shell when Halwyn finished drinking his energy. How long that process would take, Kieran had no idea. He couldn't guess how long the torment had already continued. He had lost his capacity to measure time's passage the moment Halwyn's talons had sunk into him. The only variation in the endless "now" came when the other elf's attention veered. Then the pain would stop for an interval. It always resumed, though, worse after each respite.

The enchantment had battered him with wildly varying attacks. Flames that burned as hot as any material fire. Ocean waves that crashed over him, searing his skin with salt and flooding his lungs. Mounds of earth and rocks that crushed the air out of his chest. Howling winds that lashed his face like the flailing of barbed whips.

Kieran embraced his only consolation--that Fern and Baird had escaped. The emptiness left by her absence worsened the anguish that racked him, but he thanked all the Powers of Light for that emptiness. It proved his sacrifice had been worthwhile. He would much rather have her safe and content, yet far away, than in danger but close enough to share the solace of their bond. And once enough time had passed for her memory of their union to grow dim, she would find contentment. He had to cling to that certainty, bleak comfort though it was.

The weight of Halwyn's craving descended on him afresh. It squeezed him like ripe fruit to extract his magic, drop by drop. An involuntary groan burst from Kieran. Again the needles stabbed him to drain his life. If only it would end. If he knew any way to provoke Halwyn into killing him in a single burst of power, he would do so.

Abruptly the pain ceased. Kieran gasped at the sudden release. If he could trust his sense of duration at all, the draining had stopped sooner than usual. Something must have captured Halwyn's attention.

The next moment a familiar presence brushed the edge of Kieran's thoughts. *Fern?* No, she must have reached home long ago. She should be hundreds of miles away. The sense of her nearness had to be a delusion spawned by physical and emotional agony.

Yet her aura shone in the back of his mind like the first rays of sunrise on the horizon. Surely she wouldn't return? Not after she'd escaped to her own mundane world? *Fern, go away! You don't belong here.*

He screamed aloud at the vision that engulfed him, Fern writhing under the fangs and claws of Halwyn's beasts. Convulsed by spasms of horror, Kieran rolled into a ball and struggled to lock the barriers of his mind. Dark enchantment had left him too weak, though, shredding his defenses and leaving him open to any invasion. He could only suffer his helpless awareness of her march toward the fate from which he'd tried to save her.

Go, Fern. Don't risk your life and soul for nothing.

Chapter Thirteen

Late that afternoon, Fern pulled off the interstate half an hour from Donal's place. Without the baby to tend, she'd made fewer stops and risked higher speeds. Having slept only a few hours after driving more than half the night, she would have been drooping from exhaustion if her nerves hadn't been vibrating with tension. Whenever speculation about what Halwyn would do with her if he won invaded her mind, she thrust it away. Instead, she focused on how she would persuade him to accept her proposition in the first place. He'd promised not to attack her or allow his minions to do so, but what if he ordered the creatures to block her path to the house without hurting her? Surely they had ways of accomplishing that. Or suppose other creatures lurked nearby who didn't owe allegiance to Halwyn and had their own motives for wanting a bite out of her?

During the last leg of the trip, on surface roads, she simmered with impatience. She wanted to get the confrontation over with before losing her nerve. When she reached the turn-off to Donal's private lane, she parked on the main road, locked her purse in the car to leave her arms free, and started walking. She felt mild shame at her relief that she'd arrived hours before sunset. Although most fey creatures could doubtless attack anytime, the primal human fear of nocturnal dangers made her grateful for daylight. Even so, the trees overhanging the gravel-surfaced drive formed a dim tunnel that suggested twilight rather than a summer afternoon. She momentarily toyed with the notion that Halwyn had cast a spell to darken the woods, then squelched it with a muttered curse at her own timidity. She would soon have worse things to confront than shadows.

Glittering eyes peered from the undergrowth. Leaves quivered in the windless heat. The farther she got from the car, the bolder the owners of the eyes became. They lined the lane on both sides, beings that ranged from slender women draped in cobwebs or vines to things more like animated tree stumps than miniature people. Some of the watchers looked like animals, although none she'd ever seen in a zoo or a nature program--gnarled, shaggy beasts with tusks or fangs and too many legs. A serpentine thing with three pairs of stubby wings and a tail like a scorpion's hovered in a tree. When she passed under the limb, the creature dive-bombed her. She brandished the iron filigree cross, and the flying snake veered off.

Isn't this charm supposed to make me hard to see? Not that hard, I guess, just dim. Other snippets from Ivy's favorite tales came back to her. Fern realized she must have picked up more knowledge of fairy lore than she'd intended, simply by hanging around her sister. One legend claimed you could confuse the little people by wearing your clothes inside out. *Well, it's worth a try.* She peeled off her sweat-dampened T-shirt, reversed it, and put it back on.

The flying serpent didn't attack again, and the watching faces blended into the shadows. A few paces farther on, a raccoon crouched at the edge of the path. *Raccoon? What's with that?* It took her a minute to remember the incident on the sidewalk in front of her house on Friday, which now felt like a month ago. Kieran had bespelled birds to attack Halwyn. No reason Halwyn couldn't control animals, too. Though raccoons might look cute and cuddly in kids' picture books, she knew they had sharp teeth and tough claws. Only when the animal waddled onto the gravel did she notice the spriggan scuttling beside it. *That settles it, not a normal raccoon!* Pulling off the necklace, she whipped the spriggan in the face with it. The stick-creature let out a screech like a rusty hinge and fled into the trees. The raccoon didn't budge, though.

Unsure how fast it could move or whether it could jump on her, she didn't take any chances. With the necklace tangled in her fingers, she broke into a run. The gravel crunched under her feet. She raced for the clearing where the lawn began, never looking back. Her chest and legs ached. She stumbled out of the trees panting and dripping with sweat. She leaned over, hands on her knees, struggling for breath.

A black hulk lumbered toward her. With a gasp of alarm, she stood up straight and gripped the cross so hard the points hurt her palm. The beast's fang-studded maw emitted a low woof. A hysterical giggle bubbled up from Fern's throat. The pooka. "Harvey! What are you doing here?"

He circled around her. Following him with her eyes, she saw the raccoon a couple of feet behind. The pooka snarled at the animal, which scurried back into the woods. Harvey rubbed against her side like the shaggy dog he almost resembled. She rested her hand on his massive head. *I stuck around because I owe Kieran for saving my life, so I could help in case one of his less hostile kinfolk heard what happened and showed up. But at least I'm smart enough to watch from a distance. What's your excuse for throwing yourself back into danger after he went to all that trouble for you? Just general idiocy?*

Her heart jumped. She snatched her hand away. "How come you can communicate with me all of a sudden?"

He nudged her until she touched his head again. *I could've done it anytime. You have the Sight, don't you? But with Kieran around to translate, it wasn't worth the trouble.*

"What about Kieran?" Her pulse raced with anxiety that temporarily blotted out her other fears. "Is he still alive?"

Of course. Halwyn isn't about to waste that hoard of energy by using it up too fast.

"And Donal?" She'd forgotten about the half-elf until this moment. "Halwyn said he wasn't going to kill him, either. Was he telling the truth?"

According to the sylphs, Donal is alive but unconscious. Halwyn plans to keep him in a coma until they get into the Hollow Hills. Less trouble that way.

"You're in contact with the sylphs? Doesn't Halwyn keep them prisoner or something?"

They aren't very bright, but they were smart enough not to hang around and let him get control of them. They flit inside for a quick look when his attention's occupied. The rest of the time, they stay clear of him.

"Then one of them could take him a message, maybe."

Message? What fool scheme do you have in mind, half-witted mortal? Despite the scorn in the words, his mental tone felt good-humored.

"I'm going to challenge Halwyn to a wager for Kieran's freedom." She hoped the dark elf didn't insist on a riddle game, like the fey beings in some of Ivy's ballads. Fern didn't have any faith in her ability to outwit a supernatural creature. She counted on arranging a contest that she might have a chance of winning by raw stubbornness.

Harvey shook his head. *Woman, you really are an idiot. He'll chew you into mincemeat.*

"I have to try. Will you contact one of the sylphs for me?"

A heavy sigh gusted from the pooka's jaws. *Sure, not my funeral.* He raised his head and stared into the distance. Seconds later, a sylph drifted into view. It looked ragged, like a cloud shredded by high winds. It floated up to them, and Harvey spoke to it in low growls. *She's not crazy about getting anywhere near Halwyn, but she'll carry your message. What do you want her to say?*

"Have her ask him to come out and talk to me, because I have a deal to offer him." Maybe curiosity alone would prompt the elf to parley with her.

The pooka made more growling noises at the sylph, which flitted back to the house. Harvey leaned against Fern's leg. *Here's where I bow out. If you survive, I'll be waiting for you in the woods. Good luck.*

Fern put the necklace on and clasped her hands together to suppress the tremor in them. Could she trust Halwyn's vow not to harm her? Kieran had assured her it was unbreakable, and she couldn't doubt his word. But she felt more secure with the iron cross, nevertheless. And as a last resort, she had the potion that Donal had claimed would knock out Halwyn. She took a deep breath and started toward the house.

When Halwyn emerged from the front door and strode down the porch steps, she had an impulse to throw the potion in his face the instant he came within reach. Two thoughts stopped her. First, she didn't know whether Halwyn's promise that his minions wouldn't attack her would hold if he weren't conscious to direct them. Second and more important, she couldn't count on being able to find Kieran without the dark elf's cooperation. He might have put his captive under some kind of concealment spell. Kieran had warned her that her illusion-piercing sight wouldn't work against more powerful enchantments.

"Greetings," Halwyn said, halting at the bottom of the steps and folding his arms. "What a surprise. I'm not used to unspelled mortals walking into my domain. What do you want?"

Clutching the cross, she took three strides closer to him. "I challenge you for Kieran."

He laughed, a sound like shattering glass. "I told you before that you don't have anything I want."

"I have the Sight. You like to feed on human psychic energy, don't you? If you win, you get me as well as Kieran."

"I admit the offer holds some interest, although you wouldn't provide much more than an appetizer. What do you ask for, in the unlikely event you win?"

She gulped to fill her lungs with air. "Set Kieran free and promise never to harm or harass either of us again, directly or indirectly, with the same kind of oath you took before. Not you or any of your allies. Oh, and include Donal in the bargain, and stay off his property."

He frowned at that last sentence. A fist squeezed her heart as the silence stretched. Had she gone too far by asking for the half-elf's freedom? Finally, though, Halwyn just laughed again. "Sounds like an uneven trade to me. You demand a lot more than you offer."

Fern shrugged. "It's all I have to offer. Take it or leave it."

"You haven't got a chance, so I suppose it doesn't matter how much I wager. The more you hope for, the more entertaining it will be when you lose." His eyes crawled up and down her body like stinging ants. "You tried everything, I see. Iron, clover leaves, the cross, reversed garments. Pathetic. Did you think charms against the lesser fey would have any effect on me?" He laughed. "Maybe I'll use all three of you as the quarry for a Wild Hunt. I wonder if Kieran would throw away his life trying to protect you from my hounds." He scanned her as if measuring the extent of her fear. "What type of contest do you have in mind?"

A chill trickled through her veins. *Hounds.* The word hinted at beasts far more bloodthirsty and tenacious than spriggans and redcaps. Halwyn seemed surprisingly cooperative, an attitude that confirmed how little hope of success she had. "Give me a chance to find Kieran and hold onto him. There's a precedent for that."

He shook his head with an expression of disgust. "I should have known. That blasted Tam Lin song. Well, I don't mind humoring your little plan. In this dull place, I'll enjoy the amusement. It won't be nearly so easy as you seem to think."

"I'll take that risk." She marched up to the house. From the open door, a redcap slinked onto the porch. Blood soaked its clothes and oozed from the corners of its mouth. She dragged her eyes away from it and stared at Halwyn. "Is it a deal?"

"Very well." He sprang toward her. She jumped and thrust the cross at him. "Calm down, woman, I'm only fulfilling your condition of taking the oath. Your hand, please."

Swallowing her terror, she placed her fingers in his. She half expected the scaly hide of a reptile, but his skin felt smooth and pleasantly cool. He recited a melodious phrase in the elven tongue. Light the color of honey surrounded their clasped hands, accompanied by chimes and the scent of jasmine. "I swear to do as you have demanded." Seconds later, the glow vanished. "Satisfied?" asked Halwyn.

Fern nodded. The spell matched in every respect the one she'd seen him perform with Kieran. Anyway, if he intended to trick her, she had no way of knowing or preventing him, so she could only accept the promise as valid.

"Give me a moment to prepare," he said. He withdrew into the house. The redcap, gnashing its jagged teeth, glowered at her. She cringed against the porch railing, fingered the cross, and silently prayed for strength.

It seemed like far more than a moment before Halwyn reappeared. "You have until sunset to claim your lover," he said. "If you do not succeed by then, you must pay the promised forfeit. Begin." He flung the door open and pointed at the lightless entrance.

Before taking the first step, she tucked the necklace into a pocket, for fear of hurting Kieran when she found him. She walked into a dark tunnel, as far as she could tell from the glimmer of daylight at her back. Instantly a chill replaced the humid heat of the outside world. Two strides diluted the light so that she could hardly see the outline of her own hands groping ahead of her. Two more strides and darkness enveloped her. She spun around, one hand on the wall. No sign of the door where she'd entered. The wall she leaned on felt like cold, smooth rock.

Illusion. Nothing but illusion. Surely even Halwyn didn't have the ability to magically remodel the house in one day. He did have the power, though, to create an enchantment too strong for the unguent of true sight to dispel. Although she insisted to herself that everything she saw and felt was imaginary, she continued to walk down a dark, cold tunnel. She'd have to treat this stage set as reality, at least for now.

She stopped counting steps and concentrated on placing one foot in front of the other. The temperature dropped minute by minute. The evaporating moisture on her shirt made the cold worse. Shivering, she rubbed her bare arms. Soon her lips and cheeks felt as numb as if exposed to a freezing gale.

At last she emerged from the tunnel into a lighted room, a vast chamber with a ceiling at least three stories high. *This can't be real*, she reminded herself. *This room is bigger than the whole house.* In the few minutes he had taken to prepare for her challenge, the dark elf surely couldn't have wrought a physical transformation this drastic. No matter how desperately she begged for true sight, though, the scene didn't change. Halwyn's spells overwhelmed her merely human gifts and the minor magic of the eye drops.

Mirrors covered the walls and ceiling. Because of them, at first she missed the man in the center of the floor. When her vision focused on him, a cry burst from her. "Kieran!" The word echoed over and over until the syllables decayed into a meaningless cacophony. He crouched naked with his knees bent, arms wrapped around them. He moaned, a drawn-out noise verging on a howl. She ran toward him.

She'd crossed only half the distance when he looked up, apparently noticing her for the first time. "Fern?" He sounded dazed, unsure of what he saw. "Fern, no! Get out!" Just as he shouted at her, the room fractured into a maze of mirrors. Kieran's image splintered into dozens, then hundreds. She whirled around, her head spinning. His groans of pain reverberated from all sides. Now she saw him close up and noted the haggard lines of his face, the bruises on his arms and legs. The sight stunned her. If Halwyn's abuse left him in this condition after only one day, what horrors would result after weeks or months of captivity and torture? If the draining of power had such a devastating effect on an elf of the royal bloodline, what would it do to a mortal like herself? The foretaste of what would happen to her if she lost hit her like a blow to the chest.

Too late to think about that. I have to get Kieran out of here. Charging at the nearest image, she ran into a pane of glass. It didn't feel like glass, though, but ice. Convulsed by panic, she careened from one reflection to another, bumping into shiny walls each time. The fierce cold made her fingers burn.

"Kieran, where are you?" The echoes threw her own voice back at her. She lurched to the closest mirror and pressed against it, although the ice seemed to suck the heat from her flesh. She slid her palms over the surface, dragging her feet along inch by inch. If she followed the angles of the walls, sooner or later she had to cover every part of the room. Or did she? The enchantment might channel her in every direction except the area where Kieran really lay. The "ice" wasn't even a real mirror, for she didn't see her own reflection, only blank whiteness.

Underneath Kieran's moans, she heard faint laughter. Halwyn. Of course he'd watch, enjoying the agony he caused. She paused, jolted out of her blind terror by the gloating noise. He'd given her a deadline of sunset, and he'd declared his confidence that she wouldn't make it. Time flowed differently in the elven realm. While the house lay entirely in the earthly dimension, did this artificial environment constructed by Halwyn have to do the same? Maybe his spell included a distortion of time. How many hours actually remained until sunset? She checked her watch. A row of zeros blinked at her.

With a moan, she buried her face in her arms. *No. Can't let him scare me into giving up.* She shoved away from the wall and rotated slowly, scanning the countless mirages of Kieran. He rocked, whimpering to himself. She hardened her heart against the yearning to rush to him and gather him into a tight embrace. Chasing those decoys would get her nowhere.

She closed her eyes and drew long, deep breaths to block out the distraction of sound as well. *Trust your sight.* In this case outer vision only muddled the clarity of inner vision. She and Kieran had formed a bond that Halwyn couldn't know about. She had to depend on that link to find her beloved. With one hand braced against the icy wall, she reached out with her mind. She felt his presence and inched toward him, with her eyes still closed. The cries in her ears, as well as Halwyn's laughter, receded into the background and became almost too faint to hear. Kieran's aura shone like a candle flame in her mind's eye. She navigated by that gleam, although it flickered as if a wind were trying to blow it out. When it grew dimmer, she shifted direction until it brightened. Still keeping a hand on the wall for support, she groped ahead of her with the other.

Suddenly her feet bumped into a solid mass. "Kieran?" She crouched partway to the floor, waving her hand around. It came to rest on his head.

He didn't react with any sound or movement. She fell to her knees and ran her fingers over him. He lay huddled on his side, and his flesh felt like an ice sculpture. She draped herself over his body and wrapped her arms around him. Tentatively opening her eyes, she saw the countless mirrors shatter with a loud crack. The maze of reflections vanished, leaving a huge, empty, white space. *We're not really in a snow cave*, she assured herself. *What act could dispel the illusion? Maybe if he added his psychic force to hers?* "Kieran, look at me. Can't you hear me?" Now he wasn't even shivering. She felt no emotion or awareness from him.

Before she had time to panic over the void where his consciousness should be, the floor tilted. Suddenly she lay on a steep grade, slick with ice. The slope angled to the edge of a ravine. Snatching a quick glance over the rim, she saw no bottom. She and Kieran hung suspended over an abyss. They slipped, inch by inch. With one arm flung over him and her fingers clutching his wrist, she clawed at the slippery surface with her other hand. She found nothing to hang onto. Cold air blew on her legs. Looking down again, she saw Kieran's feet dangling, too. If she let go of him, she might be able to get a grip with both hands and haul herself up. But she couldn't let go. That was the test.

This isn't real. How could I forget that so fast? She blinked, silently begging the layer of illusion to melt away. Nothing changed. She closed her eyes. *There's no ice and no bottomless canyon. We're lying flat on the floor.* Her body refused to let her reject the reality of the cold. Shivers racked her, and her fingers felt so numb she couldn't have grasped a handhold if she'd found one. She could resist the impression of falling, though. With physical sight blocked, she had no visual cues to reinforce the illusion of a sheer drop. She forced deep breaths into her aching lungs, even though the air felt so cold it seared the inside of her nose. One limb at a time, she made her cramped muscles relax. "There's nothing under us but a level floor," she said aloud. "We can't fall."

She let out a shuddering sigh when her body accepted that truth. She wasn't sliding into an abyss, and Kieran wasn't slipping out of her arms. Cautiously, she opened her eyes. Again the white walls surrounded them, but the floor, though still cold, looked ordinary. Stone instead of wood or carpet, but perfectly flat. "You see, Kieran, we're okay. Now you can wake up, all right?" No response.

Just as she started to call his name again, the floor dissolved. Green water surrounded them. She managed to grab Kieran's hand right before they both sank below the surface. She gulped air the second before the water engulfed her. Its chill numbed her fingers so that she had to open her eyes and squint through the ripples to make sure she hadn't lost her grip on Kieran. His weight dragged her down, and her chest ached from holding her breath. She kicked frantically but couldn't tell whether she made any upward progress.

If she let go, if she had both arms free, she might have a better chance to swim to the surface. If the surface existed. Since Halwyn had constructed this ordeal, he might have made it a trap impossible to escape.

That's how he wants me to think. He wanted her to treat the lake as a physical threat, when the true danger lay in letting the enchantment deceive her. *I have to remember none of this is real.* She closed her eyes and pulled

Kieran into her arms, hugging his naked body against hers. *There is no water. We aren't drowning.* She opened her mouth and drew a deep breath.

Air inflated her lungs. She found herself lying on the stone floor, embracing Kieran.

His skin felt colder than ever, scalding her like dry ice. She laid her head on his chest. She couldn't hear a heartbeat.

Her own heart raced with renewed fear. "Kieran, wake up!" She grabbed his shoulders and shook hard. Nothing. Her throat constricted with rising panic. Had Halwyn's torture done permanent damage? She sifted through her memory of the promise she'd extracted from him. It hit her that she hadn't included any mention of releasing Kieran alive. *He's not dead! No way, I won't believe it!* She clung to the hope that the intention behind her words mattered, that winning his freedom implied he would be able to leave under his own power.

If he couldn't, though, she would just have to free him with her own strength. If he couldn't stand and walk, she would drag him. If she could find the way out. Even though the mirror maze had vanished, doubtless Halwyn had other tricks in reserve. When she raised her head to look around, the blank whiteness in all directions confirmed her fears. If he wanted to prevent her from seeing the exit, he could, and he could probably distort her perception of time as well as space. She might wander in circles for days without realizing it.

She needed Kieran's power to counteract the deceptive enchantment. Somehow she had to restore him to consciousness. She remembered how their lovemaking had partly healed the fever from the poison dart. Could she pour energy into him without his active cooperation? She touched her lips to his, thinking of fairy tales where a kiss broke the evil spell. His flesh felt like chilled stone. Waking him would require more than a kiss.

"Take my energy," she whispered. "If I have any magic, use it." She stretched on top of him, willing her body heat to flow between them. She visualized her life-force as electricity radiating from a positive pole to a negative one. The more she concentrated on transmitting power to him, the more clearly she saw a pale glow surrounding him. His aura. She focused on brightening that glow, like feeding wood to a fire to make it blaze hotter. The light emanating from him flared from a wan yellow to a vibrant red. A rhythmic vibration throbbed in her ears.

His heartbeat! She covered his mouth with hers and exulted in the sensation of her life flowing into him. "You're alive," she murmured. "Wake up."

The petrified cold of his body thawed to living warmth. He stirred under her. His tongue flicked her lips, and his arms folded around her. Sitting up, she pulled him into a reclining position, his head on her breast. He didn't open his eyes.

He shivered, a reaction she welcomed as another sign of life. Remembering the flasks in her pocket, she took out one of the healing potions, uncorked it, and held it to his mouth. He drank automatically, first sipping, then swallowing faster as she tilted the bottle.

His eyes opened, and he stared blankly at her. "You're safe now," she said.

"Fern? You're here? I thought I imagined you." He touched the side of her head, stroked her hair, and traced the curve of her jaw. "You're real." Tears gleamed in his eyes.

"I didn't know elves could cry."

"When we have sufficient cause," he said, his voice husky.

"Drink this." She unstoppered the second healing elixir and pressed it to his lips.

He stopped after consuming half of it. "You take the rest. You need to restore what you gave me."

Reassured by the firmness of his voice, she obeyed. They both stood up, leaning on each other.

"Fern, you shouldn't have come. Why did you put yourself into Halwyn's power?"

"I'm not, and neither are you, now. I made him promise to set you free if I fulfilled the conditions. Donal, too." She recalled another line from the ballad, how Janet had wrapped her mantle around Tam Lin. Kieran was still shivering. Fern stripped off her T-shirt and tugged it over his head before he could protest. Size extra-large, it fitted her like a tunic, so it barely covered him.

The white cavern vanished. They stood in the middle of an ordinary bedroom. The rays of the setting sun filtered through the curtains.

She let out a long sigh. "It worked. He has to let us go." The door opened. Her heart stuttering, she placed her left hand in Kieran's right. She tucked her other hand into the pocket that held the defensive potion.

Halwyn strode into the room. "Amazing. I never actually expected you to succeed. One of the few times I've underestimated a mortal." He folded his arms and gazed at them with outward calm, but the clenched rigidity of his jaw betrayed anger.

Fern swallowed hard and squeezed Kieran's hand. "Yes, we've fulfilled the conditions. Now get out of here."

He said with a brittle laugh, "I promised not to harm or harass you. I made no promise to let Kieran profit from my defeat. There are many ways I can act against him without violating those prohibitions. Loopholes, I think you call them."

Anger radiated from Kieran, too. "What are you ranting about now? You know you've lost any chance you ever had of becoming king."

"That doesn't mean I intend to yield the rule of our people to half-bloods and human-lovers. I have plenty of time before Oberon and Titania abdicate and retire to the Shadowlands. I'll make sure neither you nor your mongrel nephew will inherit the throne."

Fern's stomach cramped with outrage and horror. *No! I can't stand the thought of that hanging over our heads for the rest of our lives!* She worked loose the stopper of the potion vial in her pocket. "We're going to check on Donal now. Keep your promise and leave this house."

She put on the Celtic cross, its metal cool on her bare chest in the vee of her bra. With her arm around Kieran's waist and his over her shoulder, they started for the door. Halwyn backed into the corridor. She pretended to ignore him, as if she had no doubt he would clear a path for them. When they passed from the doorway into the hall, she uncorked the flask, pulled it out of her pocket, and flung the potion at Halwyn.

It splashed directly in his face. He emitted a high-pitched shriek and collapsed to the floor. Startled, she clutched at Kieran, who wrapped his arms around her.

"Don't worry. The potion worked. He is stunned."

Fern took a cautious step closer and poked Halwyn in the ribs with one foot. He lay paralyzed, with his sightless eyes fixed on the ceiling. "Donal said he'd stay that way for hours. What should we do with him?"

"First, we find Donal, as you said. He can bind Halwyn more permanently, and then we'll send a message to the king and queen. Halwyn has to be turned over to them for judgment."

"But the nearest portal doesn't open for two months, right?"

"In this emergency, I predict they will send their guards through one of the more distant gates to travel here overland. In any case, this traitor will no longer be our problem."

Just as she began to tremble with relief, a wind swept along the hall, bearing the smell of dust and dry leaves. A troop of spriggans scuttled into view. Three redcaps shambled at the end of the pack. A rotten-meat odor drifted from their blood-soaked clothes.

Fern stifled a cry and brandished the necklace like a shield. Kieran raised his right hand, flame glowing in the palm.

Sylphs glided near the ceiling. One of them swooped down to Kieran and sang at him with obvious urgency. He lowered his arm, and the miniature fireball vanished. Fern pressed closer to him. "What's going on?"

"Look at them." He nodded at the creatures. They made no attempt to attack Fern and Kieran. Instead, they swarmed over Halwyn's prostrate body. "The sylph says they've come for him, not us, and it appears that's true."

Dozens of thorn-like claws ripped off Halwyn's clothes and tore at his skin. One redcap fastened its fangs in his throat, while the other two gnawed his torso, one on each side. Shuddering, Fern hid her face on Kieran's shoulder. "Why?" she whispered.

Kieran spoke a question in elven, and the sylphs' voices sang a lengthy reply. "These beings served Halwyn only because he forced them," he said. "He used them almost as brutally as he did his human prey. At the gate, when he summoned spriggans to free him, he forced them to break his chains in total disregard of the pain it caused them. Then he crushed four of them and drained their energy to revive his own. It gives their kin great satisfaction to find their master helpless."

Fern kept her eyes shut, wishing she could block her ears to the noises of snarling, chewing, and sucking. After a nauseating few minutes, the dusty, carrion-scented wind blew down the hall again. Silence followed.

Kieran rubbed the nape of her neck. "They've left. They're sated now, so they have no incentive to challenge my power."

She opened her eyes, looking first toward the ceiling, where a pair of sylphs hovered. Reluctantly, she forced herself to look downward. Halwyn resembled a shriveled mummy, with shards of bone exposed where the creatures had devoured flesh with the blood. "They drained him." She felt lightheaded. That fate might have overtaken both of them.

"Yes." Supporting her with an arm around her waist, Kieran guided her around the corpse and into a bathroom a few doors away. "Wait here while I get dressed. My clothes are in that room where I was confined."

She leaned against the sink, her head reeling, and washed her face with cool water. It wasn't long before Kieran came back, wearing his silver-gray outfit. He returned her T-shirt, which she put on, covering the necklace. "Now we look for Donal?"

Kieran chanted a question at the sylphs. They floated along the hall to a bedroom at the far end. Kieran and Fern followed them inside, where Donal lay on a four-poster bed.

The half-elf sat up as they entered. "So there you are. I should have known to stay out of royal feuds. I'm surprised you have the gall to face me."

Stung, Fern said, "What about thanking us for getting rid of Halwyn?" Donal scowled.

"He's dead?"

"Yeah, I used that potion you brewed, and then his monsters...well...ate him."

With a snort, Donal hauled himself to his feet and put on a shirt lying over the headboard. "Sure, thanks for getting rid of him after you lured him here in the first place."

"You do have a point," she said. She couldn't see any way of making it up to him at the moment, though.

"I figured he had to be dead, or the spell he had me under wouldn't have broken."

"We won't trouble you much longer," Kieran said, "but I do have to beg your help to send another message to the king and queen."

"So what do I get for all this help?"

"What do you want? As you said earlier, wealth means little to you."

"I'll think it over." Donal stomped into the hall, and the other two followed him downstairs.

In the office, he switched on the computer and activated the communication program. Or spell, maybe. Fern's brain whirled when she contemplated the interface between the two. She watched the curtains fluttering in the evening breeze with grateful wonder. It hardly seemed possible that the house had changed back to normal, with the frozen maze erased as if it had never existed. *In a way it didn't, except in a shared hallucination, I guess.*

Fenella appeared on the screen, this time wearing a butterfly on her wrist instead of the dragon. "What do you want now, Kieran? Have you come to your senses?"

Ignoring the question, he said, "Halwyn is dead."

The elven woman's eyes widened in astonishment before she got her reaction under control. "Did you kill him? That won't strengthen your case with Oberon and Titania."

"He attacked us and tried to steal the child. I traded myself for Baird, and Fern made a bargain with Halwyn to win my freedom."

This time Fenella made no attempt to hide her surprise. "Donal, is there any truth to this tale?"

"That's how it happened," her brother said. "Halwyn's own minions killed him after these two defeated him."

Fenella surveyed Fern with a cool smile. "Apparently some mortals have unsuspected depths."

Fern clasped her hands together behind her back, fighting the urge to spit out a retort to the female elf's supercilious tone. Donal beat her to it. "Come off it, Fenella. My father was human, and you liked him all right, so don't give us that bull."

"True," she said in a friendlier tone. She nodded toward Fern. "Please accept my apologies, consort of the prince."

"Consort? No, it's not like that." She blushed. What was their relationship, anyway? The gulf between their worlds remained as wide as ever, no matter how many individual elves tolerated or even liked mortals.

Kieran interrupted, "I need to speak with the king or queen as soon as possible. Please report Halwyn's fate to them and ask one of them to meet with me."

"I daresay they will look with favor on that request, given the changed circumstances." She flicked the butterfly off her arm and stared hard at him. "But remember, they will expect you to return home with their grandson, regardless. They are not likely to relent on that condition."

"We'll discuss that later." Kieran reached for the keyboard and cut the connection.

Fenella's glade vanished, replaced by the screen saver.

A chill constricted Fern's chest. The question of Baird's destiny was one barrier between them that hadn't changed. Kieran clasped her hand in both of his. "Don't be afraid. I will not allow you to lose him." He turned to Donal. "Now, how can we repay you?"

The half-elf settled into the desk chair and frowned up at them. "I've been thinking about that. I want something harder to get than a sack of fairy gold or even bankable human cash."

"What?" Kieran asked. No hint of impatience crept into his voice.

"There's no guarantee Halwyn doesn't have allies who might nurse a grudge, is there?"

Kieran shrugged. "Life holds few guarantees, even for our kind."

"I want protection. You set up stronger wards than I'm capable of producing, and you make regular visits to reinforce them."

Visibly relaxing, Kieran said, "I have no reservations about promising that. If you wish, I'll cast the first spell before we leave."

Leave? We? Together? Where does he think we're going? Kieran talked as if he expected the two of them to share a future, but how could they? Another question almost more frightening sprang from Donal's comment about "allies". *Halwyn wasn't the only elf who objected to human "contamination" of elven bloodlines. Suppose others resented a half-elf heir to the throne? What if growing up in the human world left Baird powerless to protect himself?*

To distract herself from that anxiety, she asked about something else that had popped into her mind. "What happens to Halwyn's body? You can't leave it lying in the upstairs hall." She swallowed against a spasm of nausea.

Kieran said, "That's a minor problem. Donal can place a spell of preservation on it and store it in an unused room until the king's guards arrive."

"Yeah, that'll work. Say, do you think that pooka friend of yours would be interested in sticking around?" Donal asked. "I could use a watchdog, and he might like living in my pond."

"He might," Kieran said. "You're welcome to extend the invitation. I have no claim on him."

"Okay, as long as he promises not to give the ducks heart failure. He'll be more entertaining than the sylphs. Let's face it, they're decorative, but they aren't great conversationalists."

Kieran thanked him for his help. When Fern expressed her gratitude, too, Donal shook her hand and said, "That's all right. You just go home and take care of that kid."

Her throat tightened, and she had to blink away tears.

Kieran put an arm around her waist. "We won't impose on you any longer. If you'll just notify us when Fenella's next message arrives, we'll be waiting outside." He guided Fern through the corridors to the front door, which she knew she wouldn't have found on her own. A purple sunset tinted the sky when they emerged onto the porch.

Harvey trotted up to them and nudged Fern's hand. When she scratched behind his ears, he spoke inside her head. *You did good. The sylphs filled me in. Nobody will be sorry to get rid of Halwyn.*

"As far as that part is concerned, I didn't do much. About like Dorothy accidentally melting the wicked witch."

The way you saved Kieran, though, that took guts. What are you guys doing next?

She sagged against the porch railing. "I don't know."

Kieran addressed the pooka in elvish. After a few seconds of silence, he said for Fern's benefit, "He's prepared to accept Donal's offer."

"That's nice. Good luck, Harvey."

Thanks. Drop by and say hello sometime. The pooka strolled in through the open door, presumably to settle the details of his bargain with the half-elf.

"We need to talk," Kieran said, taking Fern's hand and walking toward the pond. She managed a weak smile. "That's traditionally supposed to be the woman's line."

They sat together on the bench under the honeysuckle-festooned trellis. The buzzes and chirps of crickets vibrated in the humid air. Lightning bugs flickered in the grass. In the thickening twilight, Fern caught glimpses of the larger, brighter globes of light that she now recognized as wisps. A tiny, blue-skinned man darted across the lawn to hide behind the oak tree that shaded the pond. "That's a pixie?"

"Yes." Kieran captured her hand in both of his. "Fern, I do not want to part from you."

"I want to be with you, too, but I don't see how we could make it work." He traced spirals on her palm, sending tremors along her nerves. Her pulse raced at the memory of those long, delicate fingers exploring her body. Shoving the image away, she focused on spelling out her qualms. "You want your aunt and uncle to welcome you home more than anything, don't you?" Although his face didn't change, she felt a surge of longing from him. "If you lost that chance so you could stay with me, you'd end up resenting me. Not only that, they won't take you back without Baird, and you know I'll never give him up."

"I would never resent you. If you would allow me the opportunity to prove that vow, you would discover the truth of it. But is there no chance you might reconcile yourself to living in my world?"

"Be honest. How would your friends and relatives treat me? I haven't forgotten what you and Donal said about their attitudes toward half-elves, not to mention the way Fenella acted. Can you tell me with a straight face that they'd think of me as anything better than your pet?" His eyes slid away from hers. "I can't spend my life that way, no matter how beautiful it is inside the Hollow Hills."

"If that is your final decision, I'll defend it," he said. "I will not permit anyone to take Baird from you. If you think it best for him to live as a mortal in this world, I shall help you evade any agents the king and queen might send after him in the future."

"Do you think they will?" Her shoulders drooped with the weight of that foreboding. "Why am I kidding myself? Of course they will. They'll never give up, and if you help me, you'll end up a permanent exile. Never mind returning to Oberon and Titania's court, you wouldn't be allowed to go back to Elfland at all, would you?"

"That is one possible outcome." He stroked her hair, while his other hand kept a tight hold on hers. "I could enjoy the wild variety of this world."

"Temporarily, maybe, but if you were stuck here, you'd get tired of it and me. If nothing else, wouldn't all that iron and steel cause you problems?"

"Adair learned to live with it." He cupped the side of her face.

She turned her head to brush her lips against his palm. When she realized what she was doing, she pulled back. "I don't much like the idea of becoming a hunted fugitive, either."

"If you're determined to bring up Baird as an ordinary child," he said, "you will be hunted regardless of whether or not I'm with you."

"Another thing, what happens to him after I die? I won't live forever, and if he doesn't learn about the magical side of his nature, how can he protect himself against those hunters? But if I let him join his elven family, I'll lose him, and I can't stand that." Tears welled up in her eyes.

Kieran drew her into his arms, her head leaning on his chest. "I know. I've seen how much you love him. I won't let anyone come between you."

She yearned to relax into his embrace and bask in his caring. That surrender wouldn't solve anything, though. "Am I being selfish, trying to keep him away from his father's people? Doesn't he deserve to experience both worlds?" Half unconsciously, she snuggled closer to Kieran, while he massaged her back in widening circles. "I just don't see any way out of this."

"We shall find a way." His breath ruffled her hair. Delicious shivers trickled down her spine. "Listen to me, Fern. Open your heart to our bond. Believe that I would rather spend my life in exile than leave you. While Halwyn held me captive, it wasn't the memory of my home that I clung to. It was you."

She started to answer, and her breath caught in her throat. He stopped her with a finger on her lips. "Wherever you choose to dwell, I'll stay with you, even if it is in this world, where I'll lose you after a normal human lifetime."

She tilted her head to look into his eyes, which gleamed in the deepening shadows of evening. "That's one more glitch. You won't age, right? I'll get sick and old." She had trouble believing he wouldn't get tired of her long before her normal human lifetime ended.

"If you joined me in the Hollow Hills, you wouldn't suffer illness, and old age would be postponed for a very long time. But you have already rejected that choice, and I won't try to persuade you otherwise."

The quiet determination in his voice almost convinced her. *Open your heart to our bond*, he'd said. With her head on his chest, his pulse beat reverberated in her ears. She closed her eyes and let the glow of his aura envelop her. The strong, steady rhythm of his love echoed the pounding of his heart.

Love? Yes, that was what she sensed through the bond. He hadn't used that word yet. Maybe elves didn't think in those terms. Considering how much he risked in offering to leave his home world for her, she could do no less than match his courage.

"Kieran, I love you." He froze to stunned stillness. "I don't know how we can possibly stay together, but if you find a way, I'm ready."

"And I love you." He laughed softly. "How strange that sounds, yet I know love is the true name for this need that consumes me. In some ways our kind have much to learn from yours. I will not lose you, Fern." His lips skimmed her hair. She rested her head on his shoulder, letting her eyes drift shut. For just a few minutes, she wanted to pretend his promise could come true.

She wasn't sure how much time passed before Donal's voice interrupted them. "Fenella's back at the mirror pool," he said, "with the queen."

Kieran stood up. "Titania has come? So quickly? That sounds hopeful."

Fern had her doubts. Maybe the queen had rushed to confront him because she couldn't wait to disown him once and for all. Or maybe she felt confident she could coax or bully him into delivering Baird to her.

When they followed Donal into his office, the computer screen showed a closeup of a woman with silver hair and golden eyes. A grass-green snake coiled around her head like a tiara. By now, Fern wasn't shocked to see the serpent's jaws gape in a hiss.

In a voice like water rippling over rocks, the queen said, "Kieran, Fenella and Donal have told me what transpired between you and Halwyn. Is it true that he is dead?"

"Yes. His own minions destroyed him." He squeezed Fern's hand. "This is Fern MacGregor, sister of Adair's consort. She saved me from Halwyn."

Titania's eyes shifted to Fern, who hoped her nervousness didn't show. "Consort? I have not yet decided whether the mortal woman deserved that title. Nevertheless, I thank you for your service to my nephew and grandson."

A flash of anger momentarily overrode Fern's qualms. "It wasn't service. I love Kieran, and Baird belongs to me."

"Love?" Titania said with a cool laugh. "That feeling did not save our son and your sister from catastrophe. As for the babe, Kieran, have you not made it clear to her that Adair's child belongs with us?"

Kieran cast a reassuring glance at Fern before he answered, "I've changed my mind about that. I've come to realize that she and Baird must not be separated."

On the other side of the screen, thunder rumbled. "Surely you do not presume to dictate to us."

Fern spoke up. "I don't want to cut Baird off from his father's heritage, but I won't let you take him away from me. I'm not sure about Kieran, but you bet I'm dictating to you. If you want any part in Baird's life at all, you'll have it on my terms." She trembled under the fairy queen's icy stare, but she had to make her determination clear. "I want him to have a normal human family life. I want to make him Halloween costumes, throw birthday parties for him at fast food restaurants, watch *Sesame Street* and decorate Christmas trees with him, teach him to catch lightning bugs and take him to the beach in the summer. I want to put him in Sunday school, Cub Scouts, and Little League."

Donal interrupted, "I get it. The life you didn't have, right?"

She flinched at the direct hit. "Exactly, the life I never had, in the kind of home Ivy would have wanted to give him if she'd lived."

"If she were alive," Kieran said, "she would also allow him to enjoy the gifts and talents he has inherited from Adair." He stared into the queen's glowering eyes. "I would prefer him to have the benefit of both, but if you reject Fern's right to bring him up, I support her."

"Do you imagine she can keep possession of the boy if we send our warriors to take him?"

Firm resolution emanated from Kieran. "If you do, I'll fight them as her champion."

Titania shifted her attention from him to Fern. "Young woman, can I do nothing to change your mind?" Her eyes darkened with what looked like genuine pain. "We have lost our only son. Would you rob us of our grandchild and foster son?"

"The way you want to rob me? I could accept sharing him, but you want to take him away completely."

Miniature lightning bolts flashed behind the queen. "We can give him a life you could never imagine. Can you not see that yielding him to us is for the best? You will not lose by that decision. I can grant you the wealth to fulfill any desire you may dream of."

Fern couldn't stop herself from laughing at that offer. "You're trying to bribe me now? All I want is a safe, happy life with Kieran and Baird. As for wealth, if you're talking about fairy gold, forget it." She imagined buying a half share in Bev's bookstore with money that would wither into dry leaves the next morning. She wouldn't cheat the IRS that way, let alone her best friend.

"Very well, I propose another solution." Titania's lips compressed in a thin line and the snake around her brow hissed. "Dwell inside the Hollow

Hills with Kieran and the child. You will enjoy comfort, safety, and a long life."

"As a pet? No, thanks."

Thunder crackled, and the violet sky in the fairy garden seethed with threatening clouds.

Fern's pulse raced. Kieran squeezed her hand. "Nor would I condemn her to live as such, your majesty. And I will not let you separate the two of us."

"Now that Oberon and I know the truth of Adair's murder, we are eager to welcome you home. You would give up your rightful heritage to live in the world of change and death with this mortal? Where she and the infant might be in danger?"

"If I must. She already knows some methods of protecting herself against dark magic, and I'll teach her more. Adair and Ivy found happiness in this world. So can we."

Fern drew a shaky breath, reminding herself that Titania couldn't cast a spell through the screen to strike her down. "If you try to tear us apart, you'll never see your grandson at all."

"Fern MacGregor, you said you would not object to sharing the babe. Did you mean that sincerely? Could you reconcile yourself to a compromise to prevent his being cut off entirely from his elven blood?"

"I trust Kieran. I'll agree to any compromise that he endorses."

His affection and reassurance enveloped her like a cloak. "Fern and Baird must live in the human realm," he said. "To ensure that Baird forms bonds with his elven family and learns to use his powers, I'll bring them to visit the Hollow Hills several times each year."

"I wouldn't mind visiting now and then," Fern said, "but what about the time difference? I can't stay away for what amounts to months or years on this side. I'd lose contact with my human friends."

Titania's voice hardened again. "You claimed you were willing to compromise."

"If you spend only a few days in the Hollow Hills each time," Kieran said, looking at Fern rather than the queen, "you will lose at most a month per visit. I will make sure you are honored as a guest, not treated as my plaything."

"Okay, I can trust you for that."

His gratitude surged over her. Facing Titania, he said, "Do you accept that plan?"

The sky in the fairy garden cleared. "If your consort is willing, we accept the bargain. Understand, young woman, this arrangement does not mean Baird will stay with you forever. When he reaches maturity, he will have to assume his role as our heir and eventually become king."

"I understand." Fern swallowed the unshed tears clogging her throat. "Children grow up and move away. If that's what he honestly wants, I'll accept it."

"Very well. I swear to abide by this bargain." The glow of the truth spell shimmered around the queen. "Kieran, I rely on you to ensure that your consort keeps her vow as well. We shall look forward to the first visit soon."

He bowed, and her image faded away.

Donal, whose presence Fern had almost forgotten, reached across to switch off the communication program. "Do you two realize what you've done? You've made sure the next king of Elfland will be human-friendly. I hope I live long enough to see what happens when he takes the throne."

"Yeah, that's a good side effect I hadn't even thought of," Fern said.

"True, Baird's reign should be...interesting." Kieran bowed to Donal. "Again, you have our thanks for your help. I'll return as soon as I can to repay you as I promised."

Outside in the balmy night, Kieran and Fern strolled beside the pond, whose surface sparkled with dancing wisps. With their arms around each other's waists, she felt lightheaded with wonder at how secure she felt in his embrace. "She called me your consort."

"Yes, she has resigned herself to welcoming you as my mate."

"Is this really going to work? Can you stand living in our world year after year with only short breaks?"

"If you can abide the adjustments you'll have to make, so can I."

Adjustments? "Good grief, I just realized this is going to wreck my career."

"You regret your promise?" He lifted her hand to his lips.

"No. You and Baird are the most important part of my life. But how can I be Bev's partner when I'm gone a month at a time?"

"You could share the truth with her."

"Tell her a secret this big?" Fern's head reeled at the thought. Most of her life she'd made hiding her second sight a top priority. Revealing her odd gift, plus the fact of an enchanted other world only one step away, would mean a complete turnaround. "Bev is a good friend. I'm sure she can handle it." If her partner put up too much resistance to believing in elves, the true-sight eye drops would solve that problem. Fern felt an unexpected relief at the prospect of confessing her strangeness to a friend after so many years of caution. It occurred to her that all this time she'd been alone despite that friendship, because she'd withheld the deepest truth about herself. "Actually, you're giving up more than I am."

"I don't view the change as a sacrifice. After all, I'll be able to visit my home regularly and share it with you. There are elixirs, if you're willing to drink them, that can guard you against illness and extend your life. As for our life on this side, we can build a haven like Donal's."

She glanced at the house, a dimly outlined shape with lights shining in the front windows. "That'll take a lot of money, and don't even think of using fairy gold."

He laughed softly. "I suppose a spell to induce folk to buy your shop's wares would be against your principles, too."

"You bet."

"What about a subtle aura of magic to lure shoppers into the store?"

She mulled over that suggestion. "Sounds okay, as long as they're not actually being forced to buy anything. More foot traffic would be a definite plus." Another practical problem occurred to her. "What are you going to do with yourself stuck in the mundane world for several months straight? Unless you plan to sell potions like Donal or sing on stage like Adair, you probably don't have a lot of marketable skills."

"Why, until I discover one of those skills, I shall tend to Baird while you work at the shop."

She laughed at the image of Kieran as Mr. Mom. "Okay, you teach him basic magic, and I'll read him fairy tales and play Ivy's tapes to put him to sleep every night. Maybe this will work after all."

He gathered her into his arms, their bodies pressed together, his lips skimming the top of her head. "I called Adair a fool when he chose this changeable world and a short-lived human mate over his own kingdom. I wish I could tell him how mistaken I was."

She blinked away tears. "Well, we short-lived human types believe in an afterlife. Maybe, somehow, Adair and Ivy know we're together and taking care of their baby."

"If you believe this, I have faith in the truth of it." He kissed the droplets from her cheeks.

With a quavering sigh, she basked in the warmth that radiated from him and encircled them like a glowing mist. She trembled at the thought of how alone she would have remained if he hadn't stormed into her life to crash through her barriers. "I'm glad you made me believe in magic."

His lips brushed hers. "And I thank you for making me believe in love."

Marked for life by reading *Dracula* at the age of twelve, Margaret L. Carter specializes in the literature of fantasy and the supernatural, particularly vampires. She received degrees in English from the College of William and Mary, the University of Hawaii, and the University of California, with her dissertation published as *Specter or Delusion? The Supernatural in Gothic Fiction.* Her other works include *Dracula: The Vampire and the Critics*, *The Vampire In Literature: A Critical Bibliography*, and *Different Blood: The Vampire As Alien.* She is also the author of a werewolf novel, *Shadow Of The Beast*, and four vampire novels, *Dark Changeling* (2000 Eppie Award winner in Horror), *Child Of Twilight*, *Sealed In Blood*, and *Crimson Dreams*, along with a fantasy novel, *Wild Sorceress*, co-written by her husband Les Carter, and a horror novel, *From The Dark Places.*

Margaret and Les, a retired Navy Captain, have four sons and several grandchildren. For fans of "Vamp Tales", please do not hesitate to visit her website: The Vampire's Crypt at:
http://www.margaretlcarter.com/

You can keep track of all Margaret's books on her author page at Writers Exchange E-Publishing:
http://www.writers-exchange.com/Margaret-Carter/

If you enjoyed this author's book, then please place a review up at the site of purchase, and any social media sites you frequent!

If you want to read more about books by this author, they are listed on the following pages...

Crimson Dreams

The summer when Heather was eighteen, her dream beast's nightly visits warded off loneliness and swept her away in flights of ecstasy. Now, returning to the mountains to sell her dead parents' vacation cabin, she finds her "beast" again. But he turns out to be more than a dream. She meets Devin in the flesh, apparently not a day older. His first human lover, centuries in the past, died horribly because of her devotion to him. Does he dare expose another mortal woman to that risk?
Publisher: http://www.writers-exchange.com/Crimson-Dreams/

Passion in the Blood

Cordelia and her twin sister don't realize the mother who left them soon after their birth bequeathed them a dark bloodline. They're half vampire. Although human in most respects, they possess certain psychic gifts. A friend of their late father's, Karl, also a vampire, has been watching over their family for generations in honor of his love for their distant ancestor. When her sister is kidnapped and Cordelia must beg for help from Karl, she learns the truth about his vampirism and her own heritage. In the process, she and Karl form a blood bond that leads to deeper intimacy than either one could have anticipated.
Publisher: http://www.writers-exchange.com/Passion-in-the-Blood/

Different Blood: The Vampire as Alien

Different blood flows in their veins--but our blood quenches their thirst. From Bram Stoker's 1897 creation of Count Dracula, portrayed as a foreign invader bent on the conquest of England, the literary vampire has symbolized the Other, whether his or her otherness arises from racial, ethnic, sexual, or species difference. Even before the bloodsucking Martians of H. G. Wells' *War of the Worlds*, however, popular fiction contained a few vampires who were members of alien species rather than supernatural undead.

Even more intriguing than interplanetary invaders are humanoid and quasi-humanoid beings who have evolved to live on Earth among us, often camouflaged as our own kind. The boom in vampire fiction that began in the 1970s engendered a variety of "alien" vampires, many of them portrayed as sympathetic characters. The science fiction vampire is especially suited to the presentation of vampirism as morally neutral rather than inherently evil.

Different Blood surveys the literary vampire as alien, whether extraterrestrial or a different species evolved on Earth, from the mid-1800s to the 1990s, and analyzes the many uses to which science fiction and fantasy authors have put this theme. Their works explore issues of species, race, ecological responsibility, gender, eroticism, xenophobia, parasitism, symbiosis, intimacy, and the bridging of differences. An extensive bibliography lists dozens of novels and short stories on the "vampire as alien" theme, many of which are still in print.

Publisher: http://www.writers-exchange.com/Different-Blood/

From the Dark Places and Against the Dark Devourer

From the Dark Places

When Father Michel Emeric and Dr. Ray Benson warn young widow Kate Jacobs of occult danger stalking her, she dismisses them as deranged fanatics. The eerie disappearance of her four-year-old daughter, Sara, changes her mind. Ray and Father Mike rescue Kate's child, but the fight has only begun. Dark powers from beyond our world want to destroy Kate and Sara and prevent the birth of a future child foretold to have extraordinary psychic powers and a destiny as a great warrior against evil. Kate must develop her latent wild talents and allow Sara to do the same, in a universe weirder--and more dangerous--than she's ever imagined.

Publisher: http://www.writers-exchange.com/From-the-Dark-Places/

Against the Dark Devourer (Sequel to From the Dark Places)

All her life, Deborah has known she and her older sister have extraordinary psi powers. When their mother dies suddenly, Deborah learns she's meant to use her gift against the forces of darkness in some special way. How, she doesn't have a clue, but she wants no part of this alleged fate. Yet with evil forces stalking her, can she avoid the battle ahead?

All his life, Victor has known he and his twin sister have a unique destiny. Bred to serve inhuman entities from another dimensional plane, he's instructed to either seduce a strange young woman who poses a grave threat to the cult he belongs to...or destroy her.

Unexpectedly, he finds Deborah not only attractive and intelligent but his equal in psychic power. Although his cult views religion with contempt-

-and she's an unabashed Christian--he's helplessly drawn to her. For her part, Deborah finds in Victor a kindred spirit. For the first time, someone other than her sister can empathize with her differences from "normal" people. Is prophetic destiny written in stone, even for two potential foes falling in love? A paranormal romance inspired by C. S. Lewis's *That Hideous Strength* and the cosmic horror of H. P. Lovecraft.

Publisher: http://www.writers-exchange.com/Against-the-Dark-Devourer/

Heart's Desires and Dark Embraces

When Margaret L. Carter first read *Dracula* at the age of twelve, her spontaneous reaction was to wonder how the undead Count saw the events in which he was portrayed as the villain. She's always been fascinated with the "monster's" viewpoint and relationships between human and nonhuman beings. Most of the stories in this collection can be described as romances, and all involve love and passion in some form. Here you'll encounter vampires, elves, ghosts, and at least one human-monster hybrid. The vampire stories in the first half of the book are part of an ongoing series in which the creatures we know as vampires belong to a naturally evolved, nonhuman species secretly living among us. Readers can get better acquainted with them in *Crimson Dreams, Sealed in Blood,* and *Passion in the Blood.*

Publisher: http://www.writers-exchange.com/Hearts-Desires-and-Dark-Embraces/

Prince of Hollow Hills

When her sister mysteriously dies, Fern takes over the care of her baby nephew. She has no idea that his missing father wasn't an ordinary man or that baby Baird is heir to the throne of Elfland. Two rival elvish princes invade Fern's life--one hostile, the other alluring. One wants to kill the child, the other to guard him. But both intend to take him away from her. How can Fern fulfill her promise to her late sister while falling in love with Kieran, Baird's fiercely protective and not human--cousin?
Publisher: http://www.writers-exchange.com/prince-of-the-hollow-hills/

Sealed in Blood

Science fiction conventions attract some strange people, but Sherri Hudson never expected to spend a con weekend helping a sexy man in a cape steal photos of a winged alien. When the photographer is murdered and Nigel Jamison reveals to Sherri that the "alien" is actually his sister, the situation gets intriguingly complicated. Unwillingly swept up in Nigel's quest to rescue his sister, Sherri can't help being fascinated with him. By the time she finds out he's a vampire, the fascination has become mutual--and too strong to resist.
Publisher: http://www.writers-exchange.com/sealed-in-blood/

Shadow of the Beast

After the mysterious deaths of her brother and sister at the fangs of what looks like a feral dog, Jenny Cameron develops nightmares and blackouts. The quest for the truth about herself leads to her long-lost father, who deserted the family before her birth. He seeks redemption for the curse he carries, but has his bloody past condemned him beyond salvation? When Jenny discovers the secret of her dark heritage, she's no longer sure she can trust her dangerous nature enough to be with the man she loves, and she may ultimately be forced to destroy her own father. Fearing she has inherited the violence that rages in him, she struggles to find her true self under the shadow of the beast.

Publisher: http://www.writers-exchange.com/Shadow-of-the-Beast/

Wild Sorceress Series
By Margaret L. Carter and Leslie Roy Carter

In a world where hostile nations wield magic in combat, twin sorceresses separated at birth and brought up on opposing sides of the war find each other. Together, they face persecution for using wild magic, fight against traitors and assassins, explore family secrets, and discover the hidden origins of magic itself. Above all, to protect their world, they must deal with ancient, powerful dragons that most people don't even believe exist.

Prequel: Legacy of Magic

Most people in the country of Saphradea admire sorcerers and dream of having magical powers. Not Merina, a young woman who detests magic because she thinks it ruined the life of her mother, a failed sorceress candidate who abandoned her in infancy.

When Merina's fiance, Trinames, announces he's decided to go for training as a Healer sorcerer, her personal world turns upside down. Merina is heiress to a tract of rich farmland, and she wants only to manage her own property and bring up a family in peace--a dream she thought Trinames shared. Yet events conspire to force her into a realm of magic and intrigue she never wanted.

When Trinames is kidnapped and she strikes out across the wilderness to rescue him, in company with a wandering trader who turns out to be more than he appears, she runs into a crisis that awakens magical powers she shouldn't even possess.

Publisher: http://www.writers-exchange.com/Legacy-of-Magic/

Book 1: Wild Sorceress

In a world where warring nations use magic in combat, years ago young sorceress Aetria's untamed power caused a disaster on the battlefield. Temporarily banished and retrained, she's returned to the army to redeem herself as head of a company of novice mages. She uncovers a traitorous plot by her own commander, renews her bond with her "imaginary" childhood friend, and meets her long-lost twin sister. While also becoming a trusted friend of the commanding general of the army, Aetria unearths secrets of the true nature of the magic she and her comrades wield.

Publisher: http://www.writers-exchange.com/Wild-Sorceress/

Book 2: Besieged Adept

While learning to control her wild sorcery, Adept Aetria has defeated a pair of traitors trying to kill her, found a long-lost twin, and uncovered secrets of the source and nature of magic. Now she continues her research while battling the remnants of the Neo-Aggressor rebellion and integrating raw, untrained talent into the Sorcerer Corps. Meanwhile, she discovers deeper secrets of her own family background, along with a surprising new foe and a destiny she never dreamed of. Furthermore, she learns that her "imaginary" dragon friend Rajii actually exists...but so do less friendly dragons. What does their agenda mean for the future of humanity and magic in Aetria's world?

Publisher: http://www.writers-exchange.com/Besieged-Adept/

Book 3: Rogue Magess

Sorceresses Aetria and Coleni discover that both their own births and the history of their world have been manipulated in secret by an ancient, powerful race of dragons. Some, like Aetria's lifelong friend Rajii, have benevolent intentions toward humanity while others want to restore the people of the Domains to total slavery. All, however, have their own agendas with human beings and mortal magic as pawns.

Emerging from their long-lost mother's hidden home in the deserted Non-Lands, Aetria and Coleni find themselves targeted by assassins under control of the dragons. While the sisters' powers continue to grow, so do the magical gifts of Coleni's baby daughter, but will their magic provide adequate protection?

Meanwhile, still viewed with suspicion for their "wild sorcery", they can't convince most of their rivals and allies, including Aetria's old mentor and the commanding general of the army, that the dragons and the danger they pose are real.

Publisher: http://www.writers-exchange.com/Rogue-Magess/

Series Page:

https://www.writers-exchange.com/wild-sorceress-series/

Upcoming Books

Sealing the Dark Portal

Almost nothing Rina remembers about her life is true. Rather than the ordinary librarian she believes herself to be, she's actually a sorceress who fled from another world to ours when creatures from an alien dimension devastated her home and killed her family. Now they've pursued her to our world, summoned by a sorcerer who plans to open a portal and invite monstrous entities from the void between dimensions to overrun this planet. Rina's former bodyguard, a cat shapeshifter who was once her lover and still yearns for her, helps her true memories to awaken. She must come to terms with the truth about her past so that together they can save their new home from the fate of their old one.

Windwalker's Mate

Shannon's little boy Daniel has disturbing psychic powers. He talks to the wind--and it listens. All Shannon wants is a normal life. She wants to forget the cult of the Windwalker, a dark god from another dimension, and the terrifying night when her child was conceived. But her first love, Nathan, son of the cult leader, contacts her for the first time since that horrific ceremony. He claims his father is stalking Shannon and Daniel. Whose child is Daniel, Nathan's or the Windwalker's? Nathan's father plans to use Daniel to open a gate between dimensions and unleash chaos on our world. To save her child and become reconciled with her first love, Shannon may have no choice but embrace the strange powers she previously rejected.

www.ingramcontent.com/pod-product-compliance
Ingram Content Group UK Ltd.
Pitfield, Milton Keynes, MK11 3LW, UK
UKHW021905190726
13853UKWH00002B/516

9 798201 275129